NEXT OF KIN

NEXT OF KIN

A Tami Vaduva Novel

V.J. FITZ-HOWARD

Published by Bloodwilde Press

Published in the United States of America

ISBN (Paperback): 978-1-955039-11-6
ISBN (Hardcover): 978-1-955039-12-3
ISBN (E-Book): 978-1-955039-10-9

The screen door slammed behind me, announcing my entry. From the living room Mama shouted over the FOX News broadcast: "Fifty times a day them boys slam that door, like it's the hood of a '56 Fairlane. If you'd got a aluminum one like I told you, it wouldn't make all that racket. But Miss Princess had to get a custom-made mahogany door." Mama pronounced the word contemptuously, enunciating every syllable: "*Mo-hog-o-NEEE.*"

"I'm just trying to make a nice home for our family, Mama."

I detected, and despised, the apologetic tone in my voice. I removed my beret, tossed it on the kitchen table, and entered the living room, where Mama, installed in what she called "the fluffy chair" was all dolled up: hair sprayed; cheeks tinted orange; eyes done up like Cleopatra's. A bloodred velvet tracksuit clung to her recently renovated size four frame. The tracksuit's top was unzipped to mid-chest, revealing too much of her new 52-Ds. "That's some get-up, Mama."

Mama, eyes fixed on the TV screen, made a disparaging remark about immigrants, muted the TV, and fingered the diamond-and-ruby Cartier necklace I inherited from my most recently deceased husband, Gonzalo Fernandez. She turned to me, grinned and blew a smoke ring. "Ain't no man with a pulse—I don't care if he's eighteen or eighty—immune when I'm turned out like this," she said.

"Except that you reek of tobacco."

"And fancy perfume."

"Mama, 'Lucky You Body Mist' is not 'fancy.' There's a reason they stopped making it in 1993."

"Which is why I bought ten cases, when Merle's Department Store went out of business."

"I'm trying to say this as gently as I can, Mama. 'Lucky You' isn't elegant or sophisticated; it's cheap. Even if it was a three-thousand-dollar Amorem Rose Parfum in a Lalique bottle, it still wouldn't smell good decades on. It'd smell stale—like your lifetime supply of 'Lucky You'."

"You just don't get it, girl. The same way they keep the recipe for Coca-Cola and Big Mac special sauce locked up in vaults, I too have a secret recipe—just the right mix of fine tobacco smoke and perfume—that gives me my allure. It's been my signature fragrance since I was twelve." She raised a red lacquered finger, the nail sharpened to a point, like a talon, and brushed it over her painted cheek. "When the two aromas meet on my skin, it's like knockout gas to a man."

"Were you wearing 'Lucky You' when you met my daddy?"

She snorted. "Lucky for him. Unlucky for me."

"If you say so."

"I say so!"

Best to change the subject, I reckoned, as Mama did not welcome discussion about my daddy. "So, who's the guy?"

She winked. "I met a new gentleman friend today, at the Bob Evans."

"Mama, you don't have to take all your meals at Bob Evans.

You know you're welcome to eat here, in your home, with me and the boys."

"I ain't eating that foreign slop you sling: chicken mumbo jumbo and cuckoo."

"Chicken Morocco and couscous."

"It's un-American. Bob's fried pork tenderloin with mashed potatoes, gravy and coleslaw is good enough for me, which means it's good enough for your boys, too."

"That's what you ate today? You probably ingested thirty-five hundred calories. You're going to put back all the weight they cut out of your middle and off your backside."

"And you're gonna pay to get it all cut off again!" she brayed. "I took two bullets for you in Palm Beach, girl. Don't you forget that!"

"You make sure I don't," I hissed as I stomped towards the kitchen, regretting that I had allowed her to rile me up yet again. Truth is, I think it's more accurate to say that Mama took two bullets for her country. When Ernesto "el Libertador" Estrada, an Argentine terrorist whose evil plot I had thwarted, tried to kill me at Little Jack's birthday party, Mama had gotten in the way. While she didn't exactly get shot on purpose, she did take those bullets like a champ, and even seemed proud, not only of having inadvertently saved her daughter's life, but having contributed to Ernesto's ultimate demise at my hands. He was a man no one would mourn, and surely one who would have killed again and again.

"There's KFC in the bucket if you want a break from cooking," Mama shouted from the living room.

"Thanks, but I was planning to make"—I hesitated before I spoke—" . . . chicken noodle soup," mindful to omit the word

Thai before uttering 'chicken noodle soup.' "But I can't find the star anise in the spice drawer," I added.

"I threw it out."

"Why, Mama? That stuff is expensive. It's ten bucks a jar."

"Those boys shouldn't be eating anything that has 'anus' in its name."

"It's *anise*—not . . . *that other word.*"

"It'll put dirty ideas in their heads. You'll thank me one day."

I was just about to enter the living room and inaugurate the second argument of the afternoon when the doorbell rang, compelling Mama's dog to emerge from the ground floor bathroom, barking furiously as she rattled towards the door.

"Shut up, Bitch!" Mama yelled.

Confined to a doggie wheelchair since having lost the use of her rear legs, Bitch was hardly the spry leaper she had been in her youth.

"That must be your gentleman caller, Mama. You gonna answer the door?"

"You answer it, child. I don't want to look too eager." Her lighter clicked. "Keep him out on the porch while I have a smoke."

I turned on my heel. "What's his name?"

"Harlan Stuhl," she said. "Fancy name, ain't it? Like the name of an associate manager at the Dollar Store, which he just happens to be. Since I become alluring again, I am attracting a higher caliber man."

I was tempted to say, 'If you say so, Mama,' but held my tongue instead.

"I say so," she mumbled, apparently reading my thoughts.

I approached the screen door but saw no gentleman

caller—or anyone else—on the porch. Bitch, scratching furiously at the screen door, growled. I shushed her, scooted her aside, pried open the door, and squeezed through.

"Surprise!" shouted the Crabtree brothers, Dalton and Dustin, who were hiding off to the side.

"What are you two doing here?"

"Kidnapping you on your birthday, Command Sergeant Major Vaduva."

"Bless your heart, fellas. Really. But not tonight. It's Friday. I'm plum tuckered. We got a whole new batch of candidates in this week for summer session. Flabby and undisciplined. It's a R.O.T.C. program these kids have joined. But they seem to think they've been invited to a kindergarten birthday party. I'm getting fifty texts and calls a day from their helicopter mamas. I'm staying in tonight."

"Nope," said Dustin. "You're going out.

"See that?" asked Dalton, who pointed at an idling white limousine. "We're taking you to Lewisburg for drinks and dinner. That's an order, Command Sergeant Major Vaduva."

"I give the orders around here," I said to my employees, both of whom worked as general managers at the AutoMotives franchise locations I owned in Beckley and Dawson, West Virginia. I purchased the small businesses after my first husband, Colonel Cletus Bland III, died unexpectedly, just to give me something to keep my mind off the grief.

The identical twin brothers stood at attention and mock-saluted me, which they knew would hit my soft spot. As I sized them up, I recalled other parts on those brothers that, during a particularly lonely stretch between husbands, I had also summoned to attention—before I swore off men.

"It was sweet of you to do this, but I just . . . can't. The nanny leaves in a half hour. And even if my mother was competent to watch the children—which she is not—she's on her way out the door."

"Nice try, Tami, but you're not getting out of this," insisted Dustin. "We worked it all out with Rhandi; she said she'd be happy to stay overnight and put the boys down. We promised her double wages, and she jumped at the chance to earn some extra money."

"I don't want a nanny raising my boys. I took the university job precisely so I could be close to home. And I don't want my boys seeing me leave the house with two handsome strangers. They're not toddlers anymore. Sends the wrong message."

"Nice second try," Dalton said. "Kandi and Dondee are in the car. So, you'll be chaperoned."

Dalton turned and whistled. From the limo's moonroof, the two heads of their wives–one blonde and puffy and the other black and curly—popped up. "Get your ass over here, Tami!" Dondee shouted.

I shot a stern look at the general managers of my other two AutoMotives franchise stores, the ones located in Ronceverte and Burnwell. The girls stiffened up. "No disrespect intended, boss."

"None taken," I replied with a smile. I loved those girls. Still, I really did not want to go out.

"You're not backing out, Tami," Dustin said, with more than a hint of *and I mean it* in his tone.

I grunted, realizing that if I didn't go, the four of them would stay. "Let me change and say goodnight to the boys."

"Nope," said Dalton. "We go now. FaceTime the boys from the car. The Crabtree men and their brides are ready to rumble."

Despite how tired I was, a smile crept up on me.

"Hold tight while I go and fetch my gear."

On the drive over to Lewisburg, Dalton, Dustin, Dondee and Kandi provided business updates.

An hour later, we were gliding through historic downtown Lewisburg, West Virginia's version of Worth Avenue in Palm Beach: artisan jewelry shops, artisan glassware studios, artisan cookware stores, artisan bakeries, art galleries, and so on. The limo pulled up in front of an old warehouse that was all done up fancy: polished copper trim, hand-hewn reclaimed beams, wavy glass windows. The name of the establishment was spelled out in huge, rusted iron block letters: HOOCH.

"You're taking me to a distillery? You know I don't drink."

"With a fancy restaurant attached. Nobody's going to force booze down your throat, boss. Though you're crazy if you don't try their moonshine. Besides, we'll get you a great meal," said Kandi. "Fresh Oysters from the Chesapeake Bay." She scrunched her nose. "Comes with a weird vinegar sauce."

"Mignonette," I said. "It's a dipping sauce made of white vinegar, minced shallots, and white peppercorns. But you've got to crush the peppercorns yourself; pre-ground pepper—even if you use white pepper—makes the sauce cloudy."

"Oh," Kandi said.

"Get the crispy pork belly," said Dondee.

Dustin and Dalton, I was told, were pals with the co-owners, ex-Army fellas the Crabtree brothers knew from their time in service, as members of the 76th 3rd Stryker Brigade Combat Team, 2nd Infantry Division.

"Jeremiah does the cooking," said Dustin. "He apprenticed

in the original Hell's Kitchen—as a mess sergeant in Afghanistan. Rusty, his business partner, makes the moonshine, which he's won a bunch of awards for. But that's just a hobby. His real skill is metalworking. Handcrafted pots and pans. Copper, iron, tin—you name it. He sold the pots and pans business a year or so back to some big cookware company in California. Made a killing. That's what's funded the restaurant and distillery."

Kandi shot me a puzzled look. "You look sad, Tami."

"No, not sad." I smiled. "Just a little wistful, I suppose. It'll pass."

"You can talk about it," Kandi continued.

"Oh, there's not really much to say. Honest. When I was a little girl, my great-grandmama, Charlene, used to talk about the tin-smithers' art, which she held in high regard. The tradition was passed down, she told me, from each successive generation of fathers to sons in Petreşti, the little village in Romania from which the Vaduva clan fled some twenty-five generations back."

"Did your great-grandmama inherit any copper pots? Those would be worth a fortune now," Dustin said.

"No pots. Charlene had a tin cigarette case, though, which she claimed somebody smuggled out of Romania. The tin was all dented up and rusted. But on the back of the case, in tiny letters, it said Made in China. So, I don't think it was authentic—but I never told her that. She was so proud of our heritage."

Enough family history, I thought, then shifted the conversation back to the night's festivities. "Tell me more about your two buddies, the owners."

"Aside from being serious artists," said Dalton, "they're also serious drinkers. Especially Jeremiah. I watched him guzzle an entire bottle of Black Jack once."

"I'm not sure that's something to boast about," I said.

"He's single, Tami," said Dondee. "And singularly *fine.* Besides," she added, "all single guys drink too much. But once you get a ring on their finger, they can be tamed." She smirked at her husband. "Ain't that right, Dustin?"

Dustin, who had lost whiskey privileges the year before and was, except for special occasions, a beer-only man two years into marriage, scowled.

"Good husband-hunting opportunity for you, Tami," said Kandi.

"I'm not on the market."

"It's been fourteen months since Gonzalo died, girlfriend," Dondee said. "You've got to get on with your life."

"I'm not on the hunt for Mr. Right tonight."

"Who said anything about finding Mr. Right? Just look for Mr. Right Now," Kandi said as she climbed out of the limousine.

2.

The girl who greeted us at the door ushered us through the mob. The smells, I had to admit, were making my mouth water. And soon enough, I discovered why: a server whizzed past me carrying two goat-meat hamburgers. That restaurant, it smelled like Afghanistan—but in a good way.

We entered a private V.I.P. room. "Is this really necessary?" I asked.

"Nothing but the best for Tamsin Venables Bland Capers Fernandez," Dalton said.

"Knock it off. I'm just plain old Tami Vaduva when I'm not undercover on a mission."

"In Charlottesville or Charleston or Portugal or Palm Beach or Paris or Buenos Aires," Dalton added.

"I'd love to visit those places," Dondee said, tugging on a hoop earring.

Kandi heartily agreed.

"They're overrated. Trust me on that, girls. As far as I'm concerned, there's no place better than West Virginia."

~

For the next ninety minutes, we feasted. It was after ten p.m.

when the co-owners appeared to say hello. The girls weren't lying: They were fine looking men. After the Crabtree bothers were done razzing them on prices and wait times, introductions were made.

Jeremiah Tibbs, the chef, demanded to know exactly everything we ate, and nodded approvingly at our choices. "I hope I don't sound like a showoff," I said, "but I've eaten at some of the finest restaurants in the world. Roast chicken at Chez l'Ami Louis in Paris. Double breast frogs *á la provençal* at a Michelin-rated hunting lodge in the Andes foothills. But that goat burger and fries was the best meal I've ever eaten."

Jeremiah, whom I reckoned was a serious power lifter, could not contain his pride. "It's not for everyone; that goaty smell is a bit intense," Jeremiah said as he kneaded a cement-hard bicep, whose approximate circumference rivaled the muzzle on a M1 Abrams tank.

"Not to me," I said. "I ate a lot of goat when I was on my tours. Though, if you don't mind my saying, your sales might improve if you tell your butcher you only want girl meat."

"That's exactly my problem," Jeremiah said as he took a big swig of clear liquid from a jelly jar. I don't think it was water he was guzzling. "They only slaughter the boys and keep the girls alive for their milk."

"Girl meat is better?" Dondee asked.

"Duh," snorted Kandi.

"Let's keep the conversation focused on goats, ladies," I said in a not very convincing maternal tone.

"It's a lot less goat-y," Jeremiah answered. "Or 'aromatic,' I suppose I should say. At least that's how a food critic would put it. Bucks emit a super-stinky pheromone. Smells horrible to humans but drives girl goats wild." He lifted up his arm and took a deep niff of his armpit, letting out a big *aah*. "Triggers some sort of hormone chain reaction in does' brains; they start ovulating instantly."

"Dustin's B.O. did that to me," said Dondee as she patted her pregnant belly.

"Maybe the smell of moonshine on my breath will do that to you, Tami," said Jeremiah's flirty business partner, the distiller and iron cookware-maker, Russell "Rusty" Riddle.

"I doubt that. I don't drink," I said.

"Ah," said Rusty, "I'm beginning to see the light. Let me quote Proverbs, 23:20: 'Be not among drunkards or among gluttonous eaters of meat.'"

"It's not that. I'm not a non-drinker on religious grounds. I was an Episcopalian for a spell, though. Twice. A Roman Catholic, too—but only for a couple of days, as it turned out." Images of my deceased husbands—Colonel Cletus Bland III, FBI Special Agent Jack Capers, and failed *coup d'état* architect Gonzalo Fernandez—flooded my memory. "I simply don't like the taste of alcohol."

Rusty grinned. "It's time for some after-dinner moonshine."

Me and pregnant Dondee declined. But Kandi, Dustin and Dalton were all in.

Dondee told her husband he'd already had plenty to drink. But Dustin reminded her that we had a limousine outside—which came with a designated driver.

"Tami, I'll be deeply insulted if you refuse to taste my moonshine," Rusty said.

"I really don't want any."

"You're obligated."

"No, I'm not."

"Yes, you are: I comped your dinner."

There was something charming about this Rusty Riddle. An angle-worker, he was. Rusty was handsomer than Jeremiah, too: coal-black West Virginia eyes, wild black beard. That leather cowboy hat. But I do not as a rule find men who wear their hair in buns alluring—even if they are ex-military. "I told you, Rusty, I don't drink."

"Never taken a sip?"

"One or two."

"I knew it," said Jeremiah.

"I didn't like the taste."

"What did you sip?" Rusty asked.

"Horsebit bourbon."

Rusty spoke in a pompous voice, like a wine sommelier: "'With its subtle notes of burnt rubber and kerosene.' No wonder you stopped. What else?"

"Champagne."

"You're too earthy for that. What else?"

"Campari."

"Oh, *puh-leez!*"

"I guess that explains why I don't drink."

"Just stay put: I'll be back in a minute."

"Oh, sweet Jesus," Kandi said after Rusty went to the bar, "one sip won't kill you, Tami. It's your birthday! At least take one, and pretend you like it. Rusty takes his moonshining very seriously and makes every flavor of it you can think of. Throw the man a bone."

Two hours later, it shames me to say, I was, for the very first time, drunk. *Roaring* drunk. I reckoned the moonshine would taste like battery acid. Instead, Rusty served the liquid equivalent of my most cherished childhood memories. We started with cotton candy-flavored moonshine, followed by pizza roll moonshine, followed by pimento cheese spread moonshine, then bologna moonshine. Rusty boasted he used only natural ingredients in his elixirs—real peperoni, pimentos, and so on. I am equally ashamed to say that after each tasting, as Jeremiah and Rusty got increasingly touchy (a finger tap to my shoulder, a brush of my forearm, a gentle hand on my thigh), I grew increasingly frisky—and got a bit handsy myself. Indeed, people who know me well know I am not inexperienced with men. Nor have I ever regretted having had various goes with various men in my ongoing quest for True Love. But I always undertook the quest clear-eyed and of sound mind, which after a final shot of Mounds Bar flavored moonshine, I was definitely not. With fingers extended, Jeremiah and Rusty each separated the strands of hair covering my eyes, tucking them behind each ear. Such a gentle gesture by two raw and rugged guys. I looked up at both, wondering which one I was going to have a go with. For, by that time, I was certain a go was in the cards.

"Eeny, meeny, miney, mo," Kandi teased.

"No," said Dondee, the only sober person at the table. Directing her comments to Jeremiah and Rusty, Dondee said, "She's wasted. There are rules against that." She shook her head disapprovingly. "And you two are supposedly gentlemen."

The boys elbowed each other.

"Besides," Dondee added, "Tami's cursed with men."

"I wish she'd curse me," Rusty said.

Jeremiah, his face blazing red and glistening with sweat, raised an eyebrow. "You could always choose both of us."

I could not but help emit a sigh of regret.

"Those days are over for me."

Dustin elbowed Dalton as I directed an evil, albeit blurred, eye towards the twin brothers, indicating they had better keep our secrets from the old days to themselves.

Kandi pointed at Rusty and Jeremiah, looking them up and down good and slow. "Dondee, you haven't had a drop of hooch tonight. If you weren't a married woman, would you walk right out that door with one or both of these boys tonight?"

Dondee grinned mischievously. "Both."

Rusty and Jeremiah hooted and hollered.

"Give me that bottle," I said to Jeremiah. He handed me the empty liter of Moonpie Moonshine. "Sit down," I said to Jeremiah and Rusty. "Best of three. And stay still, the both of you."

I spun the bottle three times, as promised, but the darn neck kept landing right between them.

"Well, I guess that settles it. Being that it is my birthday, the both of you it is."

Jeremiah leapt from his chair, overturning it. "Woah!" He fist-bumped Rusty, then reached for the bottle of Hash Brown Hooch, and guzzled the remaining half in one swig.

The party broke up fast, with the Crabtree boys and their wives razzing me as they climbed into the limousine.

As the proprietors of HOOCH and I staggered down the block to Jeremiah's loft, Rusty shouted: "'He drank of the wine and became drunk and lay uncovered in his tent.'"

"That's the plan!" Jeremiah hollered back.

"That's Genesis 9:21, in case you were wondering," Rusty said.

"I wasn't," said Jeremiah.

3.

I was seated on Jeremiah's iron bed. Rusty was in the bathroom, where he'd been for a while.

"What's in the munitions box?" Jeremiah asked.

I set it on the nightstand. "Nothing of particular interest. At least not anymore."

I heard the shower turn on, and Rusty start singing Merle Haggard's "The Fightin' Side of Me."

"Come on, what's in it?" Jeremiah coaxed. "Now you've got me curious."

I shrugged. "It's just my version of a purse." There was a time when what I carried in my munitions box would have been of great relevance to a gentleman that I was about to have a go with, but that time had passed. "Wallet, phone, car keys, kid-related gear. Some lady-specific products. And my Glock."

Jeremiah frowned. "Damn. I thought you were going to say sex toys. Want another drink?"

"No. And if we're about to do what I think all of us are about to do, you don't want another either."

"And what's *that*?" he asked coyly.

"A surprise," I said.

"I love a surprise," he said, slurring the *s*. He then leaned in and kissed me. The pizza roll moonshine on his breath smelled good and tasted even better. He peeled off my top. He yanked his t-shirt off next, with one hand. He wadded the shirt and tossed it on the floor. His power-lifter's body reminded me of those gigantic tires you see at monster truck rallies: thick, bulky, rubbery, indestructible. He even had treads: thick muscle scarring—earned both in combat and at the gym—was visible across his pecs, along the deltoids, and across his abdomen, where he'd been shot.

He reached for the moonshine bottle on the nightstand, tilted it and poured half its contents down his throat.

Then he unfastened his belt. "Let's rumble, darlin'."

After we had our go, Jeremiah commenced more moonshine-guzzling. I decided not to intervene, as he'd had no problems with his performance. None at all, in fact, as he seemed able to hold an ungodly amount of liquor, which is not an unusual skill for a combat veteran of his caliber. And since he and I had just met, I figured it was none of my business to judge how much he drank anyway.

"Behind your munitions box," he said, pointing at the nightstand, "is a pack of Marlboros. Light one up and hand it to me, darlin'."

I handed him the packet of smokes and the skull-and-cross-boned Zippo. "Light it yourself; I don't want that taste in my mouth."

"I still got your taste in my mouth," he said, winking.

I shivered a little. With some dewy perspiration on my chest after our exertions, I was feeling a little cold. Jeremiah noticed and grabbed a rag wool throw blanket that lay at the foot of the bed. He covered me with it, and gave me a nice, long kiss.

The shower turned off. Rusty was in the middle of his next number: Loretta Lynn's "Don't Come Home A-Drinkin' (With Lovin' on Your Mind)."

I was feeling frisky again.

Jeremiah lit up. He blew a big smoke ring. "I've got one of those, too," he said, pointing at my munitions box.

If his munitions box contained the same "coaxing equipment" I had deployed to prepare my deceased first husband Colonel Cletus Bland III for the go that resulted in the conception of our son, Cletus Bland IV, that sounded good to me. "Show me what you've got," I said.

"I already did."

"In the munitions box," I clarified.

"It's not a munitions box exactly." Jeremiah swung his legs and stood, unsteadily, on the concrete floor. From the top shelf of a bookcase, he retrieved a leather satchel. "My uncle took this off a Viet Cong, at the Battle of Khe Sanh, in '68," he said. He rubbed his meaty thumb along the cracked leather pouch, directing my attention to a series of Chinese characters. "You can tell by the markings it's ChiCom—Chinese Communist-made."

I know what 'ChiCom' means."

"Holds forty rounds," he continued.

"What's inside?"

After Jeremiah apologized for hiccupping, he said, "Spy stuff. After 'Nam, Uncle Roy joined the C.I.A. He spent the nineteen seventies and eighties slithering around Eastern Europe: Czechoslovakia, Hungary, Poland and"—hiccup—"the Baltic states." Jeremiah unfastened the pouch. "He picked these up in his travels."

Like a first grader at show and tell, Jeremiah presented the KGB disappearing-ink pen, a camera wristwatch, a hollowed-out silver dollar, inside which messages or microfilm could be concealed, a tin flask-bomb. "This is my favorite," he said as he reached for the tube of lipstick. "Proof—not that anybody needs it—that women are more ruthless than men." He unscrewed the lid. "Single-shot pistol."

"Caliber?"

"Forty-five millimeter." He presented the tube of lipstick to me for inspection. I twisted the cherry-red tip. Out popped the muzzle. Jeremiah batted his eyelashes and made a come-hither look as he retrieved the tube from my hand.

Just then, the bathroom door creaked open, and a poof of steam preceded towel-clad Rusty Riddle. The bun he'd worn before had been taken down, thankfully. His hair was wet, black, and tussled—just the way I like it. His body was hard, damp and chiseled, though not nearly as bulky as Jeremiah's. He smelled heavily of sandalwood and his beard had even been trimmed. I had to admit that I was touched he'd gone through so much trouble. While the smell of hard work on a man had always made me friskier than a jackrabbit, I was no less aroused by good hygiene. My late husband, Gonzalo, who was fussy about his appearance, came briefly to mind, flooding me with a lustful sadness.

"Y'all started the party without me," Rusty said, his hands thrown up in the air. I noticed he'd even clipped his fingernails.

"Well, well. If it ain't Miss America!" said Jeremiah. "How long did you expect us to wait while you primped yourself up?"

"I was scrubbing the stench of emulsifiers and corrosion inhibitors out of my hair and off my person. I spent my day in my shop, making a cauldron for a museum client over in Staunton, Virginia." He eyeballed me. "And judging by the look on the beautiful Miss Tami's face, she doesn't seem to mind that I went through the trouble."

Jeremiah, naked and all, stood up and began to sashay around the room in the poorest imitation of a woman I've ever seen in my life. "Excuse me, Miss Tami," Jeremiah whispered in his best attempt at a dainty female voice, "but the bloom on my rose is fading." He puckered his lips and sat down on the bed again, then crossed his legs. "I hope you won't mind," he said as he traced the tube over his upper lip, "if I just apply a fresh coat of lipstick, so as not to be outdone by Mr. Rus—"

As he hiccupped, the weapon's discharge sounded less like a shot fired from a pistol than the kind of instant, crisp burst heard on the Fourth of July, when a kid tosses a snap'n pop onto the driveway.

"Jeremiah!" I screamed.

"No!" Rusty shouted.

That sweet hulk tilted onto the mattress and his head sunk gently into the pillow. Surrounding the indentation of his head was a pool of blood.

I grabbed my phone from my munitions box and called nine-one-one.

"Hold tight," Rusty whispered, taking his friend's hand.

Jeremiah was silent.

"Can you hear me?"

Jeremiah moaned.

"Say something, buddy!" Rusty pleaded.

Jeremiah's eyes went from glassy to distant. I had seen those eyes before. It was unlikely he was coming back. He looked up at Rusty, then turned his eyes to me.

"Thank you, Tami . . . " Jeremiah moaned.

"Hold on!" I said.

"For . . . "

"Don't give up on us, Jeremiah!" I shouted.

". . . the . . . best . . . "

"Fight, Jeremiah!" commanded Rusty.

". . . go . . . of . . . my . . . life."

Three days later, I found myself way downstate, in a place I had been before. The mist was heavy, the surroundings grim. McDowell County had the highest rate of drug-induced deaths of any county in the United States. McDowell County: a place that haunted me with unpleasant memories. A place to which I had sworn I would never, ever return.

The gravel crunched beneath the tires of my El Camino as the vehicle approached Those Who Seek Refuge in Christ Church.

Rusty Riddle stood like a sentry, motionless, in the weed-infested cemetery adjacent to the church. He was staring blankly as I approached. The silence was eerie. I was fidgety, more nervous than I had ever been before, even in combat situations.

"Sorry I'm late," I said, my voice cracking as I surveyed the church's missing eastern wall, which was draped in a mud-caked blue plastic tarp. "Drama at home." I took a deep breath and prepared to enter that church, for which my memories were unfond.

"I guess we should go in." The dread on my face must have registered with Rusty.

"The service is already underway, let's just stay out here," he said. "Nobody's going to miss us. We'll attend the burial."

Beneath a lightning-struck oak tree, one of its once-mighty limbs dragging on the ground like a paralyzed arm, two men were digging Jeremiah's grave.

"The Crabtree brothers and their wives are inside?"

Rusty confirmed.

"You sure the family wants me here after what happened? I still can't forgive myself for letting him drink so much."

"Tami, there wasn't anything he was doing that night that he hadn't done before. Well, almost anything. And you were the last person to see Jeremiah alive," Rusty said. "That matters. Besides, there's no family here; he has none."

"Then why is he being buried here?"

"Jeremiah was a congregant here as a kid."

The palms of my hands moistened. Jeremiah Tibbs was my age, give or take a year or two. I tried, and failed, to visualize him as a boy. Did we overlap for a spell at this bizarre, sinister place?

Rusty grabbed my elbow and steered me towards a row of tombstones. "I'll introduce you to his kin." He pointed out one Tibbs family member after another:

GEO. W. TIBBS, BORN AUG. 7, 1843 – DIED AUG 25, 1863, MEMBER OF BRICKETT STROTHER'S CAMP NO. 25, CONFERERATE VETERANS OF WEST VIRGINIA, "BLESSED ARE THE DEAD WHO DIE IN THE LORD" . . . DAISY MAY TIBBS, DAUGHTER OF P.E. & A.B. TIBBS, BORN DEC. 15, 1851 – DIED DEC. 15, 1851 . . . ELMER TIBBS, HERBERT TIBBS, FLORENCE TIBBS, JESSE TIBBS, NETTIE TIBBS, CLAUDE TIBBS, CHESTER TIBBS, THEODORE TIBBS, PAULINE TIBBS.

Rusty lit a cigarette. "It's too quiet in there," he said, waving the cigarette at the church.

I heard the sound of a muted piano and tambourine inside the church, but not much in the way of clapping or singing. There was a tepidness to it. Well, I reckoned, if the "congregants" were indeed Jeremiah's friends, and were anything like him—smokers, drinkers, cursers, fornicators—it was unlikely they were well versed in Pentecostal funeral rites.

We executed a turn at the end of the Tibbs' row, entering a new chain of family tombstones.

"You look like you've seen a ghost," Rusty said.

"I have," I whispered as I gazed down at the headstone of Gladys Grymes.

"You knew her?"

"Yes."

"How."

"I've been here before."

"*Here?* In the ninth circle of hell? When?"

"I was a girl."

"When it was—?"

"—Yes, when it was the Pentecostal Tabernacle of the Holy Ghost's Testimony Church."

"*Damn!* You attended services here, in its heyday, with those—"

"—snake handlers. Yes."

"'They shall take up serpents; and if they drink any deadly poison, it shall not hurt them,'" Rusty intoned. "How'd you get mixed up with those lunatics?"

"My mama brought us here."

"She was—or is—a Pentecostal?"

"Hardly."

"I'm confused."

"I'm not. Can we just leave it at that?"

He seemed taken aback. "Sorry for prying."

"Sorry I was so sharp."

"Do you mind me asking who was Gladys Grymes?"

"My mama, Velvet—that's the affection name we use for my mama; her real name is Luludja, which was my grand-mama's name and my great-grand-mama's name and is my real name too—wasn't what you'd call a very 'hands on' parent. During our stay here, when Mama had bigger fish to fry, Gladys was my minder. A sort of surrogate mama to me."

"It was not a happy time?"

"No."

I stared at the headstone, overcome by memories of Gladys. I recollected her dire predictions of the coming apocalypse, which had to be updated every New Year's Day; her deep-fried squirrel doused in vinegar-marshmallow sauce; her curly twig collection. The faintest trace of a smile came over my face.

"What?" Rusty asked.

"She was always trying to keep me on the straight and narrow. 'Keep your mouth shut and your legs crossed,' she was always warning me—despite the fact that I was nine."

"That was good advice. Especially in these parts, where it's not a case of *in spite of* being age nine, but *because* of being nine." Rusty studied the dates on Gladys's tombstone. "How'd she die?"

"I don't know. Snakebite, I reckon. That's how most people here met their end back then. Mama almost met hers here; a snake bit her, too. She was lucky: she only lost a finger." Poor Gladys, I thought to myself. I never heard about her death; nobody told us. After me and Mama left—which we did in a hurry; Mama *always* leaves in a hurry—we were never in touch with anyone from down in McDowell County again. When Mama leaves a place, she leaves no trace of herself.

"Where was your daddy during this period?"

"I don't know my daddy. Never met him. Never will. I don't even know his name; my Mama still refuses to disclose it. She proclaimed him dead to her. It's a pattern in my family among our women: unhappy endings with men. My grandma Marlene refused to disclose the name of the man who begat Mama. And my grand-mama Charlene likewise refused to disclose the name of the man who begat Marlene."

Rusty didn't seem to know what to say next. Finally: "Was it tough for all you Vaduva women, being fatherless?"

There was no sense harkening back five centuries to Petrești, Romania, dredging up details of the curse put on the women of the Vaduva bloodline. That through black magic we had been fated to never be able to keep a man we loved. Not alive anyway. I simply said, "I come from a long line of single mothers"—and left it at that.

We turned and entered the next row.

"I never knew my daddy either," Rusty said.

"That stinks. It's hard, isn't it?"

We walked in silence. I didn't like getting personal with people too quickly but felt an obligation to say something. "Where's your mama?"

"She died in childbirth."

"I'm truly sorry. My Mama's a handful, I can assure you of that. But I love her. And she's the only family I've got left, other than my boys. I don't know what I'd do if we lost her. What was your mama's name? Hopefully something beautiful, like Leigh or Margaret-Rose. If I had a daughter tomorrow, I'd give her a name like one of those."

"I don't know her name. Never learned my daddy's, either. And not for want of trying. After I ran away from my adoptive parents' home, I combed through every birth record in Doddridge County, where I spent my childhood, looking for a trace of myself—and them. But to no avail. The third poorest county in the state, it wasn't uncommon back then for babies to be born in galvanized water troughs in barns, surrounded by midwifes and the prayerful. The people of this state were off the grid long before it was cool to be off the grid."

"Your adoptive parents didn't even know your birthparents' names?"

Rusty laughed bitterly. "Of course, they did. But refused to tell me. They said they found me one morning outside their trailer, that I was their 'Baby Moses floating down the Nile in a basket'." He squashed the cigarette beneath the heel of his cowboy boot.

"Tell me about them, your adoptive parents."

"Clyde and Glodene Riddle, from a town called Big Isaac. They were in their sixties, I think, when they took me on."

"Did they abuse you?"

Rusty stopped and looked out on the field of crab grass beyond the cemetery. Perhaps I shouldn't have asked.

"Not in the way you're thinking," he finally said. "They were religious fanatics, like a lot of people down here. We went from one Pentecostal church to another."

"Including this one?"

"All of them *except* this one. Clyde and Glodene drew the line at snake-handling."

"The Pentecostals taught you scripture?"

"For twelve hours a day I was forced to study and recite passages from the Bible." Rusty laughed, but not bitterly this time. It was in that way one laughs when looking back on something they survived.

"Where did you attend services? In Big Isaac?"

"Big Isaac, at first, then Smithburg, Ashley, Blandville, and about a half dozen other places. There was no town in Doddridge County—or no church—too small or too destitute to accommodate us."

"You moved a lot," I said.

"There was never any money: Daddy was a dog groomer; Mama mopped up crime scenes. But she was a secret drinker, which made her work unsteady."

That made me think about poor Jeremiah again. "You say I couldn't have done anything about Jeremiah's drinking the other night, but I'm not so sure. I can tell you as a woman that there was one thing he valued more than alcohol."

Rusty Riddle placed his hands on my shoulders. "There's nothing—absolutely *zero*—you could have done to save him. Jeremiah had a death wish."

"You're saying he shot himself on purpose?"

"No. I'm saying he had really bad PTSD. And a happy ending was not in store for him. He had to drink a quart of booze every night before bed to stave off the nightmares."

"He didn't have to die on my watch."

"You will *not* blame yourself for his death, Tami. Hell, if anything, you gave him one final great night before going off into the unknown. He said as much as he lay dying, and I saw the look on his face as he thanked you. You obviously did him right more than any other woman ever had, so this conversation is over."

We were silent again.

"You were telling me about your adoptive parents," I said,

respecting his decision to change the subject. "Where are they living now?"

"They're dead," he said unsentimentally as congregants spilled out of the church.

A few minutes later, the Crabtree brothers, along with several pall bearers I didn't know, brought the body to the burial site.

The pastor, who was not a well-spoken man, muttered a prayer as the casket was interred.

"How old was that woman playing the piano? One hundred five?" asked Dondee afterwards, as the crowd disbursed.

"One hundred twenty," said Kandi, who surveyed the tombstones. "God, I could use a cigarette. Give me one, Rusty."

"Thanks for reminding me I can't smoke," said Dondee, who sneaked a puff of Kandi's cigarette when her husband turned to speak to one of the servers from Jeremiah and Rusty's restaurant.

The skies, gray when we arrived, were blackening.

"Let's get out of this godforsaken place before the storm hits," said Dustin.

"And we're showered with hail, locusts, and what not," added Dalton.

Rusty Riddle escorted me to my car. "Can I ask you one more thing?"

"Anything you like," I said.

"Could I, um . . . "

"What?"

"Could I hold your hand?"

I'm not sure why I hesitated given that I had intended to do a lot more than hold hands with Rusty Riddle on the night Jeremiah died.

Rusty noticed my delay and put his hands in his pockets. "I hope I'm not being inappropriate, this being Jeremiah's funeral and all. I just feel like there's something between us, Tami. Something—and it's eerie, I'll admit—that *connects* us. We have lived parallel lives, I guess. Pentecostal churches as kids. We both went into the army. You were even there the night my best friend died." He ground the toe of his boot into the mud. "I just hope that after we've had time to mourn, we can become real friends." As I climbed into the El Camino, he continued, "I didn't tell you this when I met you for dinner and moonshine, but—"

"—I will never take another drop of moonshine—or any other form of liquor—again. Ever. I'm going to A.A."

His big white teeth lit up like a neon sign. "A.A. is for quitters, darlin'! Now you just pick yourself up and climb right back on that barstool, like a big girl."

"Not funny," I said as I fastened my seatbelt.

His tone became serious. "Look," he said as he drummed his fingers on the door, "I know this is a weird time, a weird situation, but I thought I should tell you I have never been so happy to win a chance at a girl—especially in a game of chance like spin the bottle—as I was the other night. Even if it meant I had to share. It feels weird to say this, but it's the honest-to-God's truth: I felt a special connection to you the second we met."

Though I had no intention of saying so, especially after what had transpired on the evening of my birthday, and particularly because of my track record with men, I felt the same way.

"This is hardly the time to ask a girl out. But I'd really like it if we could see each other again. Even if it's just to have a mutual shoulder to lean on."

"I'm not sure that's such a good idea."

"I realize the timing is horrible," he said. "But you've got to admit: we've got a lot in common. Jeremiah. Busted-up families. Pentecostal churches."

"From which we ran screaming."

"Exactly."

"We were just tourists, Mama and I, when we were down here. In and out in about a year. I had never been in a church before that time and, truth be told, not since, except to get married."

He lit another cigarette. "Boy, you're good at shutting a conversation down."

"Sorry."

"But I don't give up so easily. I like talking to you, Tami. That's all. It's easy and natural." He looked away. When he looked at me again, his stare was intense: "Would it hurt just to go have a coffee sometime, or grab a burger? Some place up in Beckley or Lewisburg?"

My intention was simply to graze his hand with mine—just to prove I had a beating heart and to acknowledge he had one too. But I found myself squeezing his hand—harder than intended. "Rusty, I'm a black widow spider. Every man I couple with dies. I'm cursed. You don't want to be with me."

"I'll take my chances."

"Last Saturday night, when Jeremiah died, I decided I'm done with men. Forever. My first husband died only months after we were married, trying to rescue our son, who was being attacked by a swarm of yellowjackets. My second husband died in our bed, of heart failure, on our honeymoon. Want to know how my third husband died?"

"No."

"I'm retiring. Hanging up my spurs. From now on, the only men in my life will be my boys. Please understand that I intend no cruelty towards you when I say what I'm about to say—because you're a bright, fine looking, charming man—but we're never going to see each other again. We can't. For your sake and mine. I wish you much success with your restaurant and distillery. And your life. You deserve the best—which you won't get if you're with me."

He just stood there, biting his lip, trying to summon, it seemed, the right words to say.

I looked down at the gearbox. I needed to get out of there double quick, before I changed my mind. But my hand was numb; it was like it was asleep. I pulled it away and turned over the engine.

"Tami, just give me a—"

I jerked the stick shift into reverse, kicking up a cloud of dust as I backed out.

5.

Later that same day, as I was preparing chow for the boys, Mama walked in and deposited onto the kitchen island the spoils of her daily hunt: boxes of Little Debbie snack cakes, apparel from Walmart, bouquets of artificial flowers, battery-powered dinner candles, tissue-paper tablecloths from the Dollar Tree store, and "treasure" procured from her favorite junk shop in Beckley: a porcelain figurine that showed a cluster of cherubs encircling a plump piglet; a painting of a big-eyed kitten; a rhinestone chandelier earing (with no mate).

"I bought you something fancy," Mama said as she fished through one of the bags.

I was still raw from the funeral. "Please stop buying clothes for me, Mama. If I want clothes, I'll buy them myself."

She ignored my protest. Like a matador waving a cape, she spun around and presented an orange-hued woman's hoodie sweatshirt for my inspection. Printed in 3D, across the front, back, sleeves and hood, were gigantic squares of Cheez Its, each cracker about the size of an 8x10 picture frame.

"Look at me. I'm a grown woman, Mama," I barked. "I don't want to wear Cheez Its sweatshirts."

"You don't have to be an ungrateful bitch about it."

Mama's dog scuttled out of the bathroom, reckoning she was being summoned.

"Not *you*, Bitch," Mama said. "Her," she said as she pointed at me. Mama was no apologizer. *Ever.* But I knew she regretted the tone she deployed when she unwrapped the Little Debbie. Though the message was intended for me, she directed it to the dog. "Mama's sorry for talking mean to you," she said in a baby voice as she crammed the oatmeal cake in the dog's mouth.

I needed to soften my tone of voice, too. "I'm not ungrateful, Mama," I said, placing my hand on her forearm. "I just want you to stop wasting money on this junk." I should have stopped there but couldn't restrain myself. "*My* money."

Mama yanked her arm away. "You've got plenty, girl. Hundreds of millions."

"At the rate you spend it, not for long. You spend seven hundred fifty dollars a month on your so-called 'imported' cigarettes."

"If I could get my Eve Ultra-Light Menthol 120s in West Virginia, I would. But I can't, so Royce drives down to Alabama to fetch me a fresh supply once a month. You can either pay for his gas, or build me one of those humid rooms, like they keep cigars in, and I'll buy a year's supply. But you won't buy me a humid room, will you? Well, I'm entitled to a few dollars for raising you. Besides, you've spent a thousand times what you share with me on this house." She waved her arms theatrically, as though we were standing in a grand ballroom at the Palace of Versailles. "Them big glass windows that look out on the river. That chandelier with the deer antlers you had shipped from Wyoming."

"Elk."

"Deer antlers from West Virginia ain't good enough for

you. And how much did you spend restoring that El Camino of yours? That fancy paint job and electric motor from Tulsa."

"*Tesla.* And, yes, I have money, which you are a beneficiary of every day. I spent forty-nine thousand dollars on that ninety-eight-inch TV you're parked in front of every day. I buy fresh food—and always enough for you. It's healthy and delicious, but you refuse to eat it."

"There'd be a few pennies extra for me if you hadn't given all Gonzalo Fernandez's money away. I'm your mama, the one who made you alluring to him in the first place. I got a claim on my share of that $2.4 billion."

"No, you don't, Mama. Neither do I. Nor do the boys. It was blood money."

"Bullshit. It was *green* money. And you gave it all away. Showoff. Putting your name above the door of every new get-off-opioids clinic and veterans' charity in the state."

"My name's not on any of those buildings, Mama. And you know it. Every penny I donated anonymously."

"Everybody knows it come from you, that money—which is just as you intended it."

"You know nothing about me, Mama. And nothing about honor."

Images of my most recently deceased husband, Gonzalo Fernandez, intruded upon my mind: him galloping down the polo field; Gonzalo's enthusiasm for imported Italian cherries in his Manhattan cocktails; the look on Gonzalo's face, moments before his death, when he released his grip on me and plunged to his death in the South Atlantic Ocean. "Let's drop this conversation before one of us says something we'll regret," I said.

It was silent as we went about our respective tasks: Mama

unloading four new ice cream scoopers to her existing collection of some two dozen; me assembling Cleet IV's meal, which Mama paused to inspect, disapprovingly. "That looks nasty," she said.

"No, Mama. It looks *healthy.* There's a difference. It's a Greek chicken keto bowl."

"What's that green shit in there?"

"It's called zucchini. It's a vegetable." I shook a bit of salt over the bowl. "Not that you'd know."

She stuck out her tongue and repeated what I said. "'*Not that you'd know.*'" She fiddled with her ponytail, which had loosened while she was shaking her head at me. "I'll tell you what I *do* know, child: He'll never eat that."

I should have bitten my tongue. "You're right about that, Mama. He won't. And he'll be fifty pounds overweight instead of the current twenty if you keep feeding him fried chicken, 7-Up, Little Debbies, Nilla wafers and Cracker Jacks."

"He's growing."

"Yes. He's growing *wider.* By the minute. And I'm sick of it!" I grabbed an ice cream scooper and hurled it at the window, shattering the glass.

Mama startled.

I slumped to the floor and put my head in my hands.

Mama, not by disposition a nurturing sort, lowered herself as best she could and did her best to comfort me. "What's wrong with you, child?"

I did not as a habit share with my mother details of my personal life, as her feedback was generally unhelpful. But I told her how, in a moment of weakness and loneliness, I had the previous Friday acquired a new "gentleman friend." I admitted to sleeping with him. I admitted to exposing him to the family curse.

She stroked my hair. "It's a stubborn curse, child," she whispered. "We've all suffered under it, us Vaduva women. I reckon if I had a man who ever stuck around longer than a night, I wouldn't shop so much. But I'm bored. And lonely, like you. I need something to occupy my time."

"Sorry about the ice cream scooper, Mama."

"We got plenty."

"Look at that window."

"We could use a little fresh air in here."

I told her about the funeral, about my venture down to McDowell County, to what was once the Pentecostal Tabernacle of the Holy Ghost's Testimony Church.

The muscles in her face clinched up tighter than a miser's fist. "You've no business down there, child."

"I met a man down there."

"Who?" Mama asked suspiciously as she lit a cigarette.

"Technically, I met him last Friday night. He is—or was—best friends with Jerimiah, the man they buried."

"This man you met, the surviving one: Young fella?"

"About my age," I said.

Mama looked skeptical.

"You'd like him, Mama. His name is—"

"—Don't say it! You're liable to curse him, too." Mama flicked cigarette ash in the sink. "That boy you met with today, he was a member of that church, back in the day, before they shut it down?"

"No, but he was well acquainted with it."

Mama looked relieved. She walked over to the closet to fetch a broom and dustpan. She was silent, absorbed in her thoughts. Finally, as she began to sweep up the glass shards, she said, "I reckon you told him stories about rattlers and copperheads."

"We didn't talk much about that."

"What, then?"

I looked at her with a combination of resentment and longing. "Actually, we talked about our daddies. He didn't know his either."

Mama, head cocked, was about to say something but held her tongue.

I walked over towards the hole in the wall where the window once was. "When I was growing up, every time I ever tried to get information about Daddy, you shut the conversation down. I gave up by the time I was sixteen. But I'm not a little girl anymore, Mama. I'm a grown woman. A mother myself. I've got a right to know who my father is."

"That subject is closed," she said defiantly.

"I've no men in my life other than my boys. No father. No husband. And it dawned on me today—for the first time—that I never will. I have a right to know about the man who brought me into this world."

"*I'm* the one who brought you into this world, not that jackass!" She leaned the broom against a chair and approached me. "He's gone, child. Forever," she said as she placed a hand on my shoulder.

"You've hidden a lot from me."

"To protect you," Mama said.

"I don't need protection."

After she removed the carton of rocky road ice cream from the freezer, she turned to me. "I've told you things. Taught you things. Don't you forget that."

"Like what?" I asked.

"When you were a teenager, I told you about that secret muscle every woman's got in her private lady parts area." She arched her eyebrow. "I reckon you put that learning to good use once or twice."

"You really want that to be your legacy, Mama?"

"I taught you our Gypsy arts, too," she said as she dredged a spoon through the carton, daring me not to correct her and say "Romani," a descriptor she hated. "Taught you to read palms and cards."

"And pick pockets."

Her mouth tightened. "Which I ain't ashamed of. Our people have been discriminated against for centuries. Mastering that skill meant we could eat. And let me remind you of something: My passing that skill down to Cleet IV helped you stop a terror attack masterminded by your third husband," adding, after she removed the spoon from her mouth, "whose money you gave away."

I would not take the bait a second time.

I meant only to talk to myself, but the words rolled out of my mouth, albeit as a hushed mumble. "I want my daddy."

"No, you don't, child," Mama whispered.

Presently, I was visited by an idea. "Mama, I've got a question."

"You ask too many questions."

I pressed. "There's one other dark Gypsy art you never taught me, Mama. One I know about that you don't think I know about. One that great-grandmama Charlene and grandmama Marlene told me you were the best in the family at."

Unable to resist flattery, Mama replied: "What's that?"

"Talking to dead people."

"The most dangerous art of all."

"I want to talk to my daddy."

"Who says he's dead?"

"Is he?"

"He's dead to me. That's all you need to know."

"If he's dead, I know you have the power to summon his spirit. I just want five minutes with him."

"That's about all I had with him. And that was five minutes too many."

"What makes talking to dead people so dangerous?"

"Remember when I had that mix-up in Charleston a few years back?"

"Which one?" Over the course of my lifetime, my mother had been drawn into dozens of "mix-ups," many into which I was conscripted to get Mama out of. Of course, none of them were ever her fault, according to her. There was that "mix-up" at that convenience store on Maccorkle Avenue, where she was caught trying to redeem counterfeit lottery tickets; the "mix-up" on the parking lot next to the greyhound racetrack, where she was photographed removing another motorist's license plates; the "mix-up" at the Food Lion, where she was caught pretending to scan a family size bag of Funyuns at the self-checkout; the "mix-up" at the Heermann Mobile Home Park, where she was caught posing as a realtor to gain entry into a former gentleman friend's home.

Mama continued. "Remember that lawyer you found for me after the manager at the Food Lion falsely accused me of shoplifting?"

"Dixie Somebody," I said.

"Dixie Ates."

"What about her?"

"She told me: 'A lawyer should never ask a witness a question the lawyer doesn't already know the answer to.'"

"What's that got to do with talking to dead people, Mama?"

"You can ask dead people anything you like. But there's a good chance you won't like the answers you get. Which is why I think everyone's better off if they just keep their mouths shut and get on with their lives."

"I have a right to know, Mama."

After she swallowed another spoonful of ice cream, she scanned me up and down. "Ain't nobody braver than you, girl. I'll give you that. You fought them Arabs; you tracked down the father of your child; you rescued a girl who wasn't even your own kin from sex-kidnappers; you stopped a terror attack on Argentina. But it ain't brave to ask deceased loved ones questions you don't want to hear the answers to. Or *shouldn't* hear the answers to." Then, unexpectedly, she dropped the bravado and moved in closer. Her black eyes were moist. "Loneliness comes with our curse, child. Once a Vaduva woman realizes—once and for all—that she'll never have a man in her life, she's got to learn to cope with it. And not ask questions. You can have a man for a night, or a month, or maybe even a year. You can have lots of men—even at the same time, if you can take it. I reckon you've had your share; I know I've had mine. But they can't and won't be around permanent. Never."

"I just want a man to talk to, Mama."

"Shh," she said. "No tears, child." Mama embraced me and rocked me gently. "I can see you're still too young to understand all this. The pain don't ever go away. But, if it's any relief, it don't sting as bad by the time you're my age, either."

"Introduce me to my daddy. I promise I won't ask a single question. I just want to see his face."

Mama tossed the empty ice cream carton in the garbage bin. "I ain't arranging a meeting with your father—dead or alive. Never. But . . ."

"But what, Mama?" I eagerly asked.

"I shouldn't do this."

"Do *what*?"

Mama looked at me empathetically. "If you want someone to talk to, to bring you comfort now that you're facing the hard truth about your future, maybe that can be arranged."

"Who?"

"You had a few good men in your past. Maybe they can offer you some comfort—provided you keep the conversation light. But I warn you: Don't ask questions you may not like the answers to. Instead, just talk about good times and fond memories together." She shrugged. "Maybe it'll lift your spirits."

"You'd do that for me, Mama?"

She dislodged a spec of walnut lodged between her front teeth with a fingernail. "Against my better judgment."

I hugged Mama, squeezing her so hard I reckoned she might pop. "Who am I going to talk to?"

"You just hold your horses," Mama said as she shooed me away. "Go and fetch that nanny woman. We need four participants to get the best spirit reception, but we can make do with three."

"I'll rustle up four bodies."

"Meet me in that fancy room you go to, that dark one."

"Why won't you ever call it by its name: the library?"

Mama snorted. "Ain't nobody but a showoff ever had a 'library' in their house."

"What's that smell?" Rhandi asked.

"Incense," Mama whispered as she directed us to our chairs.

The baby was fussing. Mindful that my baby-whispering skills were superior to hers, Rhandi handed him off to me as we entered the library. I sang my nursery rhyme: "From his nose to his toes—"

"—Shh!" Mama barked.

Sheets were draped over the TV screen, as well as over the new *trompe l'oeil* mural I had recently commissioned: a deer hunter in fluorescent orange bibs, loading his prize 47-point buck into the bed of a pickup. On the round table in the center of the room stood three blue candles, which flickered intermittently, their batteries apparently dying. A still pendulum, situated at the middle of the table, dangled from a chain. The chipped Ouija board, a slab of weathered, uneven oak, was placed before Mama. It was decades old—perhaps even centuries. On the board, beneath a wide magnifying glass, were symbols, pictures, letters, numbers, and words. Also displayed on the table were three mementos Mama had procured from my bedroom, each sentimental to me: a big picture book once owned by my late first husband, entitled *Remarkable Trees of*

Virginia; a compact disc, entitled *This is My Beloved*, which my second husband played on our honeymoon, before his untimely death; and a paisley Charvet ascot, a favorite accessory of my late third husband.

"Why the Little Debbies?" I whispered to Mama.

"A food offering to the spirits."

Mama instructed everyone to hold hands and close our eyes.

"Time for the music," Mama said. "Push the button on the cassette player, child."

I pressed play. The muffled, synthesized sounds of violins exploded into a throbbing disco beat, followed by vocals, which Mama lip-synched. *"The fortune queen of New Orleans was brushing her cat in her black limousine . . . "*

I was no expert on traditional Romanian folk music, but I knew enough to know this wasn't that. "What is this, Mama?"

Mama, clearly irritated, whispered over the song. "Cher. Now keep quiet!"

When the song ended, we sat in silence for what seemed an eternity.

"The séance will now begin," Mama finally said. "Repeat after me, girls: *We summon the spirts of Cletus Bland III, Jack Capers, and Gonzalo Fernandez.*"

We repeated the chant: *"We summon the spirts of Cletus Bland III, Jack Capers, and Gonzalo Fernandez."*

Mama said the chant again, her voice higher pitched this time, almost like she was trilling.

We repeated the chant again.

And again.

And again.

"If you can hear us, spirits, rap once," said Mama.

There was a scratching sound. I opened my eyes.

Rhandi, visibly spooked, asked, "Did you hear that?"

"That's just Bitch," Mama said. "She wants in. Don't let her. She'll annoy the spirts with all that racket she makes."

After Bitch gave up and left, we began chanting again. "*We summon the spirts of Cletus Bland III, Jack Capers, and Gonzalo Fernandez.*" Rhandi and I continued chanting in our normal voices, but Mama's was like a screech now. Feral, animal-like. I've never ever heard her sound like that. Not even when she was telling a fortune to some sorority girl about her latest crush.

And then we heard it: a first rap, then a second, and, finally, a third.

All of us looked upward, into a sort of blurry, blue-gray mist. Then, the first image appeared: a human head. My mouth opened and I heard a gasp come out of it. For the image that appeared above me was undoubtedly the face of my most recent late husband, Gonzalo Fernandez. Next, the head of my other deceased husband—Jack Capers—appeared. Tears were streaming down my cheeks by the time I saw the head of Cletus Bland, my first husband, floating above the table.

Mama introduced herself to Gonzalo Fernandez and reminded Colonel Bland and Jack Capers that they had met before.

"I remember you, Velvet," husbands number one and two said in unison.

I was shaking. The sight of the three of them, together, jolted me. "I'm Tami," I said like an idiot, as if we'd never met.

"And I'm Rhandi Lee Taudrey, the boys' nanny."

The men nodded. A few moments passed. Then Colonel Bland asked, "Aren't you going to introduce us to that baby at your breast, Tami?"

"A naked cherub, sent from God," said Jack Capers, who, of the three, was the only man of true faith.

"The child suckles with unrivaled *élan*," Gonzalo Fernandez said.

I cradled the baby's head. "This is Maximo. He's your son, Gonzalo."

Gonzalo, lover of all things beautiful, choked back a tear. "My dream was to become a father. A dream denied—or so I thought. Hold him up, *amor*, so I can get a better look at him."

I pulled the baby away from my breast. Maximo cried.

"Turn him around, *amor,*" Gonzalo said.

I turned Maximo around, planted his feet on the table, and tilted him backward, at a forty-five-degree angle, so Gonzalo could examine his progeny from his nose to his toes.

Maximo, intrigued by the three faces floating above him, stopped crying.

Gonzalo smiled approvingly. "Oh my," he said, beaming as he surveyed the naked infant. "Maximo is his father's son. An apt name you gave him, I daresay."

Colonel Bland and Jack Capers frowned.

"There isn't a lot of time, child," Mama said to me. "Make your conversation."

I didn't know what to say. I put Maximo back on my breast, then stammered and looked down at the board in search of clues.

"Go on," Mama said as she moved the magnifying glass over various letters and numerals.

I looked up at my first husband. "Are you in pain, Cleet, wherever you are, after all those yellowjacket stings?"

"I'm at peace, Tami."

"You did the bravest thing for our family that anyone has ever done."

Cleet smiled serenely but did not reply.

I gazed up at the image of my second husband. "I want you to know, Jack, I honored your wishes. Gatuh Island is now a nature preserve. Nobody will ever develop it."

"I know."

I choked back the tears welling up in my eyes. "I'm sorry I killed you on our honeymoon, Jack."

"You didn't kill me, Tami. My heart did. It would have failed eventually. And there was no better time for that to happen than during the first and only time in my life I made sweet love, to my first and only wife."

Cleet and Gonzalo frowned this time.

I next directed my gaze to Gonzalo. "You died nobly," I said to deceased husband number three. You put my life above yours. You sacrificed yourself for me. I'll never forget that."

"It was my honor—and duty—to preserve a work of art like you, Tami," said Gonzalo.

My boys' fathers requested updates on their sons.

"Cleet IV is a guitar prodigy," I told his father. "He's obsessed with a Hungarian-Romani jazz guitarist these days, a fella named Gábor Szabó. Someone at The Juilliard School in New York saw him perform a Szabó tune on YouTube and invited our son to audition for a place at the school."

Cleet III said he was proud of Cleet IV. I then updated him on his daughter from his first marriage, Augusta, as well. I told him that she was a fine young woman about to graduate from West Point Military Academy. He was enormously pleased, of course.

To Jack Capers, my second husband, I said, "Little Jack

just took the blue ribbon in his age category at Nationals, the silat tournament they hold every year in San Diego. The world's leading silat instructor, a fella from Malaysia, was so impressed he invited Little Jack to Kuala Lumpur for one-on-one instruction."

Jack Capers beamed, as he too had been a black belt in silat.

To my third husband, I said, "It's too soon for me to tell you what Maximo's going to be good at, Gonzalo. All I can tell you is he loves his mama. I know I'm not supposed to say this, but he loves me even more than the other boys did at his age, though I never thought that could be possible. All he wants to do is suckle and stare up at me with those big black eyes. He'll nurse for three or four hours at a time. After I'm certain he's had his fill, I try to take him off me. But he doesn't like it one bit."

"I could tell the second I laid eyes on him that Maximo is a lover of women, an admirer of beauty, and endowed with a special gift," Gonzalo said. "You will not be the first woman to surrender to his disarming charm and gentility, of this I assure you, *amor*."

I didn't know what next to say. "Thanks for being with me, you three," I stammered. "I had a tough day."

My late husbands nodded sympathetically. "We know," they said in unison.

"I'm not a believer in self-pity, but I never felt so lonely as I do today. It dawned on me that there was no man in my life when I was a girl. No daddy to teach me. Or tickle me. Or protect me. Or rescue me from harm. And you three, whom I loved, each in your own special way, visited me only briefly. I realized today that I will have no man in my life in the years ahead, when my hair turns gray." I wiped a tear from my eye with my sleeve. "I'm sorry. I'm making this all about me. Tell me more about how you three are doing? What are your days like up there?"

"We may be on the other side, Tami," said Jack Capers, but we're on *your* side. And your daddy, wherever he is, is on *your* side, too."

"What do you mean, Jack? Have you met my daddy? Is he up there with you?"

I looked over at my mother, who was not pleased with the direction the conversation was taking.

"Thank you, spirits, for coming today," Mama said abruptly. "Tami's son needs to be put to bed. So, we'll sign off now."

"Maximo slept before the séance, Mama—and you know it. Cleet, Jack, Gonzalo: Don't leave! Tell me about my daddy. How do I locate him?" I pleaded.

Mama, grimacing, folded her arms across her chest.

"May I reveal an uncomfortable truth, Tami?" asked Cleet.

I looked at my mother. Fearful of denying a spirit's request, she nodded that I would be wise to let Cleet continue.

"I can't speak for the other men gathered here today," Cleet said, "but physical intimacy with a man —which you are very, *very* good at, Tami, let there be no misunderstanding about that—is not the same as *emotional* intimacy. You are clad in emotional armor. I don't presume to know anything about curses, but it seems to me that if you find your daddy, and forgive him, and allow him to love you, and love him back, perhaps it will heal your heart. Who knows, maybe your luck with men will improve."

"That ain't gonna happen," Mama said.

Cleet's likeness flickered.

"Wait, Cleet! Don't go. Where is he, Cleet? Where's my daddy?"

"You must locate him on your own," said Gonzalo.

"Lead me to him!" I begged.

"It's a bad idea, Tami! You don't want to talk to that joker. I'm warning you for the last time!" Mama said.

"How do I locate him?"

"The answer to your question is in here," said Jack Capers.

A vibrating Bible floated above the table.

"You know I don't know a word of scripture, Jack," I protested.

"You will go on a pilgrimage," Jack said.

"Where?"

"Seek the Canaanite in the valley," said Cleet.

"Who?"

"Read Genesis, 10:19," said Gonzalo.

"You will locate him," Cleet said. "You are resourceful. You are determined. You have grit. But you must now acquire a new skill: faith. You must have faith, Tami."

In unison, my husbands chanted:

"Have faith, Tami. Have faith, Tami. Have faith, Tami."

As they repeated the chant, their voices, and their images, slowly faded.

And then, at that moment, all three of Mama's battery-powered candles died.

The room went black.

Mama sparked her lighter. In the pale glow, I saw that her hands were shaking as she lit her cigarette. "Don't listen to them, child. Let sleeping dogs lie. He was nothing but trouble, your daddy was."

I rose, handed off Maximo to the nanny, and headed towards the door.

"Where you going, child?" Mama asked.

"To Bible study class."

Rusty Riddle was behind the bar at HOOCH, polishing a shot glass with a towel.

"I thought you never wanted to see me again?" he said when I slapped the Bible on the bar.

"It wasn't personal. You know that." I climbed onto a bar stool.

"So, you're taking my advice? Back in the saddle again, like a big girl?"

"Not exactly."

"What'll it be, bologna moonshine? You fancied that one the most, if I recall."

"Water. No ice. No fruit. And don't spike it with anything; I'll know."

"Comin' up."

He returned with the beverage.

"Rusty, I need you to interpret a Bible passage for me."

"I'm a devout atheist these days, sugar. You're better off getting your preaching from somebody else."

"I'm not looking to be preached at. It's a clue."

Rusty raised an eyebrow. "To what?"

"A Bible passage will lead me to my daddy."

He rolled his eyes. "Bullshit."

"Just help me, this once. And I won't bother you again."

"What if I *want* to be bothered again, Tami?"

"Will you help me or not?"

He smiled. "Only if you join me for some goat sliders. In honor of Jeremiah."

"Deal."

Rusty summoned the assistant manager to cover for him at the bar. He took a seat beside me. "Which passage?"

"Genesis, 10:19." I reached for the Bible.

"Don't bother." Rusty took a swig of water from my glass, swallowed, then recited the scripture. "'And the border of the Canaanites was from Sidon, as thou comest to Gerar, unto Gaza; as thou goest, unto Sodom, and Gomorrah, and Admah, and Zeboim, even unto Lasha.'"

"What does it mean?'

"Basically, the verse is defining the boundaries of the territory occupied by the Canaanites. God has a real estate deal in the works, unbeknownst to the Canaanites: He's about to give their land—what will soon become known as the Promised Land—to the people of Israel. The Israelites will show up in Canaan, conquer the Canaanites, then take possession of the place. The Canaanites will surrender to their fate and become the servants of God's chosen people. The wicked ones who resist—and there were some *very* naughty boys and girls in Sodom, Gomorrah, Admah and Zeboim—will be destroyed by fires sent down from heaven."

"So, this place, Canaan, is modern day Israel?"

"Maybe. God made the real estate deal of a lifetime, the ancient world's equivalent of the Louisiana Purchase. His chosen people got not only what today we call Israel, but the West

Bank and Gaza, Jordan, and the southern halves of Syria and Lebanon to boot."

I pried open the lid of my munitions box and retrieved the keys to my El Camino.

"What are you doing?" he asked.

"I'm leaving."

"Where?"

"To Canaan. To find my daddy."

"Now?"

"Yes."

"You promised to stay for sliders."

"Raincheck." I stood. "I can't wait one more minute."

"Yes, you can. Sit down. For Jeremiah Tibbs's sake."

I sat.

Rusty instructed the bartender to pour him a beer. "Let me get this straight," he said when the mug was placed before him. "Based on a Biblical passage you're dropping everything and going to Israel, the West Bank, Gaza, Jordan, Syria and Lebanon? To locate a man you've never met? Whose face you've never seen? Whose name you don't even know?"

"I've done it before." I told Rusty how I located three terrorists in Syria—Abdulaziz Farooq in Manbij, Radwan Bouazizi in Kobanî, and Hafez Al-Dimashqi, who was hiding beneath a butcher's shop in the town of al-Shaddadah.

"But on this mission, you won't have access to Uncle Sam's satellite footage and tracking technologies."

"When I set my mind to a task, I cannot be stopped."

"When I go after a woman, neither can I," Rusty said as he sipped his beer.

"You are one of the kindest persons I've ever met, Rusty Riddle. It's weird, the connection I feel towards you. Like I could drive cross county with you without a word ever being exchanged and feel totally comfortable with the silence. Or, after five hours of silence, say, 'I'm hungry, what do you say we stop for—'"

"—Korean barbeque," Rusty interjected.

He could tell by the look on my face that I was spooked. "How'd you know that's what I was going to say?"

"Maybe we're soulmates. And maybe you should stop fighting that."

"Rusty, I'd give anything to get to know you better, but—"

"—Same from my end."

"But until I find my daddy, I'm done with men. I just can't take the risk. My daddy will help me and sort out my issues. When I find him—and I *will* find him—I'm convinced he'll be able to help me break a curse I have lived under my entire life. A curse that has negatively affected my relationships with men. If and when that happens, you'll be the first person I call. Hopefully, you'll not have slipped away."

"I'll be waiting." He eyed me head to toe. "I'm not kidding, Tami."

I rose hastily. "I've got to go now."

As he leaned in and attempted to kiss me on the cheek, a flash of heat surged within my body. I rebuked him. "It's just not right."

I guzzled the pint of water before me in one gulp, as I was keen to douse the red-hot embers of friskiness glowing inside me. But I could not—and would not—surrender to his affections; this man was special, and I wasn't about to make him dead husband number four to Tami Vaduva.

"I'm sorry to bother you, General Loehr—I mean Director Loehr," I said as turned onto Interstate 64. "I still can't get used to calling you 'director.'"

"Call me whatever you wish, soldier. And despite the fact you're no longer under my command, I'm in the habit of taking your calls, Command Sergeant Major Vaduva. A habit not easily broken given the extraordinary work you've done protecting this great country of ours from enemies foreign and domestic."

I thanked the director for his praise as I aimed the El Camino eastward. "Sir, I was wondering—"

"—Does this mean that after rejecting a dozen appeals to come work for me at the Bureau you've come to your senses and changed your mind?" he interrupted.

"I need peace and quiet at this juncture in my life, sir. That wouldn't be in the cards if I was working at the Bureau of Alcohol, Tobacco, Firearms and Explosives."

"I need your unique set of skills—now more than ever, soldier. I've got five different cases I could use you on, starting today. Your firepower is wasted at a desk. You know it and I know it. You need to be in a combat zone, Command Sergeant Major Vaduva."

"I took the R.O.T.C. job because I needed to focus on my family, sir. On my Mama and my boys. I didn't have the greatest childhood, and I want to ensure my boys' is a good one."

"Send them to boarding school. Best thing that ever happened to me, and I thank my parents for it every day."

"I need to be present, sir."

Director Loehr snorted. "You can't tell me you like that job. What are you doing at that college? Something in H.R?"

"Something like that, sir."

"I've got Antifa anarchists in Oregon looking to burn down police stations; I've got white supremacists in Alabama building bombs; I've got illegal firearms dealers in Philly; I've got a beer wholesaler down in Florida who's cheated the United States Treasury out of tens of millions of tax dollars; and I've got an end-of-days cult leader holed up in the Allegheny Mountains, stockpiling guns and sulfur inside a compound."

"They sound like interesting assignments, sir. But not for me. Not at this stage of my life." I swerved to avoid a deer as it leapt out onto the highway. "Permission to speak freely, sir?"

"Granted."

"As difficult as these domestic matters will be to resolve, they've got to be easier than taking out bad guys across the Middle East, aren't they, sir? Seems to me there'd be plenty of talented law enforcement people here in the U.S. for you to lean on."

"You're wrong, soldier. Our government arms, equips and trains our fighting forces to win—by any means necessary—when deployed overseas. But on the domestic front, nobody's allowed to get hurt. Not civilians. Not the bad guys. All we do is stand on the bad guys' front lawns, month after month, and watch them. 'The bad guys have to make the first move,' I'm always told. 'No more Ruby Ridges!' the bureaucrats say. 'No more Wacos.' Like they expect us to knock on these thugs' front doors, hand them a Bundt cake, and get them to surrender peacefully."

I endured about five more minutes' ranting from Director Loehr—the new presidential administration, Congress, funding reauthorizations, bureaucrats, the news media—before he finally ran out of steam. I seized my opening. "I need a favor, sir."

"Name it, soldier."

I explained my predicament, how I had before telephoning Director Loehr just concluded a call with my boss at the college, who refused to grant me an emergency leave of absence to resolve an urgent family matter.

"One of your boys is in trouble?"

I told him they were thriving.

"Your mother, then? Velvet, right? Complications from the shooting down in Palm Beach?"

I explained that she was better than ever, like brand new after her surgeries.

"Then what's the problem?"

"It's my daddy, sir."

"I didn't think you had a daddy."

"Neither did I. Mama told me he was dead. But I have it on good authority that he may be alive. I have a lead on where he is. It's important I find him."

"You sure you want to, soldier?"

"We may reconcile. We may not. I am not starry-eyed, sir. But either way, I need closure before I start the next chapter of my life."

"And this boss of yours, he's being recalcitrant? What's this fella's name? I'll make some calls."

"It's a woman, sir." I furnished her name.

"Expect authorization within the hour. For as much leave as you need. Paid."

"That's kind of you, sir."

"I wish you well on your mission."

"I'm sorry I can't help you, sir."

The phone went dead.

8.

Across the villages and cities of the land once known as the Canaan Valley—from Beit Shean, to Megiddo, to Mehola, to Ma'aleh Ephraim, to Jericho—I searched for Daddy. I scoured teashops. I snuck onto farms. I visited hospitals, prisons, and brothels. I hung around tourist sites, reckoning Daddy might want some English-speakers to consort with. I descended upon various government agencies.

All to no avail.

I was driving my rental car through a particularly dusty, barren stretch of roadway when I realized I had not eaten in three days.

I pulled up to a roadside falafel stall in a place called Ghor es-Safi, situated between the governorates of Karak and Tafilah, near the southern shores of the Dead Sea. I adjusted my niqab, making sure none of me was visible other than black eyes peering through the letterbox opening. I approached the stall humbly, mindful that I was an unaccompanied woman, an unusual sight in this part of the world.

The Jordanian falafel man wore a heavily stained *gallebaya*, the traditional long shirt, and a white turban. Initially, he was rude to me. He was certain, I reckoned, that I was a prostitute, or a woman who had otherwise shamed her family and was on the run. After I greeted him, I turned on the tears. "I am distraught," I said in Arabic. "My husband, he is missing. Lost for six days now. Have you seen him?" I described a plump, round-headed, ill-tempered man with five days' worth of stubble on him. As expected, the falafel man said I was describing his previous hundred male customers.

In an intentional act of deception, I swayed dramatically, explaining that the smell of the food made me dizzy. I had been so concerned about finding my husband that I had simply forgotten to eat. Would the falafel man make for me a hearty feast? I had money, I told him. He agreed.

As he prepared the food, I consulted my map. I was somewhere near Lot's cave. I asked the falafel man if knew about it or had been there. He did not, he said, as he uncovered two large metal bowls, one with chopped eggplant and one with the light green falafel mix. As he formed the falafel balls and dropped a half dozen of them into the hot oil, I realized we were not far from the ancient cities of Sodom and Gomorrah. I pulled up the ancient site on my phone, hoping I might be able to tour the ruins. It was now home to something called "Dead Sea Works"—an industrial site where salt was harvested from the Dead Sea.

The falafel man plucked the balls from the oil and replaced them with eggplant. While the eggplant sizzled, he chopped tomatoes and cucumber in uniform squares. I attempted to engage him in conversation, but he had no interest in conversing with me—just like every person I had encountered since I landed in the region.

It was silent as he laid out three rounds of pita bread and put two falafel balls and a few bits of eggplant, tomato, and cucumber cubes in each before wrapping the food in newspaper.

After I paid, I took a seat at one of the three "tables" nearby, which consisted of one big rock surrounded by a few smaller rocks to sit on. As I chewed, I contemplated what I was about to do next. I was overcome by shame: I had never traded my affections with men for personal gain. Ever. Not for diamonds or furs, nor for promotions or money. To be sure, I had had my share of intimate encounters with men. But all I wanted in return was True Love. Nothing more, nothing less. I never used a man in my life—not once—unless it was to extract information that would save American lives.

Nonetheless, I took a deep breath and dialed the number.

"Well, this is a welcome surprise," Rusty Riddle said. You said you wouldn't be in touch with me ever again the first time we met. Then you reversed yourself and said you'd get in touch if you found your daddy. You must really be the legend people say you are you if you found him after only three days in the Holy Land."

"I'm no biblical expert, Rusty. I'm a military expert. Tell me to find a one-eyed mullah hiding in a cave in Afghanistan, and I'll find him. And bring him out, dead or alive. But I'm over here looking for a faceless West Virginian in a land of Arabs and Jews. I don't know what his job is, or if he even has a job. My daddy could be as young as fifty and as old as one hundred. When I track men here, my nose is trained for terrorists, not old hillbillies."

A rusted-out 1971 Mercedes-Benz 200 sedan rolled up. It was one of those urine-colored numbers prevalent in the region, usually as taxis. A portrait of Saddam Hussein was etched onto the rear windshield.

"You'll never find him."

"Yes, I will," I said as a traditionally dressed man in a red and white *kuffyeh* and ankle-length *thawb* put on a pair of oversized sunglasses as he stepped out of the car. For some reason, I couldn't take my eyes off him, despite the fact that, as he approached the falafel-vendor, he pressed his index finger against his right nostril, and with a fierce snort ejaculated a stream of snot from his nose.

"Where are you now?" Rusty asked.

"Just east of the Dead Sea, in Jordan, not far from the Israeli border." I hated myself for what I was about to say. "I have a question."

"Shoot."

"Were you serious when you said you'd like to really get to know me?"

"Yes."

I couldn't get the next series of words to come out.

"You still there, Tami?"

"I'm still here." I stared at my food, not knowing what next to say.

"Is there something you want to ask me, Tami?"

"Rusty, what if I told you I'd like to get to know you in the Biblical way?"

"I'd say, 'Praise Jesus!' darlin'."

"But what if I told you there's a catch?"

"Name it!"

"You have to come over here and help me find Daddy. I'm out of my depth with this Bible stuff. I'm running in circles."

"Those terms suit me."

"What if I told you there's a second condition?"

"Go on."

"We've got to find Daddy before you can take me. No Daddy, no me."

"Tami, I'll look under every rock, ruin, salt pile, sand dune, or whatever. But first, I'd like to ask you a question."

I paused. "Go on."

"You know damn well I'd help you without any kind of trade. Not that I'm complaining about the terms. What's this really about?"

I wasn't about to tell him about the way my heart crackled like a mosquito-zapping lamp every time I thought of him. I didn't even like to think about it myself. Or that despite having voiced my concerns about my family curse having something to do with Jeremiah's death, I was actually fairly certain it didn't. I had had lots of goes with lots of fellas who had lived to tell about it. But Jeremiah's accident did remind me just how dangerous loving me could be. Especially if I loved back. "Pack up your gear and get to the Greenbrier Valley Airport. Be there in ninety minutes. There'll be a chartered plane waiting for you."

There was a long moment of silence on the other end of the line. Finally, Rusty spoke. "Just one thing," he said.

I felt my stomach drop.

"I want more from you than just a go."

"Oh?"

"I want you to promise that you'll give *us* a try. A real one. A proper romance. One that may or may not end in marriage. I'm done fooling around. I'm ready. I knew it the moment I met you."

"I'm not; I'm a three-time widow."

"I want kids."

"I've already got four."

"Who is the fourth? I only know about your boys."

"I have an adult step-daughter, Augusta, from my marriage to Colonel Cletus Bland, my first husband."

"I want a brood of kids, *Inshallah.*'"

"'If God wills it'? I thought you didn't believe in God?"

"I don't. But nobody's an atheist in a foxhole, darlin'. Would you ever consider it again? Having kids? Having *me*?"

That he even had to ask the question was absurd. Would I consider a U.S. military veteran who wore a tobacco-colored leather cowboy hat perfectly and looked like he just rode out of the Utah desert on a fine Quarter Horse? In a heartbeat—were it not for my curse with men. But I wasn't about to tell him that. "Right now, my top priority is to find my daddy. I told you that already, Rusty."

"Then your answer is no?"

"No. My answer is *not* no. But it's not yes, either. At least not now."

"At some point you're going to have to get back in the saddle again," he said.

"I'd like that very much," I said. And I meant it.

"In the saddle with me?"

"I just don't want to lead you on, Rusty."

"Just a shot, Tami. That's all I'm asking."

9.

After I chartered Rusty's flight, I stared blankly at the two maps before me, an ancient map with ancient city names and a modern one, which included highway routes and updated city names. I was trying to imagine what my daddy could be doing in those modern-day places. What skills would a man born and raised in McDowell County, West Virginia, have to offer in this part of the world? Were they short of men who knew how to drag a doe with a stick, or organize mega mud truck races? I chewed a wad of falafel as I read about the ancient city of Lasha, a city famous, in Biblical times, for its thermal springs. Called Callirrhoe today, the pictures on my phone revealed nothing but a big pile of rubble. Archeologists, over the span of decades, had picked the places clean. The cities of Admah and Zeboim—also in the Canaan Valley—were equally desolate.

At the falafel stand, the snot-shooting customer who had rolled up in the Mercedes argued over prices with the owner. The falafel man, visibly enraged, but clearly intimidated and reluctant to get into a fight, agreed to his customer's terms and served the man his food—then promptly packed up his gear, loaded it into his truck, and left.

I returned to my phone: Only two images of the ancient

city of Gerar popped up, both of poppy fields; not a human in sight.

From the rock behind me, the customer unwrapped his meal, bit into it, and chewed loudly, lips smacking as he gorged on his lunch. Good thing I had scarfed down all my food, as my appetite would have been diminished.

I resumed my investigations. The ancient city of Sidon, the third largest city in Lebanon, where I would rendezvous with Rusty the next day, looked most promising. As I scrolled through pictures of crusaders' castles, the man behind me belched, then began punching numbers on his phone.

When, for the first time, I actually listened to him speak, the voice made the hair on the back of my neck stand up. Without the growl of anger he had used in his argument with the falafel stand owner, his voice was unmistakable. His was the brittle, but casual, voice of death.

A decade previous, one of my comrades in Afghanistan, Captain Delmar Jorn, a dentist attached to DENCOM—the U.S. Army Dental Command—was kidnapped and brought to a terrorist's hideout, a cave in Sari Pul Provence. Inside was terrorist Waheed Yousufzai, who required emergency dental care.

I never met Waheed Yousufzai in person. Nor did I ever see his face, as it was covered when I watched him on video—moments before he repaid the dentist's kindness by executing him on live television. But I remembered every word of the five-minute diatribe Waheed Yousufzai issued against "The Great Satan, America." All of it delivered with the same even tone he was exhibiting on the phone now. He could get more riled up about falafel prices than the murder of man who had done nothing but help him. The churn in my stomach returned as I recalled seeing him in that video, conversing in a high-pitched, almost birdlike Arabic, spittle flying out of his mouth in every direction, like buckshot. For Waheed Yousufzai had a horrendous—and unmistakable—lisp.

I rose and squared my shoulders. My chest inflated. I gathered my trash and headed towards my car, careful to avoid eye contact. He took no notice of me, engaged as he was in yet another belligerent exchange, most likely with a pimply teenage suicide bomber. Quietly, I released the hood of my car, loosened the timing belt, and re-secured the hood. But I consciously made a racket as I entered my car, making certain he heard the car door slam. I inserted the key and made about a half dozen attempts to turn the engine over. By the third time he turned and looked in my direction, I could tell the noise was irritating him.

Phase one of my mission was accomplished.

After three more attempts to start my car, he terminated his call and stomped over towards my vehicle, knocking hard on my window. I lowered it. He interrogated me for about five minutes, wanting to know if I was a prostitute, scolding me for being unaccompanied, looking at the backseat of my car for luggage or other evidence that I had fled my husband. I explained I wasn't running from him, but *to* him. My husband was missing, I said, turning on the waterworks. And now my car was broken down, I complained. The battery light was blinking just before I pulled over, I told him. Was there any chance he might have jumper cables in his car? "I'll compensate you," I said.

"How?"

"I have money."

His nose twitched. "How much?" he asked.

I offered one hundred fifty dinars.

Spittle shot at me as he spoke: "You are a rich woman!" said Waheed Yousufzai. "I have boys working for me who will never see that much money in their lifetime. What does your husband do?"

I had never been more grateful to be wearing a niqab; at least the saliva he sprayed was absorbed by my face covering and not clinging to my cheeks. "Can I trust you?" I asked.

"No," he said with a titter. "But you must if you want my help."

I darted my eyes back and forth like I was nervous about someone overhearing us, despite the fact we were in the middle of nowhere. "He sells arms to rebels," I whispered. "In Syria. In Afghanistan. To Sunni insurgents in Iraq. He will reward you even more handsomely if you help me find him. I only have one hundred fifty dinars with me. He'll give you five thousand, or more, if you help me locate him."

He asked my husband's name.

I invented one.

"I don't know him."

"No one does. This is why he is a success in a very dangerous—and for most people, brief—career."

He squinted his eyes at me and I wondered if I should turn on the waterworks again. He leaned in. "I want weapons, not money. And I don't negotiate with women. We'll start your car. And then I will help you find your husband."

He climbed in his Mercedes and rolled it up to my hood. After he retrieved the cables from the trunk, he popped his hood and mine.

I pretended to be helpless.

After the cables were hooked up, as energy my car didn't need was being transferred to its battery, we stood between the kissing cars. As awkward silences are common when two strangers assist one another roadside, I engaged him in small talk. "It is not my custom to complement men who are not my husband," I said.

"Nor should it become one," he said as he inserted his hand into his trouser pocket and made some sort of adjustment.

"But aside from helping me get out of this desolate place as dusk approaches, may I say that you have a fine set of teeth. It's remarkable that you still have them all. An uncommon sight in our region."

He smiled proudly, displaying his braces.

"My children wear braces, too," I continued. "One of the many blessings Allah has bestowed upon me—in addition to my four children—is to have a rich husband who has provided excellent dental care to our family."

"An American dentist put these on for me for free," he said, tapping his front teeth. "Gave me six fillings, too."

"That's first-rate dental work."

The proud smile morphed into a sad frown. With his index finger, he tapped the braces. "They won't come off."

"Why not? Orthodontists put braces on and take them off every day."

"The dentist who put them on . . . went out of business," he said.

I contained the rage boiling in my chest. "Surely you could visit another dentist," I said evenly.

"Not possible."

"You could see a non-American dentist? There are many good ones in Amman. Our family dentist, Dr. Khatib —"

"—Too dangerous."

"He trained in London, and—"

"—No!"

I moved in closer. Though I'd have preferred to have been doused in jasmine perfume, it's a no-no for Muslim women to smell alluring, unless they are being chaperoned by husbands or sons. Instead, I "accidentally" brushed the sleeve of my niqab against his. "I have an unusual request, sir. I have never seen a filling. My daughter, Nahla, has to get one next month. She is the first member of our family to require one. Might it be possible for me to see one of yours?

"Why?"

"I promise not to touch it. I just want to see what it looks like. Was it painful, when they filled it?"

Waheed Yousufzai mumbled something about the noise being worse than the pain as he tilted his head back and opened his mouth, but I couldn't understand him, as it is hard to understand people who speak with their mouth open, as every dentist knows. "Can I trouble you to open wider?"

He opened wider.

"Just a little further?"

He tilted his head back further, his eyes trained on the clouds above.

"Nahla wants gold for her fillings, but the dentist says silver is preferable," I said as I reached behind me and disconnected the jumper cable from the battery. "Gold is far more attractive. Especially since the silver they use isn't even pure silver; it's an alloy composed of silver, tin, and copper," I said as I jammed the live jumper cable into his mouth and clamped it against the top row of metal braces.

Sandwiched between the two cars, he could not escape.

About three seconds—and one thousand amps—later, he slumped backward, his head landing on the engine block. Little puffs of smoke floated out of his mouth. Despite the fact that he was undeniably dead, I let the motor continue to idle after his red-checkered *kuffyeh* got caught in the fanbelt. His head swirled in a rapid, circular motion, slamming into the engine block every few seconds. The stench of dead, burnt flesh never smelled so good.

I separated Waheed Yousufzai and his jumper cables from my car, hopped in, and aimed the vehicle in the direction of Sodom and Gomorrah.

10.

The next day, after I arrived in Lebanon, Rusty Riddle and I visited the ancient Sidon Synagogue. Built in 833, the synagogue was dilapidated and people-scarce, as many local Jews fled Sidon after the Lebanese Civil War began in 1975. No clues were offered there. Nor were they at the many mosques, Evangelical Christian Alliance Churches, Maronite Christian churches and Greek Orthodox churches we visited, including Nicholas Cathedral, where Saints Peter and Paul, whom I had heard of despite not having ever been much of a churchgoer, once met. We even went to someplace called the Eshmun Temple, which predated the Christian era by some twenty-five hundred years.

We interviewed clergymen; we inspected texts; we attempted to decode artwork and icons; we interviewed congregants. But to no avail: No clues pointed us in the direction of Daddy.

Sweat-soaked, our faces as moist as glazed pigs, we walked through Sidon, along the Mediterranean coast, in South Lebanon. “We’re near the Soap Museum,” I said, pointing down at my guidebook. “It’s about the history of the soap making.”

“I can’t think of anything less interesting,” said Rusty. “You really think your daddy is working in a soap museum?”

"We should look behind every door."

We went in and did what we always did: First, we surveyed the place, from end to end. As I was an expert in detecting the various ethnicities of the region—skin tone, eyes, build, comportment, dress, and so on—it was relatively easy for me to identify, and disqualify, natives of the Levant, be they Jewish, Christian, Arab and so on. Next, was there a male on the premises over fifty who looked like an American? During our brief time on the ground, we had questioned hundreds of American-looking men. The Irish, British and Canadians were promptly disqualified. The Americans we found were religious pilgrims, mostly. Devout Mormons, Catholics, Protestants, Evangelicals, and Seventh Day Adventists, usually roaming in herds. I listened for regional accents. Many Southerners were among the ranks, but none spoke with the distinct accent of West Virginia. My ears were tuned to the frequency of familiar slang: But I heard no one say, "Look out the 'winder' at that sunset." Or "Did you 'warsh' your hands and feet before entering the mosque?"

I had no illusions this search would be easy, given that I had no name for my daddy, nor did I have a photograph of him. "He's an American. He'll look like me, or at least look half like me," was all I could say.

The men I spoke to just shrugged and said they were sorry, but they couldn't help.

"All I need is a sign. Just one sign," I told Rusty.

After we left the soap museum, we walked through the Old Souk Walk, for about the tenth time. Dusk was upon us. "Are we ever going to eat?" Rusty asked as the aromas of roasting lamb and fresh-baked *manakish* were pulled, steaming, out of ancient ovens.

"We don't have time to sit down and take a meal. Pop in that sweets shop over there," I said, "and find something to tide you over."

While Rusty bought food, I interviewed passersby. Still no leads.

We resumed our trek through the winding stone pathway of the ancient market district, past the hookah-hawkers, spice vendors, and fruit stands. "Want one?" Rusty asked as he opened the sweets box. "It's called a *ma'amoul*—a little cookie filled with fruits, dates, walnuts, and pistachios."

"No. I want my daddy."

We passed a butcher's shop, where about five animal hearts, roughly the size of human heads, were suspended from J-hooks. "Cow hearts, I reckon," Rusty Riddle said.

"I doubt it. You won't find much cattle in these parts. More likely Nubian ibex."

"Never heard of that."

"Goat species, desert-dwellers. Got those big curvy ram horns." I told Rusty how, a few years prior, my C.O. sent me to al-Shaddadah, a town in Syria, to take out an ISIS leader named Hafez Al-Dimashqi. "Finding and killing him was the easy part," I told Rusty. "It was getting out of there that almost got me killed." I told Rusty how I hid inside a rubble of incinerated Iraqi Army Humvees, all of them captured by ISIS after the fall of the Mosul in 2014. They were scattered across the hard mud, those Humvees, piled up like corpses. Around four in the morning, several days in, a Nubian ibex wandered by. After I broke its neck, I carved it up and ate everything, raw, including its heart.

"I think I lost my appetite," Rusty said as he closed the lid on the box.

Yellow streetlamps flickered to life as dusk gave way to nightfall. We traversed the ancient alleyways in search of Daddy: we prowled the stone corridors of the Sidon Sea Castle, a fortress built by the Crusaders in the early 13th century; we investigated the "Caravanserai of the French," an ancient and now abandoned inn built in the seventeenth century to accommodate French merchants; we got lost inside the Qalaat Al Muizz, the "Castle of St. Louis," where we struck out yet again. Rusty said it was time to call it a night; we returned to the hotel.

Inside our room, Rusty collapsed onto his bed. As he lay there, he angled his nose towards the damp armpit of his denim shirt. "I've definitely gone native," he said. "Time for a shower." As he peeled off his grime-coated shirt and jeans, I occupied myself with the contents of the suitcase on my bed. But I stole a glance out of the corner of my eye, as his jeans fell to the floor and he stepped out of them. I snuck a second peek at his backside, when he walked towards the shower.

Within me, the embers of friskiness began once again to glow.

At the entrance to the bathroom, he suddenly turned—and caught me staring. "What are you looking at?" he asked as a grin swept widely across his face. I heard him turn on the shower.

He left the door open.

11.

The next morning, inside the hotel's restaurant, we were tearing into the big breakfast spread laid out before us—concrete-thick yogurt and olive oil, fried cheese, olives, zaatar, cucumbers, tomatoes, fresh mint leaves, Lebanese bread, honey, and tea—when Rusty said, "Usually women who gorge at breakfast are coming off a night of wild sex. If this is what you eat after you shut a guy down, how much do you devour after you've done the nasty?"

"Sorry," was all I could muster.

"When I caught you looking at me on my way into the shower, I reckoned it was an invitation."

The memory of his muscular backside occupied my mind. "I shouldn't have done that," I said as I picked up my phone.

"You check your phone every five minutes."

"I'm waiting for a reply."

"Your nanny?"

"No. The boys are in good hands with Rhandi. I've got about five gallons of pumped breast milk in the freezer for Maximo, so he won't starve."

"Then why the obsession with the phone?"

"I'm waiting to hear from my old boss. But he hasn't replied, which is unlike him."

Rusty poured me, and then himself, more tea. "Where's our wild goose chase taking us today?"

I listed our destinations. "Maybe he'll turn up."

"No, he won't."

"I don't give up. Ever."

"So, I've discovered," Rusty said on his way to the latrine.

I sat there picking at my fried cheese, thinking about my mission. A mission—if accomplished—that would change my life and the lives of my children, making it possible for me to love again. Make a life and a home with a man. Break the curse that had bedeviled the Vaduva women for centuries.

I took a sip of my tea, sweet and hot. It seared the back of my throat. "Daddy," I whispered, like a prayer.

My phone pinged, alerting me to a text message. Rusty Riddle's name appeared. I worried for a minute that something was wrong. Bad things were known to happen in men's rooms in the Levant. Had Rusty been jumped by a band of Arab teenagers, robbed, beaten up and left half dead? This had happened to a soldier I knew years before, when he was in Yemen. Was he balled up on the floor, the victim of food poisoning? I tapped the message icon and gasped, like some refined Southern Lady. For, inside the men's room, Rusty had taken a photo, a self-portrait, as it were—and a very intimate portrait at that. His appendage stood at attention. "First Sergeant Russell Riddle reporting for duty, ma'am," the text caption beneath the photo read.

I cupped the phone in my hand, shielding it from the waiter's view. The family at the next table looked at me suspiciously. I knew it was a mistake to reply. I should simply have ignored it. But he needed to get the message. "Stand down, soldier," I replied. I placed the phone on the table, screen-down. The phone pinged again. A second photo of Rusty Riddle's gear popped up on my screen. "Please stop," I said, despite the undeniable fact that I was becoming increasingly frisky.

"It's your turn," read his next message. "Send me a picture of your honey pot."

I looked over at the next table, where one of the children, an adolescent boy, was staring at me. He could have been my own Cleet IV. I reached past the olives, mint leaves, and bread, grabbing the wooden handle of the tiny metal sauce pot. I lifted it off its saucer and placed it before me. After I photographed the pot of honey, I texted it to Rusty. "Pull up your pants, soldier," my caption read. "We've got a mission to complete."

Outside the hotel, electrical wires crisscrossed the street at every angle, like those red-laser security systems in museums. Above the wires, clouds gathered. A few minutes later, after the rains began, we wandered into yet another house of worship.

When we exited, an hour later, the rain had stopped. Steam rose from the boulevard as we entered an old Ottoman sauna. After failing there, we walked through the gates of the British War Cemetery.

"I didn't know there was a British war cemetery in Lebanon," Rusty said.

"You're a United States Army veteran and you never learned about the British Mandate for Syria and the Lebanon, when they carved up the region after the First World War?"

"When I was here, I was too busy figuring out how not to get shot rather than study history," Rusty said.

We read the bronze placard about King George VI's

1941 campaign against the Vichy French troops, then walked through the rows in silence. The fallen British soldiers, practically boys, were struck down so young: WILLIAM GORE GIBBS, Gunner, Royal Artillery, 22 years old; ROBERT JOHN GREIG, Corporal, Royal Corps of Signals, 20 years old.

And then: ALISTAIR HENRY GRYMES, Driver, Seaforth Highlanders, 19 years old.

I stopped.

Rusty looked down at the tombstone. "You know this guy?"

I crouched down, running my fingers along the young man's name, like the act alone could tell me something.

"Gladys Grymes. My minder when I was a child. Remember that tombstone we saw in the cemetery behind the Pentecostal Tabernacle of the Holy Ghost's Testimony Church?"

"Yeah. So what?"

"I was sent to Canaan to find a clue. This is my sign. Daddy's got some connection to the Grymes family."

Rusty put his hand on my shoulder.

"That's nonsense. The fact that you have found two headstones—one in West Virginia, the other in Lebanon—with the same name sounds like a coincidence to me. Grymes, while not exactly as common as Smith or Johnson, isn't exactly Gajowszczyk either, Tami."

"Coincidences are never coincidences. They're signs. Gladys is the secret to finding my daddy."

Rusty raised his eyebrow. "How do you figure?"

"That's what I intend to figure out."

Rusty rubbed his eyes one-handed, with his thumb and index finger. "English people's names are on tombstones all over the world. You said as much: in Britain, Canada, Australia and all their former colonies—including the U.S."

"The Seaforth Highlanders weren't English; they were Scottish."

"What difference does it make if they were English versus Scottish?"

"Most West Virginians' origins are Scots-Irish—not English. There's a connection. I feel it."

I was still trying to connect the dots when my phone rang. "Good morning, General Loehr. I mean Director Loehr."

"You can call me general until the day I die, Command Sergeant Major Vaduva."

"Director, I know I've been pestering you with texts over the past few days, but I thought the news I have to deliver would be best conveyed by voice."

"If you're calling to say you want to come work for me, I'm delighted."

"It's not that, sir."

"Continue."

"A few days ago, I was in Jordan."

"And?"

"Made an un-authorized kill, sir."

"Who?"

"Waheed Yousufzai, the man who killed Delmar Jorn, inside that cave in Sari Pul Provence."

The director was silent. I reckoned I was in deep trouble. "My emotions got the better of me, sir. I am in the region as a tourist and civilian, not as a member of the United States Armed Forces. I felt I had an obligation to—"

"—Were there any witnesses?"

"None, sir."

"You're sure?"

"Certain, sir. It happened way down deep in the Jordan

Valley. Desolate place, on a roadside. I hadn't seen a car in either direction for two hours."

The director was silent again.

"Sir?"

I heard him swallow. "We'll keep this between us, for now."

"Yes, sir."

"Justice is delivered," he said matter-of-factly.

I thanked the director, relieved I was not about to be put up for a court martial.

He was about to hang up when I said, "I'm sorry to have to ask, but I've yet another favor to request of you, sir. It's small, but terribly important. It's related to the search for my father."

"I'm listening."

"I was wondering, sir: Can you ask someone on your staff to run a background check on a woman named Gladys Grymes. Resident of McDowell County, West Virginia. She's deceased."

A silence fell between us, and for a moment I thought we might have lost our connection. "Sir?"

"I know all about Gladys Grymes, soldier."

"Sir? I hope you don't mind my asking, but . . . *how*? She's an old country woman who has been dead for years. She was also my minder, when I was a child. I can't imagine she was any kind of security threat to the United States."

"She wasn't. But her son was—*and is*."

"Her son?"

"A man by the name of Euple Grymes."

I mouthed the name to myself. To my recollection, Gladys Grymes made no mention of a son, or husband, or any other family member, for that matter. She was just a spinster old lady—or so Mama told me.

"Where and when did you meet Gladys Grymes, Command Sergeant Major Vaduva?"

"When I was nine, sir. When my Mama and I were congregants at the Pentecostal Tabernacle of the Holy Ghost's Testimony Church, which is way deep down in McDowell County. It was a frightening time and place, sir, filled with snake-handlers and—"

"—I know all about that church, soldier. Euple Grymes was the pastor there."

My heart pounded. During my time at the church, Mama told me to keep away from the pastor; she said a "demon" lived inside him. I feared the pastor, whose Christian and surnames I never even learned, as he was addressed, always and by everybody, and without exception, simply as "Pastor."

I took a deep breath and grew very silent and still, like the boys behind computer terminals in Langley, seconds before a drone strike is green-lit. "Can you tell me, sir, based on the Bureau's investigation, if this Euple Grymes had any children?"

"Did he ever, soldier."

According to the people interviewed in McDowell County by ATF agents, Director Loehr explained, Euple Grymes was rumored to have sired, beginning at age twelve, at least twenty children, all of them out of wedlock, all from different women. Only ten of the alleged twenty had been located and interviewed. His progeny—the ones AFT could find—were still in the county and, frankly, had not fared too well: They were on disability, most of them, living in trailers, shacks, and barns in little unincorporated communities: Jolo, Elbert, Mohawk, Lex, Yerba, Skygusty.

I was afraid to ask the next question. "Sir, do you know where he is now?"

"Solider, I track his whereabouts down to exact latitude and longitude by the second. He's the cult leader we're in a stand-off with, up in Tucker County, in the Alleghany Mountains. And I'm losing patience with him, Command Sergeant Major Vaduva. He's got a cache of weapons, three hundred 'disciples,' and a rap sheet as long as your arm. I'm not going to let this joker continue to make a mockery of my agency and the American people."

"He's got three hundred people holed up in a cave, sir?"

"He's not in a cave. He's in a compound. And it's not in the mountains; it's at ground level, surrounded on all sides by mountains." The director explained the situation: Euple Grymes was holed up in what geologists called a muskeg, a bowl-shaped bog of some sort, a wetland that accumulates dense layers of peat and moss over decades, even centuries. Three hundred million years ago, the director continued, nature carved a hole in the middle of the mountain range. The way he described it made the place remind me of an appetizer idea great-grandmama Charlene once clipped out of *Woman's World* magazine and Scotch-taped on the fridge: a big round of rye bread that was hollowed out and filled with green goddess dip. Though she intended to make it someday, she never actually got around to it.

There was only one road into the compound, the director continued. From outside, approaching visitors had to ascend the range, circling their way up to the top before circling down, from the top of the mountain, into the basin. The logistics were a nightmare, he said. But the director was undeterred. "Mr. Grymes is on federal land, on a National Wildlife Refuge. And we're taking it back, soldier. Whether my agents have to descend by chopper or navigate the interior of the bowl like water swirling down a bathtub drain, one way or another we will recapture and secure the Canaan Valley."

It was like I had been punched in the stomach. "Did you say Canaan Valley, sir?"

"Affirmative, soldier."

"'Seek the Canaanite in the valley,'" I mumbled.

"Come again, soldier?"

I regained my composure. "It's something Cleet Bland implored me to do. At least in spirit." I abruptly stopped talking, mindful that the director might not have approved of me communing with my deceased husband at a recent séance.

I was still struggling to process it all.

"Command Sergeant Major Vaduva? Are you still there?"

"Please don't take him out, sir. Not yet," I pleaded in a low voice.

"Why?"

"Sir," I said, my voice quivering, "I think Euple Grymes is my daddy."

12.

Twenty-four hours later, I was inside the Ariel Rios Federal Building, in Washington, DC, standing in front of ATF Director Peter D. Loehr's desk.

The director tapped his fountain pen on its top, a habit of his when thinking. "There's no father listed on your birth certificate?"

"Affirmative, sir."

I wasn't sure how much information it was prudent to disclose to the director. When I was a child, after Mama raided the collections basket at the Pentecostal Tabernacle of the Holy Ghost's Testimony Church one time too many, and decided her fortunes would improve if we fled, she and I moved upstate, back to Thurmond. It was there she attempted to enroll me in school—for the first time. The principal said he'd need to see a copy of my birth certificate. I didn't have one. The principal told Mama tough luck: no birth certificate, no enrollment. So that evening, Mama, an expert forger, made me an official Luludja Vaduva birth certificate, which she rendered old looking, smearing it with cigarette ash and drizzles of Mountain Dew. In the paternity section of the document, it simply said: "Father Unknown." The next morning, she brought me back to the school, slammed the document down on the principal's desk, and I was enrolled.

"Command Sergeant Major Vaduva, the chances of Euple Grymes being a relation of yours are, in my estimation, slim. I mean no disrespect when I say that I've met your mother and, given my brief interactions with her, it was my distinct impression that she never suffered for a lack of male attention. She and Mr. Grymes may have overlapped at that church where he was pastor, but it seems to me likely she may have overlapped with other gentlemen around the same time. Not only at the same church, but likely in the broader community."

I couldn't deny that. But I also couldn't deny that both my instincts as a command sergeant major in the United States Army and as a woman trained in the psychic arts by my mother—and hers before her, and hers before her—were pointing me in the direction of Euple Grymes. "Director, I'm asking you to trust the gut of this soldier."

"I can't deny you've got the best instincts of any soldier ever to serve under my command. You want in on this? I'll eagerly accept your help—provided you don't let your emotions cloud your judgment."

"That's never happened before, sir; it isn't going to happen now. I'm going to help you get him, sir."

The director leaned back in his chair. "Dead or alive, soldier?"

"I'll bring him out alive, sir. With minimal conflict. Let me make an appeal to him. If we're kin. I'm part of him and he's of me."

Director Loehr opened the lap drawer and retrieved a cigar. He rose from his desk and walked over to the window. He unwrapped the cigar, clipped it, and put the unlit stogie in his mouth. He moistened its end as he gazed out the window.

In the distance was the dome of the United States Capitol. "See that female figure? That bronze statue standing atop the dome?"

I confirmed I did indeed see the statue of the lady.

"She depicts War and Peace."

"Yes, sir."

"Notice she's holding a sheathed sword in her right hand, and a laurel wreath and shield in her left."

"Right, sir."

"Have you ever heard the expression 'war is failure'?"

"No, sir."

"People only go to war because they failed. Diplomacy failed. Negotiations failed. Accommodations failed. Threats and cajoling failed. No one in this agency—or in this government—seeks to apply force. But if, as a last resort, we must, we will. I need to know that if we run out of options, *you* will."

"With all respect, Director Loehr, if ATF lets me communicate with my . . . with Euple Grymes directly, and tell my story, my way, on my terms, I feel confident we won't be forced to pursue that option."

He approached a wall of silver-framed photographs. All of them showed him shaking hands with V.I.P.s: presidents, senators, several chairmen of the Joint Chiefs of Staff, several SECDEF's, and more bearded-and-berobed sheiks and heads of Middle Eastern states than I could count. Finally, he turned to me and said, "You're dodging my question, Command Sergeant Major Vaduva. I need to know, right here and now, if you can pull the trigger."

"Sir, I—"

"—How many confirmed kills do you have under your belt, soldier?"

"One thousand four hundred sixty-one official confirmed kills, sir."

"And the unofficial kills?"

"One hundred eighty-nine, sir, if you include Waheed Yousufzai earlier this week."

"Do you know why you have more kills than anyone who ever served under my command?"

"I reckon because I'm a good shot, sir."

"Finding a kid with twenty-twenty vision and teaching him how to sight an enemy through a scope is a detail, soldier. An important detail, but at the end of the day, simply a detail. No, the reason you are the most highly decorated female in the history of the United States Army is because you are as cold-blooded on the inside as a reptile."

His comment stung. I was a loving person. I loved my husbands; I loved my boys and my Augusta, whom I no longer thought of as a step-daughter but as a daughter of my heart; I loved my mama. I loved my comrades, especially the fallen ones. When I killed, I was just doing my duty, plain and simple.

Director Loehr must have noticed the forlorn look on my face. "That's a compliment, soldier. You are the most emotionally-detached fighter I have ever been privileged to have under my command. You don't think. You don't blink. You simply *act*. You get the job done."

"Thank you, sir."

"But I worry that your time away from regular combat has softened you."

"Sir?"

"Maybe it's the grief you've endured after losing three husbands. Maybe it's motherhood. Maybe it's that you're stationed in a R.O.T.C. unit in West Virginia rather than in a tent in the desert."

"With all respect, sir, I didn't think or blink when I jammed a hot jumper cable in Waheed Yousufzai's mouth. I just did it and got the job done."

"When you reported his capture, do you remember what you said to me?"

I did.

"And that was . . . ?"

I bit down on my lip and swallowed hard. "'That my emotions got the better of me. That won't happen again, sir.'"

"If I deploy you on this assignment, you'll have to choose a side, soldier. And I need to know it's *my* side, your country's side—not Euple Grymes's side, even if he is your daddy."

For the first time in my military career, I worried that my loyalties were divided. "I know which side I'm on, sir," I said in a tone I feared was not very convincing.

The director stared forcefully at me. "You're sure."

"Certain, sir."

He yanked the phone from its cradle and buzzed his assistant. "Tell Rohrbach and his team to meet me in the conference room for a full briefing on Euple Grymes."

13.

Special Agent Warner Rohrbach and his team were waiting when the director and I arrived. Introductions were made, then the director promptly excused himself. I still can't remember the names or faces of the dozen men and women I met, as my eyes were fixed on the five-foot-by-five-foot monitor where, for the first time in my life, I saw a photograph of the man I believed to be my daddy.

I had expected him to look like the older men of downstate West Virginia: hunched, scrawny, scarred, meth-mouthed. But Euple Grymes's fate was not the fate of men who had endured the hardships imposed by life in Jolo, Elbert, Mohawk, Lex, Yerba, Skygusty and the other the grim hamlets of McDowell County: He had a full head of lavish black hair, with streaks of gray at the temples. Impossible to age-stamp, he hadn't a wrinkle on his face, and that face was constructed of high cheekbones, full lips, and full eyebrows—features similar to mine. The salt-and-pepper stubble on his cheeks made him look like a swashbuckling hillbilly pirate. But while I had my mother's brooding Romani eyes, this man had a pair of peepers as blue as sapphires. Ones that seemed to look right through you. I couldn't help but notice that the slight curl to his lip was seductive in the way of an accomplished lady's man: withholding of affection, mysterious, full of naughty humor.

The photo of Mr. Euple Grymes was recent, Special Agent Rohrbach said, shot by an ATF agent, using a telephoto lens. In the series of images that followed, he was photographed amongst the many outbuildings that comprised his Canaan Valley compound, chopping wood and performing other chores. His sculpted frame was unmistakably the result of a disciplined diet—and a serious physical fitness regimen.

"He looks like a bodybuilder," I said.

"Gymnastics," Special Agent Rohrbach said. "Take a look at these." A series of images of Daddy outdoors flickered across the screen: Daddy outside one of the dormitory buildings on a pommel horse; Daddy gripping still rings; Daddy on parallel bars behind the barn; Daddy executing a forward somersault with a half twist on a trampoline. He seemed to be flaunting his physique for the unseen photographers hiding up in the mountains: He was always shirtless, in a pair of tight jeans; the veins on his muscular arms were visible. His waist-to-hip ratio rivaled a high school football quarterback's. This was no pear- or apple-shaped older man with Low T.; his body was built for breeding—which perhaps explained the estimated twenty children he had sired.

A full dossier on Euple Grymes, from the beginning, was presented by Special Agent Ferneau, a young female agent. She clicked a remote and advanced the photos on the screen: "Euple Everett Grymes, only child of single mother Gladys Grymes, of Jacobs Fork, McDowell County, West Virginia; paternity unknown; no school records to show; first arrested, age eleven, on one count of profane swearing and intoxication in public, put on probation; arrested age twelve, for false calls to police, put on probation; arrested age fifteen, receipt of a stolen firearm, served three months at Emil J. Koob Juvenile Center, Vallscreek, West Virginia."

It took her twenty minutes more to get through the rap sheet: probation violations, contempt of court citations, arrests for failure to pay restitutions, stalking in violation of parole, dumping trash on the highway, several more arrests for profane swearing and intoxication in public, DUI—all this before his twenty-first birthday.

It was after his twenty-first birthday, Special Agent Ferneau continued, that the real trouble started, landing him in prison for longer stretches of time: Convictions included one for sexual assault and kidnapping: he had apparently picked up some triplets on their eighteenth birthday and filmed himself having sexual intercourse with the gals. Although word around town and from witnesses was that the triplets had been enthusiastic participants, two of them even throwing a party to screen the aforementioned film for their friends, the mother of these young women, apparently an ex-girlfriend of Mr. Gyrmes, was enraged and cajoled one of her daughters into filing charges. This resulted in his first stint in federal prison. After that, there were more illegal possession of firearms charges; unlawful purchase, receipt, or processing of distilled spirits; illegal possession of explosive materials or incendiary devices; and finally, the "sexual intrusion of a person who is mentally defective." In that case, Special Agent Ferneau reported, it was a former Miss West Virginia who had sustained head injuries after falling off a mechanical bull. It was noted that she has since recovered fully and was even Mr. Grymes' live-in girlfriend for a time after he got out of prison.

He had no official employment record whatsoever, except

for six-day period when he was eighteen and part of a state-sponsored rehabilitation program: He worked at the Swirli King in Beckley but was terminated for engaging in sexual congress with a minor inside his vehicle, a 1973 Gremlin, on the ice cream parlor's parking lot, in broad daylight, during the lunch rush.

The knot in my stomach grew tighter when it was disclosed to me that the fourteen-year-old girl Euple Grymes interfered with on that fateful day was none other than Luludja Vaduva.

Special Agent Ferneau could tell I was taken aback. *"You know* Luludja Vaduva, command sergeant major?"

"I do. And her name is pronounced 'Lulu-de-yuh'—not 'Lulu-jah.'"

"You have the same name, command sergeant major. Are you related?"

I blinked. "She's my Mama. She's also known by the name 'Velvet.'"

Special Agent Rohrbach glared at the young special agent. "Why didn't we know this?"

"I thoroughly interviewed her—Velvet—sir," Special Agent Ferneau said, defensively. She scrambled through the files on her desk and flipped open a folder. "Luludja Vaduva is the daughter of a woman also named Luludja Vaduva—a woman known as 'Marlene.' And Marlene is the daughter of another woman named Luludja Vaduva—a woman called 'Charlene'. But she—Velvet—made no mention of a daughter. Or any other children, for that matter."

"It's an unusual name," said Special Agent Rohrbach. "When you ran it, Command Sergeant Major Luludja Vaduva's name didn't pop up?"

Special Agent Ferneau flipped through more documents. The young woman's face was scarlet. "It did, sir. But it was one of about two dozen Luludja Vaduvas, all with differing addresses across the state. We ran a lot of them down, but all the addresses and social security numbers were fakes, all of them tied to efforts to double dip on government payouts."

That's my Mama, I thought to myself.

"And you didn't investigate those?"

"Sir, with respect, when I interviewed Ms. Vaduva, my job was to verify that she was indeed the woman named in the criminal action against Euple Grymes. I had no reason to believe she was lying when she said she had no children. So, once she confirmed that she was indeed the victim, I thought our work was done. Again, with respect, sir, I wasn't there to investigate her family tree. Nor was it within my remit to investigate what might be social security fraud perpetrated by Ms. Vaduva, or her many relatives across the state with the same surname. Although I did alert the Social Security Administration."

Special Agent Rohrbach, unable to mask his disappointment in his agent, cleared his throat. "Shall I have Special Agent Ferneau *continue,* Command Sergeant Major Vaduva?"

"Yes, sir," I said.

After the last of his convictions, the young ATF agent, her composure regained, said Euple Grymes found Jesus when he was serving time at the Louis H. Meinhardt Correctional Complex in Mount Olive. Daddy's cellmate, Cornelius Schlarb, converted him. They studied and recited scripture eighteen hours a day, for four years. Cornelius Schlarb, she continued, was a Pentecostal who hailed from a long line of snake-handlers scattered across Appalachia. Mr. Schlarb taught Daddy that dark art, albeit with rubber as opposed to real snakes. The plan was for Mr. Schlarb, upon his release, to become pastor at the Pentecostal Tabernacle of the Holy

Ghost's Testimony Church. And when Mr. Grymes's stretch at Mt. Olive was complete, the plan was for him to follow Mr. Schlarb down to McDowell County and become associate pastor.

But Cornelius Schlarb was poisoned three days before his release and died, in a still-unresolved crime, Special Agent Ferneau said. Once Euple Grymes got out, the special agent continued, he took Cornelius Schlarb's place as pastor.

It was a lot for me to take in—which I reckoned Special Agent Warner Rohrbach and his team recognized. A break was called.

As I looked at the timeline up on the screen, I surmised Euple Grymes arrived at the Pentecostal Tabernacle of the Holy Ghost's Testimony Church about a year before mama and I did.

I went to the front of the room and picked up the clicker that lay on the conference table. I found a photo of him, from that brief moment in time when our paths crossed. The young man in the photo—rattlers coiled around both arms—I recognized in only the vaguest sense. When I was living down in McDowell County as a girl, he had made us feel most unwelcomed at the church. "Pastor" refused to make eye contact with me the entire time I was there. Though Mama never indicated in any way that "Pastor" was my daddy—or that Gladys Grymes was my paternal grand-mama—she was adamant that I should curry their favor. "That man owes us money, child," Mama said on more than one occasion.

But "Pastor" was immune to my charms. He never spoke to me. Not once. He refused to apprentice me or Mama in the snake-handling arts, which I had to learn on my own. Raising me was delegated to others, too. Mama was all too happy to transfer parenting duties to Gladys Grymes while she focused on emptying Euple Grymes's pockets.

After the ATF team was reassembled, I was asked if I had any questions.

"So how did he wind up in that compound in the Canaan Valley, as the leader of a religious cult?" I asked.

Special Agent Rohrbach brought up images of the compound, shot from a variety of angles: overhead satellite, from mid-mountain, at ground level. "The next sequence of evidence photos and short videos, I am required to tell you, will feature images of nude adults. Do I have your permission to continue?"

"Show me the pictures."

About a dozen different photos depicting the same situation were displayed. In each image, a Chevy Tahoe with blacked-out windows was shown arriving in front of the main building. From the front passenger's side emerged a gorgeous young woman, who then opened the rear compartment of the vehicle, from which emerged a succession of passengers—attractive young men and women, Black, white, blonde, brunette, redhead. Each was fully dressed upon exiting the vehicle. From a second story window, Euple Grymes spoke through a bullhorn, issuing directives. Soon, each young adult disrobed. One item of apparel at a time—hoodies, t-shirts, belts, jeans, socks, sneakers, bras and underwear—was removed and strewn about the grounds, until all the individuals stood nude.

Another image of Daddy speaking through the bullhorn appeared. "What's Daddy saying?"

"They are being instructed to fig-leaf their genitalia with cupped hands and remain still. Next, he summons 'Bosley'."

"Bosley?" I asked.

"Bosley is the driver of the Tahoe," said Special Agent Rohrbach, "and from what we can piece together, Grymes's right-hand man. Or, rather, woman."

A series of Bosely images followed. She was older than the

young people by about a decade. And a standout in Daddy's world, for she was what could only be described as ugly. Not "unattractive," which would have been the more charitable description. But ugly. Unspeakably ugly. Her face was ruddy and manly. Her body lumpy. Her bright orange hair was concealed beneath a baseball cap. She wore, in each of the photos, baggy jeans and an oversized, knee-length yellow t-shirt with the Pennzoil motor oil logo emblazoned across the chest.

"The M.O. is to deploy the pretty girls as bait—to lure new members into the cult—then Bosley delivers them to the compound?"

The ATF officials confirmed my hunch.

"What else do we know about her?"

"First, she's West Virginian. We picked up her voice on a boom mic. Definitely local, based on the accent. Second, she has some training in accounting, and appears to be the chief financial officer, for lack of a better term, for Grymes's operation. We've picked up conversations between her and Grymes. She uses terms like 'assets' and 'capital projects,' and 'lease-purchase agreements' for equipment brought to the compound."

"If she's a CPA she has to be registered somewhere, doesn't she?"

Special Agent Rohrbach shook his head. "There are no Bosleys registered—in West Virginia or anywhere else—that match her description. Bosley, in fact, may be a code name, or a nickname. And what makes this all the more remarkable is that she has a sideline business of her own, one she did before she teamed up with Grymes, doing the books for two dozen or so little mom-and-pop businesses in Beckley and Charleston—dry cleaners, restaurants, jewelry shops and the like. She's a ghost in those circles, too."

"You've interviewed the small-business owners?"

"No. Too risky. Instead, we've reviewed their tax filings. Discretely, of course. Bosley's name—and no other name, except for the owners'—is listed as the tax-preparer. She appears to be scrupulous about not leaving traces."

"These local shops hire a sex-trafficker from a cult to do their books?" I asked.

"It amazes me," said Special Agent Rohrbach. "People will hire anybody who walks in off the street to manage their books; they don't bother to conduct even the most basic background check. I can say this, though: none of her clients has ever leveled any allegations against her—and we've checked."

A new series of photos were displayed: parades of nude young adults entering the compound. Bosley, fully dressed, was always last in line. In each photo, she carried in her right hand a paper sack.

"What's in the bag?"

Special Agent Rohrbach instructed a colleague to zoom in on the image. "It's a Hardee's bag. In addition to delivering fresh recruits, she delivers lunch. She goes through the same Hardee's drive-thru and procures for Euple Grymes a Monster Double Thickburger. No fries. No beverage. Just a Monster Double Thickburger. Same order every time."

A photo of Bosley entering the compound appeared, followed by the door closing. "So what happens once all the young people go inside?"

"Are you familiar with the term 'conversion therapy,' sometimes referred to as 'reparative therapy,' Command Sergeant Major Vaduva?" asked Special Agent Rohrbach.

"No, sir."

"It is the pseudoscientific practice of trying to change an

individual's, usually a young adult's, sexual orientation—from homosexual to heterosexual—using psychological, physical, or spiritual interventions. It's especially popular among certain fundamentalist Christian sects, who view same-sex relations as abhorrent."

"Euple Grymes is some sort of counselor to gay youth?"

"No," said Special Agent Rohrbach. "To our knowledge, his focus is not on gay youth, but on straight youth. But he's applying the same principles to 'convert' the roughly three hundred young adults recruited into his compound for therapy. Most of the people inside are in their twenties."

"If not from gay to straight, then converting them from what to what, Special Agent Rohrbach?" I asked.

"From lustful and prolific fornicators into 'Prophets and Angels', Command Sergeant Major Vaduva." He cleared his throat again. "He takes in the 'wanton'—sex addicts, adulterers, prostitutes, porn addicts—you name it. Next, he 'cleanses' them. Gives them a fresh start. They come to him to be made wholesome, or so he claims. 'Before the Fall Ministries' it's called," said Special Agent Rohrbach.

"Do they all walk around naked? If so, I should think that'd make the young people lusty."

"They are naked only upon arrival. It's a symbolic casting off of the former self. The 'harlot's costume'—that might be a halter top or stiletto heels or what have you on the woman. The cocky young men shed their 'players' costumes'—the too-tight trousers that that leave little to the imagination, and so on. But once inside the compound," Special Agent Rohrbach continued, "most of the converts are made to wear white linen tunics. Some, according to our intelligence, are given haircuts that are 'more pleasing to the Lord,' whatever that means, while others—a small cadre of regularly visible cult members, all male, who work the grounds and do most of the heavy chores —are given your basic buzz cut. Once an individual's 'lust is conquered'—again, what that means exactly is unclear—phase one of the process is complete. And thus, begins phase two."

"Which is that, Special Agent Rohrbach?"

"A 'return to innocence,' a reverse-commute to the Garden of Eden, before the fall, before Adam and Eve ate the forbidden fruit."

"Are any of the disciples inside the compound minors?" I asked.

"No, which complicates matters for us. No children are endangered," a bald agent in the room chimed in. "Euple Grymes is quite familiar with the law in this regard and allows no one in who cannot prove their age conclusively."

My next thought was so unpleasant to contemplate it summoned bile from my stomach. I swallowed, then asked, "Is . . . Mr. Grymes . . . having sex with his disciples?"

"We don't know," Special Agent Rohrbach said. "What we *do* know is that apart from age, Euple Grymes is also particular about one other feature when it comes to his 'disciples.'"

"And what feature is that?"

"It would appear, at least according to our monitoring of Before the Fall Ministries, that the vast majority of Mr. Grymes' disciples are pleasing to the eye."

"You're saying he only allows highly attractive young men and women into the compound?"

"Generally, though there are a few outliers, as you could see with the Bosley woman. But those appear to be henchmen and henchwomen. Otherwise, everyone is well-groomed and well proportioned."

As much as I disapproved of the life the man who was very likely my daddy had led—and the perverted life he was in my view currently living—I didn't want to see him dead. "What's happening inside that compound is unseemly," I said, quoting a vocabulary word I had learned years before, when I was made to listen to language and diction podcasts in Charlottesville, Virginia. "But it sounds to me like these are adults engaged in consensual adult behavior. People who can leave anytime they want."

"Except they don't. *Ever*," said Special Agent Ferneau. "Since its start, only one person has ever gotten out of Before the Fall Ministries. She spent more than a year with a cult-deprogrammer and has been the source of what little we know regarding the cult's inner workings."

"Can I talk to her?"

"The forensic psychologist or the girl?"

"Both."

"Yes," Special Agent Ferneau said. "But I'm afraid you'll be wasting your time. The psychologist brought us little of value. And the girl has only a rudimentary recall of the events and experiences she witnessed while a cult member. Everyone inside the compound is brainwashed, mentally re-engineered. When she joined Before the Fall Ministries, at age nineteen, she was stripped of her former identity: Everyone inside is assigned a new moniker upon arrival. The men, who are referred to as 'brothers' are assigned ancient Biblical names: Brother Boaz, Brother Gad, Brother Phut, and so on. The women are referred to simply as 'Angels.' When the girl finally got out the Ministry, or rather, escaped with the help of her brother, a police officer, she had no idea of her previous surname, address, family history, schools attended, and so on. After that incident, security on the compound increased three-fold."

"I'm not a lawyer, sir," I said to Special Agent Rohrbach, "but it doesn't sound like kidnapping. I understand they're on federal land. But is squatting cause for a raid that might get people killed?"

Special Agent Rohrbach clicked the remote. "There's more." A satellite image of the compound appeared onscreen. He directed my attention to one of the out buildings. "They've got a ton or more of sulfur, Command Sergeant Major Vaduva."

"Sulfur?"

"They source it from Louisiana, from basins down on the Gulf Coast."

"I've never seen sulfur, only smelled it. Is it a liquid? A gas?"

The bald agent chimed in: "It's found beneath sediment. Sintered microcrystals. It's a brittle solid, with jagged formations. Pale yellow in color. Chunks about the size of a baseball. Tasteless, odorless, and insoluble in water." He saw the puzzled look on my face. "They're *burnable* rocks, Command Sergeant Major Vaduva."

"Slow burn, like charcoal? Or fast burn, like lighter fluid?"

"Both. Sulfur can be ignited by friction, static electricity, heat, sparks or flames. It slow burns—at first. The yellow solids melt; they break down into a blood-red goop, at which point, as the temperature climbs, it begins to emit a blue flame. Then, when it hits four hundred-fifty degrees Fahrenheit, the sintered rocks ignite or explode, emitting poisonous gasses: hydrogen sulfide, sulfur dioxide and sulfur trioxide."

Director Loehr was standing in the doorway. "Brimstone, Command Sergeant Major Vaduva," he said gravely. "Euple Grymes is preparing for 'End of Days.'"

15.

The next morning, I made the trek up, and then down, the Allegheny Mountains. It took a lot of convincing, but Director Loehr finally agreed to let me take my own car in, alone. I didn't want to roll into the Canaan Valley behind a caravan of M1 Abrams tanks. The El Camino, with its quiet electric engine, provided stealth. Until it didn't: Once I arrived in the basin, its bright yellow paintjob attracted notice.

After I brought my vehicle to a stop, I stepped out of the car and put my hands in the air.

Several windows in the main building opened. Rifles, dozens of them, were suddenly trained on me.

I took one step towards the main door. Three brawny young men, their thin white tunics leaving little to the imagination, cocked their weapons in unison. They didn't appear much older than twenty. I froze. While I had on countless occasions been forced to stare down the barrel of a gun, I found this unsettling. That a man who was my own flesh and blood could, in the name of God, teach a group of lost souls to train their guns on a stranger who had done nothing to provoke them nauseated me. It also made me ashamed. I got to wondering if Director Loehr was right after all: Perhaps I had gone soft.

"Hold it right here," the first young man, a tall one that

must've been six foot five, shouted. He had a strong West Virginia accent. "We've done nothing wrong and ain't hurting anybody in here."

"I believe you." I said as I began to advance.

"That's far enough!" a second young man, also tall, muscled, and local-sounding shouted. "Get back in your car, real slow, and go."

I folded my hands, prayer-style. It was a reflex developed during my time overseas, when confronting terrorists. I walked backwards, eyes fixed on the would-be shooters. When I reached the El Camino, I slowly, carefully climbed into its bed and stood up. "I want to speak to Euple Grymes," I shouted.

"Never heard of him," the second young man said.

"Yes, you have."

"We don't talk to ATF."

"I'm not ATF. I'm United States Army. I pointed to the insignia on my uniform."

"You're government!"

"Euple Grymes will want to talk to me."

No one replied.

"I'm his daughter. Tell him Tami Vaduva is here. His daughter with Velvet. Tell him that: Velvet Vaduva. Also tell him I'm the only advocate he's got on the outside. I'm the only person standing between him and a dozen tanks itching to come down that mountain and rain hellfire on this compound. Which you don't want to happen. Because you know none of you will come out alive. And I don't want that to happen, either, because my daddy is inside that building with you. I know you're listening, Daddy. Show yourself. Talk to me. It's Tami."

"You got snipers up in those hills!" one of the young men shouted.

I came down from the bed of the truck, keeping my hands well within sight, and approached the compound. "Nobody's going to shoot. I just want to talk to my daddy."

"He ain't here!"

"I know you can hear me, Daddy. I'm your baby. Don't pretend not to know me. The way you pretended not to know me when I was a girl and met you for the first time, when me and Mama came to live at the Pentecostal Tabernacle of the Holy Ghost's Testimony Church."

I inched forward.

"Stay right where you are!" one of the young men in the windows chimed in.

Everyone contemplated their next move in silence.

Finally, that guy leaned off to the side, his head out of sight. When he reappeared in the window, he said, "Take off that hat."

I removed my beret.

"Undo your hair."

I did. My long, black "wild and wonderful" mane cascaded onto my shoulders.

"Stand sideways."

I did.

From inside the compound, a gravelly voice, possibly female, declared: "She don't look like the pastor's daughter to me."

"She's got dark hair like him," the young man leaning out the window asserted.

"Shut up, Brother Boaz," the gravelly-voiced person said.

"It's Tami," I said.

"Lady, I don't care what your name is, or who you say you

are. You've got a uniform on, and you're gonna turn around and git," said Brother Boaz.

"Git!" several cult members began to shout in unison.

"I've got a deal for Euple Grymes," I shouted over their "gits."

"No deals," shouted yet another young man.

"Tell him that ATF knows all about the sulfur."

Inside the windows, several of the young men and women retreated from sight.

And then . . . that shock of black hair appeared in the window. It was Euple Grymes—Daddy!—in the flesh. I could feel the palms of my hands moistening, my heart rate increasing. He hoisted the bullhorn to his mouth. In a voice as even, sober and authoritative as the Chairman of the Joint Chiefs of Staff testifying before a hostile Congress, he said "Read the West Virginia Code, girl! We're not breaking laws here. We got exemptions to use fire for religious services."

"I don't want you to die, Daddy. But if you don't surrender, you will. I know the director of ATF. He's a decent man. He says—"

"—There's nobody in the government that's decent!" he shouted.

"I'm in the government, Daddy."

"I ain't your daddy!"

"You are. And you know it." I would not permit my emotions to overwhelm me. I got back on script. "The director says if you come out, there will be no violence. If you give up the sulfur, there will be no arrests. If you evacuate the federal land on which you're squatting, you'll get a slap on the wrist. He just wants this over. He doesn't want a standoff like Waco. Or Ruby Ridge. And I know you don't either."

Euple Grymes did not reply.

Maybe an appeal to emotion wasn't such a bad idea after all. "It's not too late for you and me to get to know each other, Daddy. You have three grandsons. Strong and handsome and talented grandsons. The oldest is a musical prodigy. He plays guitar. His name is Cletus."

"What kind of pussy name is that?"

I ignored the insult. "Your middle grandson, Little Jack, is a martial arts black belt. Your youngest grandson, Maximo, is just an infant. But I know he'll be a great man someday." I took another step forward. "Put down your arms, Daddy. Come out. Come to my home in Thurmond. Meet them. Love them."

"Pastor Grymes ain't going nowhere," the gravelly-voiced person shouted.

"You can meet Mama again, after all this time. I'm sure you have wondered how she turned out. She's more beautiful than ever, Daddy. Like a movie star."

One of the disciples pulled the lever on his lever action .30-30 Winchester. "Now get outta here! Else I'll shoot!"

"Daddy! I need you to talk to me. I'm living under a curse, and only you—"

I flinched as the bullet shattered the passenger window of my vehicle.

"That's your first warning," Brother Boaz shouted. It was followed by a second shot, which pierced the El Camino's rear quarter panel. "The third one goes through your leg!"

"Okay, Daddy, you win. I'll go now." I skulked over to the door of my vehicle. I looked up at the sky—at Director Loehr, who was watching the standoff from his office in Washington, via satellite—and mouthed, "I'm sorry, sir."

I entered the vehicle, turned over the engine, crept quietly across the basin, and slowly, shamefully, ascended the mountain.

16.

On the drive back to Thurmond, after a caravan of two dozen Harleys passed and the noise abated, I summoned the courage to call Director Loehr.

"I failed you, sir."

"Quite the contrary, soldier," he said enthusiastically. "Mission accomplished."

"Sir?"

"They discharged their weapons. Until now, Grymes and his disciples have exercised great restraint. We needed them to fire first, but they refused to be tempted into shooting. As always, you are my secret weapon, Command Sergeant Major Vaduva. You must have really got under his skin."

"That wasn't my intent, sir."

"I've already started the paperwork. The request for authorization to raid the compound is being drawn up now."

"Send me back in, sir. I'll persuade him to stand down."

"The horse is out of the barn, soldier. My request will be on the attorney general's desk first thing in the morning. Then the lawyers and the bureaucrats over at DOJ will pick it apart for three to five days. They'll move a few commas around in my memo, recommend substitute words for words that require no substitutes, just to say they weighed in. We'll oppose the nonsensical changes, just for the sake of fighting over issues with low stakes. They'll dig in. We'll pretend to be outraged, move some more commas around. It's the same playbook every time. Then, once we're aligned, the plan will be presented to the president."

"How long before you go in, sir?"

"Seven days, max."

"Sir, there's a week between now and then. Permission requested to go back into the Canaan Valley a second time and broker a peaceful solution."

"Permission denied, soldier. We started your way. We'll finish mine. Your work is done here. Go home now. Go back to your life and your job at the college. Tend to your boys and your mother. Leave this with us."

"But, sir, there's another way. If you'll just—"

The line went dead.

It was approaching eight-thirty p.m. when I loaded the boys' plates in the dishwasher. It was the first time I'd been home in almost two weeks. I was feeling sorry for myself, for failing at my job and for failing as a mother, relegating my duties to a nanny, which I swore I would never do.

Mama entered the room. She pointed to the broken window, over which several sheets of plastic garbage bags were crudely taped. The plastic rustled. Through an open slit on one side entered the evening breeze. "A bird got in the house while you were in Egypt—or wherever it was you went cavorting. A sparrow. Cleet got him. Lured the critter with a palm load of Cheez-Its crumbs, then wrapped his fingers around the bird.

Took him outside. Cleet opened his hands real slow, like a flower blooming. Let him go. He's a gentle boy, Cleet IV is, when he's not making a racket on that guitar."

I mumbled something along the lines of "That's nice, Mama," as she opened the refrigerator.

After procuring a can of pumpkin cheesecake dip, she turned to me and scowled. "What you so moody about?"

I threw the rag in the sink. "Guess who I met today—for the first time?"

Mama raised an eyebrow as she plunged a spoon into the can, but said nothing.

"My daddy."

"Your daddy's dead."

I heard thumping on the stairs. The basement door flew open. Cleet IV and Little Jack rushed into the kitchen. "Mama, take us out for ice cream," Little Jack pleaded.

"Not tonight, baby, Mama just got home."

"You got to go on adventures, Mama," said Cleet IV. "We've been cooped up here."

"Pleeeease?" Little Jack pleaded.

"C'mon, take us to the Swirli King," Cleet IV continued.

I protested, but the battle was lost before it began. "Tell Rhandi to get Maximo ready." The boys hooted. As I did not want to discuss the matter of my father in front of my boys, I was not keen to have Mama join us. Nonetheless, she was a member of the family, albeit a trying one, and I felt obliged to extend an invitation. "Mama, you want to come?" I asked half-heartedly.

Mama licked a spec of dip off her upper lip. "No. Bring me home one of them peanut butter sundaes. Extra whip cream. And sprinkles."

The boys ran to the basement to fetch Maximo and Rhandi. After I was certain they were out of earshot, I resumed the debriefing with Mama. "Daddy's very much alive, Mama. He's up in Tucker County, in the Canaan Valley."

"He's dead to me."

"I had to learn about him—his name, his life, and his life with you—from the director of the Bureau of Alcohol, Tobacco, Firearms and Explosives, in Washington, DC."

"And what name is that?"

"Grymes. Euple Grymes, Mama."

"Euple Grymes," Mama snorted. "In trouble again, is he? That ain't no surprise. That idiot couldn't steal a glance without getting caught and thrown in jail."

I told her what I had learned about Daddy's life, after he and Mama split up. She claimed to be uninterested. She requested no details, asked no questions. She just stood there in the kitchen, her arms folded across her new, ample breasts. But I could tell she was listening to my every word. After she had processed all I had to say, she gazed out the window. "Stay away from him, child," she mumbled.

I approached Mama. She didn't like being touched, much less hugged, so I simply laid a hand, very gently, on her shoulder. "I know he took advantage of you. It took everything within me not to cry when I heard that story, Mama. I'm sorry. Truly. It broke my heart when I heard what happened to you."

Mama jerked her shoulder out from under my hand.

"Took advantage of me? You mean like a rape?"

I nodded solemnly.

"That fool couldn't rape a chicken." She tossed her head back defiantly. "And with his looks didn't even need to try. He had a whole bunch of girls following him around every day, like groupies at an Ernest Tubb concert."

"And you were one of those girls, weren't you? Waiting. Hoping he'd notice you?"

Mama curled her lip up like she'd just sucked a lemon.

"What kind of nitwit you take me for?"

"Mama, I wasn't . . . "

"First of all, at that age, I didn't wait for nobody. I looked like a Gypsy version of Elizabeth Taylor, or so I was told. I had my own line of gentleman callers waiting for me wherever I went. And Euple Grymes was one of them." She inspected her fingernail. "Took advantage of me? He *wishes.* I got to him—and during his lunch shift, not when all the trashy girls showed up, after school. We had our little rendezvous—you didn't know I knew fancy French words, but I know a lot more than I let on—in his car, where I lifted his wallet, a half-pint of Virginia Gentleman whiskey, a Zippo lighter, a half-smoked joint, a pack of Juicy Fruit, a coupon for free fries at Burger King, and a Conway Twitty cassette. He wound up getting fired from his job at the Swirli King and thrown into jail. Me: I got baked, drunk, and fed."

"Mama, you were barely in high school!"

"So, sue me: I was a late bloomer. 'The Virgin Mary' your grandmamas Marlene and Charlene used to call me when they found out I was still a virgin in the eighth grade. Did you know that when I became a real woman, they got me a cigarillo and a box of Dunkin Donuts to celebrate? Not the plain ones neither. They bought me the jelly-filled kind."

Mama turned away. She never liked anyone to see her cry. "Sometimes I sure do miss them girls, despite all the trouble they caused."

"I miss them, too, Mama," I said. "I miss them, too."

Outside our cabin, the fireflies were just beginning to appear. The Northern red oaks, their branches swaying gently in the light summer breeze, shimmered beneath the full moon.

We approached the minivan, on whose windshield a buzzing cicada crawled. Little Jack stepped out of his rubber sandal, approached stealthily, and slapped the bug with his heel, splattering it.

"Why'd you do that?" Cleet IV protested.

"Why shouldn't I?"

"They're cool. A million insects, all of them singing in the same key. There's a composer in New Jersey, a clarinetist, who records duets with cicadas. His stuff is awesome. I'll show you a video in the car."

"I'd rather watch silat master Panuta Rahmawati throw a one-finger death punch," said Little Jack.

Cleet IV, Little Jack, Rhandi, Maximo and me piled into the minivan. After Maximo was secured, we commenced the journey into town.

I wasn't on the main road more than a minute, listening as the boys bickered about which ice cream offering at Swirli King was superior, when a pickup truck appeared in my rear-view mirror. It was not an uncommon sight on rural routes in Thurmond that time of night, but what was unnerving was that the vehicle's headlights were turned off.

The truck was riding on my bumper.

I slowed to a crawl, right-signaled, and rolled onto the shoulder.

"What are we doing, Mama?" Cleet IV asked.

"Got a speed demon behind me, baby. Just letting him pass."

When his vehicle disappeared at the bend, I resumed our journey. As I approached the bend, the truck was parked on the shoulder. Its driver was not visible as we passed.

Seconds later, the vehicle again appeared in my rearview mirror.

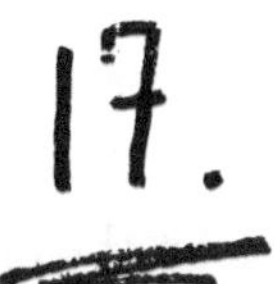

The vehicle tailed me into Beckley. I turned onto the lot at the Swirli King. The tailing vehicle did the same. I parked the minivan. The truck rolled into a parking space at the opposite end of the lot.

"Everybody stay put," I said as I sifted through my munitions box, past the diapers and baby bottle, and retrieved the Glock. "Lock the doors and don't come out until I say so."

I lowered myself to ground level, taking cover behind the minivan, and maneuvered towards the pickup. A bunch of teenagers, huddled outside the Swirli King, watched as I approached the vehicle, crouching. Upon reaching the passenger's side door, I smashed the window with the butt of the Glock and shouted, "Get out of the truck!"

Inside, a startled Rusty Riddle raised his hands.

"I could have shot you!" I said. "Don't *ever* stalk me again."

"I wasn't stalking you, Tami," he said, his eyes wide. "Well, okay," he said, "maybe a little. But lovingly, gently." He lowered his arms. "I just wanted to see you. You haven't been taking my calls. And I knew you wouldn't be pleased if I just showed up on your doorstep. So, I thought I'd hang around and, eventually, you'd go to the grocery store or something. My plan was to 'accidentally' run into you in the meat department at the

Food Lion, where we'd both reach for the last pack of hotdogs. Just before the fight was about to break out, I'd pretend to be shocked and say, 'Tami? Is that you? What are you doing here?'" He tipped his leather cowboy hat and said, "Sorry, I gave you a fright."

He leaned in to kiss me on the cheek.

I turned away.

"Look, I'm crazy about you, Tami. Are you not getting the message?"

"I'm getting the message loud and clear, Rusty. But you know the rules."

Forlorn Rusty removed his cowboy hat and traced his thumb along the crease.

I summoned my children and introduced Rusty Riddle to my crew as we entered the Swirli King. After the boys and Rhandi were installed in a booth, scooping up sundaes and biting the heads off dipped cones, I agreed to join Rusty for a walk outside, around the perimeter of the building. He insisted that he was entitled to hear the details of my encounter with Euple Grymes, classified information be damned, as I would not have located the old man without his help.

I told Rusty about Before the Fall Ministries.

"I bet the brainwashing is intense," Rusty said. "I witnessed it firsthand as a kid. Once the pastor and his helpers get their hooks into you, it can take a long time, sometimes decades, to be truly free. I was well into my twenties, years after breaking away from that world, and I was still under the church's spell. Felt like a haunting. You're lucky you didn't go inside, because there'd have been a risk you'd never come out. Or come out forever changed." He reached for my hand. "Don't ever let anybody get inside your head."

"That's not a risk."

We were well into our third lap around the building when the clang of a dumpster lid startled me. I reflexively looked in that direction, and my eyes became transfixed.

"Do you know her?" Rusty asked.

I pulled myself together. "Who?"

"That girl in the Swirli King uniform, the one standing next to the dumpster who just lit up a smoke."

I looked up at the girl, whom I hadn't even realized was there. "I wasn't paying any attention to her."

"What then?"

He must have seen the emptiness in my eyes.

"What is it, darlin'?"

I exhaled. "It appears I was conceived on this parking lot, probably next to that dumpster."

"Shut the front door!"

"In a 1973 AMC Gremlin." I told Rusty the story.

"And I thought being deposited, Moses-style, on the steps outside my adoptive parents' trailer in Big Isaac was a hard luck story," he said.

I wept.

He rubbed his thumb in the palm of my hand. "We can't control where we come from, but we can control where we go next," Rusty said.

A cluster of Harleys rolled onto the lot, circling the Swirli King like Indians surrounding a covered wagon. I pulled myself together. "I've got to get back to the boys."

Back inside the Swirli King, the boys—their faces and shirts caked with hot fudge, sprinkles, peanut dust, more sprinkles, and whipped cream—were indifferent to our absence. "They look like the crime scenes my mama used to clean up," Rusty said.

After Rhandi and I wiped the boys down, I told the fellas to wrap things up while I went to order Mama's dessert.

Rusty escorted me to the counter.

The woman who took my order said, "Still pretending you don't know me, Tami?"

"Huh?"

"When I was smoking my cig out back you acted like you didn't recognize me."

"I'm sorry," I said as I stared into her bright blue eyes. "My mind was elsewhere when we were out back." I studied her features. "You're Donna-Lynn Deneen," I said.

"Last time you saw me, a few years back, was inside the Southern Regional Jail. You pretended not to know me then, too."

"You had tattoos around your eyes then, didn't you?"

"Miniature black stars. But they're gone now."

"You look better without them. Your gorgeous eyes should occupy center stage."

"You pretended I was invisible."

"I knew exactly who you were when I saw you in that holding cell. I just couldn't say so."

"Didn't *want* to say so, you mean."

I wasn't interested in telling her the whole story—how I was ducking General Loehr, hiding out in Thurmond after becoming the widow of former U.S. Army Colonel Cletus Bland, III. Nor, I reckoned, would she have been interested. Instead, I simply said, "I was doing undercover security work back then—for the government," and left it at that. Whether she bought the explanation or not, she seemed to forgive me.

Rusty Riddle bristled. "You were in jail, Tami?"

"Director Loehr had me brought in. Trumped up charges. Just to scare me into coming back to work for him."

"Dream boss," Rusty Riddle said, rolling his eyes.

"Our relationship is complicated," I told him.

"When I met you in jail, you were pretending to be some sort of stuck-up high-society bitch," said Donna-Lynn.

"Tamsin Venables Bland was my married name. That's what I was using then. I didn't want anyone to know I was Tami Vaduva. I just hope you'll believe me when I say it wasn't personal. I remembered exactly who you were when I saw you. I remembered you from Fayette High. I knew you dated Scooter Skinner that summer between freshman and sophomore year."

"Ever see those idiots?" Donna-Lynn asked.

"Who?"

"Scooter Skinner and Ricky Ray Jeeter."

"We don't move in the same circles." I regretted using that phrase, but I couldn't take it back once it exited my mouth. I must have sounded like the snob she took me to be.

"Best thing that ever happened to my life was getting out of theirs," said Donna-Lynn. "It took long enough, but I'm all cleaned up."

I gave her the once over. "You look good." I meant it. The last time I saw her, in jail, she was gaunt and strung out, her hair stringy and unwashed. Now she looked robust. A little plump, but in a healthy way. To be sure, her hair wasn't done up in a style that would have attracted compliments in Palm Beach, but it was more stylish than any cut I had ever seen in Beckley. I complemented her on her skin, too, which was dewy. "Looks like you really turned your life around."

She couldn't mask her pride. "This isn't my real job. Just a way to pick up a little extra money. I got four kids now. My real job is being a personal stylist. I learned how to cut hair and do makeup."

"It shows," I said, genuinely impressed. I knew from experience that learning how to do hair and makeup was an art. It took time and moxie to get good at it.

"The judge told me if I didn't finish high school and learn a trade, he'd lock me up for good," she explained. "So, I got my GED certificate, then went to cosmetology school. They made me study how to contour eyebrows for a week. There are, like, twenty different shapes."

"Who knew?" said Rusty.

"I own a little salon a block from here. Though I don't know for how much longer. But I do makeovers for all the girls we knew from Fayette High, now that they're old and in their thirties. Haircuts, makeup. I sew, too. Got my own line of designer dresses. I've only made a few so far, but all of them sold out."

I congratulated her as the boys and Rhandi appeared at the counter.

"I could do you, if you want to pop in sometime," Donna-Lynn said.

The boys tugged at my arm. "C'mon, Mama!"

"A makeover's not in the cards," I said to Donna-Lynn. "I had the granddaddy of makeovers a few years back, when I lived in Charlottesville, Virginia. And again, when I moved to Palm Beach. But now I'm back to the old me. The real me. And I like the real me."

"Me too," said Rusty.

"It shows," Donna-Lynn said, smiling through bleached-white teeth. "You were always the prettiest girl at Fayette. Even prettier today."

I thanked her and we said our goodbyes.

Outside, on the parking lot, Rusty was applying pressure. "Come over to Lewisburg, for lunch."

"I have to work tomorrow."

"Then dinner."

"I need to make dinner for my boys."

"When can I see you?"

"After I rescue my Daddy!"

18.

The next morning, I was washing dishes when Mama entered the kitchen and handed me a jewelry box. "I got these for you."

"Thank you, but I already told you, Mama, I can dress myself!"

Mama looked away. She pursed her lips, then moped towards the living room, where she collapsed into her fluffy chair. She sat in silence for a minute or so, then switched on FOX News.

I felt like an ungrateful brat. She never knew how to mother me. Nor did she understand me or have any idea how to talk to me. The only way she knew how to connect with me—from the time I was a girl—was to gift me junk she had either bought or more likely shoplifted. "I'm sorry, Mama," I said as I walked in the living room. "Whatever is inside this box, I'm sure it's lovely. Let's open it up."

She kept her eyes fixed on the TV screen. "Don't do me no favors."

"I mean it. I've been wearing a uniform, or a disguise, for so many years now that I don't have my own personal style anymore—the way I did when I was in high school, when all the girls dressed like that girl in *The Dukes of Hazzard*."

Mama, still pouting, kept up the silent treatment.

"It was kind of you to think of me," I said.

Mama aimed the remote at the TV and turned up the volume.

I opened the box. "These are really fun," I said as I smiled artificially and removed one of the matching earrings from the box. I fastened the slim, dangling plastic tube to my left ear.

Icy Mama allowed herself, if only for a moment, to thaw. "They look real, don't they?" Mama said.

"I've never seen cigarette earrings before, Mama."

"Me neither. I was hoping they'd have some in the shape of Eve 120s. They'd have been longer and skinnier. A good dangle. Them shorties you got there look like Marlboros."

"The length is perfect. A lot of craftsmanship went into these," I lied as I plucked the second earring out of the box. "Great details. They could have made the tube all white, but they colored the filter tan and even put lipstick marks on it."

"Did you notice one has a red glow at the end, to make it look lit, and the other's got that long bit of ash. See how it's curving? That was smart of them. Looks real, like it'll drop off and land on your shoulder any minute."

"Right."

"Put 'em on, child."

I obliged Mama. There was a time, when I was a teenager, when I too probably would have thought the earrings were stylish. A time when my Mama's style informed—actually dominated—my own. A time when she dressed me head to toe, in one "alluring" ensemble after another. A time when she inked a zipper tattoo on my pelvis and put two "W" letters on my backside. It wasn't until years later, when I was living in Charlottesville, and introduced to the term "downmarket" by the yoga moms at Worthington Country Club, that I discovered girls like me were mocked and derided by high class people.

Mama was looking at me funny. "What's wrong?"

I reckon I must have looked like one of those eight-year-old boys you see in the New River Park public swimming pool. They're always down there, in the deep end, flailing and floundering and splashing and shrieking until, suddenly, their bodies freeze up. Their eyes go wide. And everybody knows exactly what's happening: they're peeing. Then, once relieved, just as suddenly, the flailing and floundering and splashing and shrieking resumes. Naturally, I wasn't peeing, but I was similarly distracted for a moment.

I rushed to Mama and threw my arms around her neck. "You're a genius, Mama!" I said, and rushed towards the door.

The strip mall was vacant. All the shops—the video-rental store, the shop that repaired fax machines, the fitness club for "curvy" women, the one-hour photo lab—were shuttered.

"What are you doing here?" Donna-Lynn Deneen asked when I burst into her salon.

"I've changed my mind. I need a makeover."

Donna-Lynn looked me up and down.

"When I offered you a makeover, it wasn't because you *need* one," she said as she folded an angora sweater. She laid the garment on the front table and smoothed it out with the palm of her hand. "You look better than any woman I've ever seen in my life, I swear to God. I guess I was just hoping you'd let me at least do your nails or something, so I could show you what I can do. I wanted to impress you, Tami."

"That's sweet of you to say, Donna-Lynn. And I have no doubt about what you can do. It's just that I didn't come here to look better, exactly. I want to look . . . different."

Donna-Lynn put her hand on her hip, defiantly, like she used to in High School. "I don't understand."

"You talked about the old-old me, the one you knew in high school. I'm thinking I want you to turn back time," I said. Mama, even though she hadn't intended to do so, had just provided me with the strategy to return to—and infiltrate—Euple Grymes's compound. He had seen me on only two occasions in his life: when I was a girl and the day before, as an adult woman in my thirties, clad in military attire. The latter was at a distance to boot. I was certain I could fool him on my next visit, if properly disguised, and gain entry into the compound. Of course, it was hardly my intention to share the motives for my makeover with Donna-Lynn, given that she very may well have heard of my Daddy's Before the Fall Ministry—or for all I knew, was friends with people trapped inside. I didn't think she was the type to tip them off or anything, but an innocent comment could put both her and me in danger.

"And if you do this for me," I told her. "You get first dibs on giving me the granddaddy of all makeovers in order to get me back to myself again. Head to toe."

"Alright!"

"And I'll tell everyone I know about what a wonderful stylist you are, too. Only there's one condition."

Donna-Lynn nodded fervently.

"This makeover—the one we're doing today—stays between you and me."

As I went looking for outfits and accessories, Donna-Lynn told me about her store. The woman who ran the court-mandated GED program in Beckley had taken a shine to Donna-Lynn, my former classmate told me. After troubled girls received their GEDs and job skills training, the program director and her husband, with money from their own pockets, paid for the girls to come to Donna-Lynn for cuts and makeovers and wardrobe tips, so they could present well on job interviews.

As I inspected the merchandise in the store, I feared my disapproval of the inventory went undisguised and adjusted my facial expression. Maybe I was just being overly self-conscious. But I knew I wasn't a part of her world anymore. And I had to wonder if she could smell that on me. I may not have fit in in Charlottesville or Paris or Palm Beach, but I had *been* to those places, and sat at grand tables, and mixed with fancy people, and learned (admittedly, after repeated practice) to pronounce words and phrases like *trompe l'oeil* and *L'esprit de l'escalier* and *élan*, which was the favorite word of my late third husband, Gonzalo Fernandez. Of course, I was determined, despite having inherited several fortunes, to remain "down to earth," to live simply, in an un-showy—or as they used to say in Charlottesville, "un-*shiny*" —fashion. But increasingly, I wondered if my pretentions to humility were not in fact pretentious themself, an expression of condescension.

"That's a Kasper," Donna-Lynn said, breaking the silence.

"What is?"

"A designer suit. It's vintage. From the nineteen eighties."

"Oh."

"Shoulder pads are coming back," added Donna-Lynn.

"I didn't know that." Despite being clad in couture dresses when I lived in Palm Beach, I still couldn't name a fashion designer. We needed to get down to business. I smiled and asked about all the services she offered.

"Haircuts, makeup, eyelashes, nails, body waxing, tanning, and fashion consulting," she said. "I'm like one of those stylists in Hollywood. I look at your skin tone, coloring, body type—stuff like that—and tell you what looks best on you."

"Go lock your front door, hang your 'closed' sign, and pull down the shade. We've got a lot of work to do, and I don't have a lot of time. Don't worry about lost sales. I'll make it worth your while."

"There aren't any sales to lose." Donna-Lynn said as she walked towards the front door and closed shop. "Where do you want to start, Tami?"

"Clothes."

Donna-Lynn instructed me to strip down to bra and underwear so she could start with a blank canvas, then add colors, textures, fabrics, and so on. She looked me up and down. "My God, you have six pack abs. And your boobs! They're fantastic. And real! You look better than any teenage girl I've ever known."

"I do a lot of P.T. Can we look at dresses first?"

Donna-Lynn flipped through the racks. "This is very nice," she said as she pulled a floral dress off the hanger. It's from Walmart. Like all their stuff, it's cut for big girls. But I can nip and tuck here and there and we can show off your rump and bust."

I studied the racks disapprovingly. "Everything I see in this shop—all your inventory—these are the makeover clothes you give to bad girls who want to be good. Girls who come here after the judge sends them here, right?"

"A lot of it is donated by professional women, secretaries, receptionists, girls like that."

"I don't want this stuff. I want the clothes the bad girls wore *before* their makeovers. Do you have anything like that in the shop?"

Donna-Lynn looked puzzled but said she did. In the back room. She had tried to resell them on eBay, she said, but had no takers. "I even tried to give them to Goodwill. But they didn't want them neither." She ushered me into the stockroom. There must have been three dozen Hefty bags piled against the wall. We sifted through them. The bags were filled with treasure: a sleeveless t-shirt with the words Daddy's Little Slut printed across the chest, mesh mini-dresses, fake leather corsets, sparkly ankle boots.

"Oh my," Donna-Lynn said after I tried on one garment after another. "You look like a very bad girl."

"Perfect," I cooed.

"Is this all for that handsome cowboy I saw you with at the Swirly King?"

"I'm afraid not."

"Oh," she said. I could tell she was wondering if Rusty might be available. "What's next?"

"Hair," I said.

"That's my specialty! I'm real good at it. Better than a lot of the gals at fancy salons in Charleston."

"Do you have any before and after look books of your court-mandated customers?"

"I've got hundreds of pictures," she said.

"Show me."

"I have to warn you, Tami, some of the before pictures are pretty scary."

"Good," I said as I flipped through the look books. "How about this one right here?"

It was a picture of a girl with dark, crimped hair and feather-like bangs.

"You sure you want that?" Donna-Lynn asked me.

I nodded and Donna-Lynn stepped back, folding her arms across her chest and squinting her eyes. She stretched out her arms and made her hands into the shape of a frame, presumably putting my face in it.

"Tami," she said, putting her arms down, finally. "I don't know why you want to do this. If it's not for a man, then maybe you're on a secret mission?" Donna-Lynn winked at me and smiled on the one side of her mouth. "But if you want to feel like the old-old you, but not exactly look recognizable, if you know what I mean, then the hair needs to go big. Hair changes our appearance more than anything else."

"Ok," I said.

"And you'll need to go blonde. I'm talkin' bombshell blonde."

I slumped and dropped the hair book onto Donna-Lynn's manicure table. "Not again."

"Again?"

"Oh, nothing," I said. "You do what you have to do."

After she bleached and arranged my hair, we turned to makeup.

"So, what's the look we're going for today?"

"Wanton."

"Huh?"

"Wanton."

I don't know what that word means, Tami."

"You do know what a slut is, right?"

"Sure."

"That's what I want to look like."

Donna-Lynn raised an eyebrow. "I just have to ask. Why?"

"I'm not at liberty to discuss it. But that's what I want."

"Okay, top secret it is," she said with a shrug. "The customer is always right."

"Show me your eyeshadow shades, please."

Donna-Lynn spread them out before me.

"I'm thinking a seventies shade, like something you'd see on a *Playboy* centerfold."

Donna-Lynn's face lit up. "Something Stevie Nicks: pale green or blue. Wait, I've got it: spearmint!"

"And tons of mascara."

When the eyes were done, Donna-Lynn stepped back and giggled. "You look like a porn star, only super pretty."

"That's exactly the look I'm going for. Now what about eyebrows? Should I go pencil-thin?"

Donna-Lynn put the mascara back in its case. She shook her head.

"Tami, I got one condition about this makeover."

"Go on," I said.

"I'll make you look as trashy as you want, but I'm not going to destroy your eyebrows. They're perfect. Just look at those arches." She gave me a hand mirror. "Who did those for you?"

I wasn't about to tell her a salon-owner in Palm Beach taught me how to sculpt them.

"The only women you see with those super-thin crescents are porn stars," she said. "The cheerleader who wanders into the men's locker room after the big game, and the next thing you know . . . "

"I've never watched that stuff," I said.

"The father of one of my kids was hooked on '70's smut. He made me watch the entire *Debbie Does Dallas* series over and over. Bought me a knock-off Dallas Cowboys Cheerleader outfit for my birthday one year, as if that wasn't a gift meant for him."

"If pencil-thin eyebrows are the way a porn star would look, then I want them."

"I'm not tweezing your eyebrows, Tami!" Donna-Lynn said. "But I will mess them up and shape them with a dark pencil. That'll make you look slutty alright, and it'll give the illusion of changing your facial structure somewhat. When I'm done with you, I won't even recognize you."

"Deal," I said, because I really did trust Donna-Lynn. What she lacked in exposure to style and taste, she made up for in skill.

After she was finished with makeup and eyebrows, including sculpting my lips into a shiny pink neon shape that looked like I was always sucking on a lollipop, I inquired about "off-the-books" procedures offered. "Can you do piercings?"

"I'm not supposed to. You have to be licensed to do that. But I do have lots of fake piercing type jewelry that looks totally real. Got 'em for noses and bellybuttons, eyebrows, even more private parts, if you know what I mean."

"I know exactly what you mean. But I'm afraid the kinds of people I'm going to be around in the near future will know the difference between the real thing and a fake."

"If you really want real piercings, maybe I can call someone I know? See, I'd do it, and I know how to—I did a lot of piercings for girls in the can—it's just that I can't afford to lose this shop, Tami. I'm two months' late on rent as it is, and my landlord keeps threatening to evict me. Though we both know he has no tenants to take my place."

I asked her how much rent she was behind on, and she told me. Then I retrieved my checkbook from my munitions box and wrote her a check. "Your rent is paid through the end of the year."

Donna- Lynn looked like she was about to cry. "I can't take this," she said as she set the check on the table.

"You can and you will. The service you are providing me—if we get it right—is worth all the money in the world to me."

Donna-Lynn blotted a tear from the corner of her eye with her pinky, the way I was taught to do when I lived in Charlottesville; it keeps the makeup from smearing.

"Swear you're not from the Department of Health?"

I made the Scout sign. "On my honor."

"What do you want pierced?"

"I should warn you that most of the piercings I require will be of an intimate nature."

Donna-Lynn put her hand on her hip. "I have pierced women in places I didn't even know existed."

~

When the piercing was complete, I asked, "What else can you do for me?"

"Tats. I mostly take them off these days. But I know how to put them on if you've got a design in mind. I can borrow a tattoo gun from my next-door neighbor. He's got great equipment, but he's a terrible tattoo artist. I will not do your face or your neck, however. That would be like drawing a Hitler mustache on a picture of Pamela Anderson."

"I've got my own tattoo man." I looked at my watch. "He'll be here in about an hour. No disrespect to you, Donna-Lynn, you're really good at this work, but I don't want anything permanent tattoo-wise. And my guy's a real artist. He's going to put tats on me with Sharpies, then distress them, so they look like they've been on me for years. But maybe you can offer some design suggestions."

"What do you mean by 'distressing'? Like smearing them up and stuff?"

I told her about Fabrizio, the Italian craftsman who painted *trompe l'oeils* for me at my homes in Palm Beach and Thurmond, and how he could blend colors to make anything look like it was old.

"I don't get you, Tami. The girls who come in here are distressed beyond belief. Their faces, their bodies, hell, even their souls, and especially their lives. They'd give anything to be new—to look the way you did when you walked through my door. I mean you're still beautiful and everything. Hotter than ever. But if truth be told, it's the kind of hot that would have all my exes panting on the floor with their eyes bugged out."

An hour later, I stood before a full-length mirror, transformed. I was wanton. I was trashy. I was slutty. "Donna-Lynn," I said, as I looked myself over, "That is exactly the look I was going for."

19.

I was at the grocery store, in the deli, reaching for a package of bologna, when the customer next to me snatched it out of the cooler before I could get to it.

I looked angrily up at Rusty Riddle, who was grinning. "I predicted this would happen."

"Not funny!" I said.

He stepped backward. "Show me your hair."

I removed my hot pink, White Trash Princess baseball cap and shook out my platinum hair.

"Holy shit, Tami. What have you done to yourself?"

"A reverse-makeover."

"What happened to your eyebrows?"

"They're sculpted with eyebrow gel and a black pencil. And why are you stalking me again? This time I'm bound to shoot."

"Not stalking you again, I swear. You blew past me on Robert Byrd Drive. You're pretty easy to spot. Not many people in Beckley tooling around these days in a restored electric El Camino pocked with bullet holes in the rear quarter panel." His disapproving eyes surveyed me head to toe. "*Why,* Tami?"

I seized the packet of bologna from Rusty's hand. "I'm going into that compound. Euple Grymes saw my face two days ago. So, I reckoned I'd get a new one and pay him another visit. Going in stealth this time."

He looked down at my belly, exposed between a pair of hip-hugging cut off jean shorts and fluorescent tube top.

"Those lightning bolt tattoos on each side of your abdomen are horrible. You permanently disfigured yourself for that man?"

"They're temporary, put on with Sharpies."

"Your hair: It's so . . . *not you*. But somehow—I can't believe I'm saying this—it's . . . *hot* . . . " He approached. "Can I touch it?" He ran his fingers through my hair. "You look like a . . . "

"Harlot?"

"Exactly. Yes. A harlot—who just ran screaming out of a burning meth lab."

"That's music to my ears."

He followed me into a grocery aisle. "You can't be serious about going in there."

As I loaded the cart with Maximo's diapers and wipes, I explained how I infiltrated a seamstresses' group in Ghazni Provence, when I was twenty-three, but had to look forty-three—and did, after I threw palm loads of sand into an electric fan trained on my face. I further elucidated him on my infiltrations of high society in Charlottesville, Charleston and Palm Beach. "I'm trained to blend in."

"A religious cult is different than a terrorist cell. You admitted as much to me when we were in Lebanon."

"Rusty, I believe that the man who runs Before the Fall Ministries is my daddy, and I'm bringing him out. Alive."

I was pushing my cart towards the checkout when he stood in front of it, blocking my progress. "Your boss, that director who now works for ATF, he approved sending you in there alone?"

I told Rusty Director Loehr didn't know about—or approve—my plans.

"Can't you get arrested or Court Martialed for interfering?"

"Sometimes it's better to ask for forgiveness rather than ask for permission."

"Tami," he said, wrapping his meaty paw of a hand around my forearm, "what if you *don't* get out alive?"

We locked eyes. "I always get out alive."

He put his hands on my shoulders and pursed his full lips. "Then I'm coming in with you."

"I work alone."

"You seem to forget that I'm a veteran, too."

"I honor you for your service."

"I am a proud atheist, Tami. I told you that. But there is one thing I do believe: the wiliest, sneakiest pastors are pure evil. They spin words; they wind up emotions. Rather than pretend to be God—which is what megalomaniacs do—they claim to speak *for* him. They are deceivers, those pastors. Once they trick you with scripture, no amount of willpower can undo the spell. I know scripture. I know their tricks. You don't. Let me help you. Because for God's sake, Tami, if that man really is your father, you're going to be more vulnerable to him than you can imagine."

"I have been mentally and physically tortured in the line of duty, Rusty. I've been water-boarded, bastinadoed and denailed. I've been hooked to electric cables. I've been starved, sleep-deprived and Ta'liq-ed. I'm not afraid of a silver-tongued preacher. Even if he is my daddy."

"Men in there will try to have sex with you. Maybe women, too."

"I'm prepared for that possibility."

"Including Euple Grymes—if he doesn't know the fornicator on his doorstep could be his daughter. Or hell, maybe *because* you're his daughter."

I told Rusty about the horse- and mule-riding training I received for six weeks in the Pamir Mountains, in the Gorno-Badakhshan province of Tajikistan. "Three teen-aged stable boys pinned me down and tried to have a go at me. They're singing in a boys' choir somewhere now. I'm not afraid of an old man."

Rusty opened a box of wooden matches and placed a matchstick between his upper and lower teeth. "I helped you look for your daddy in Lebanon. If he's in the Canaan Valley, I'll help you bring him out —alive."

"I'm not going to be responsible for putting you in jail, Rusty," I said. "Or bringing you out in a body bag."

I thought about my curse.

"You made a promise to me: If I helped you find him, you'd give us a chance. Do you remember saying that to me?"

"I do."

"I have skin in the game."

"You've got a restaurant to run. People rely on you for jobs."

"I make moonshine and burgers. There are higher callings in life. Helping you is one of them." Rusty took my face in his hands. "Let me come with you. If you get killed in there, because of your ego, what happens to your kids?"

"How would you know what it's like to be a parent?"

He gripped my hands. "Fact: There are dozens—maybe hundreds—of people inside that compound and they're armed. Fact: They've got brimstone and are preparing for End of Days. Fact: You don't know shit about scripture."

"I'm going in as a wanton harlot. No one expects me to know scripture."

"No, they don't. But if you think you can just waltz in there and snatch the pastor and founder of that ministry, then tiptoe out of there, you're nuts. You'll meet an unhappy ending. If you're going to get him out peacefully, minus some bullet holes, you need to master his own language—the Bible—and use it against him. Matthew 26:52: 'Then Jesus said to him: Put your sword back into its place. For all who take the sword will perish by the sword.'" He grabbed me by the forearm. "You've got to be one step ahead. And the only way you'll get ahead is if I'm there at your side, marching in lockstep. You can't do it alone, and you know it."

I extricated myself from his grasp, albeit gently. I pushed the shopping cart onto the parking lot. He followed me and said, "I may not be as decorated as you, but give the Devil his due: I did two tours. I know how to use a weapon." He loaded Maximo's box of diapers into the bed of the El Camino. "You're not going in there alone and that's final."

20.

Our trek commenced pre-dawn. It took us some four hours to descend the gray, canopied interior of the Allegheny Mountain range, on foot. We sliced through spider webs the size of TV screens; waded through calf-deep streams; slid on our hindquarters down ravines, the mud-coated husks of dead cicadas stuck to our backsides.

A light rain greeted Rusty and me as we entered the Canaan Valley basin. Our clothes were sopping, our bodies coated in grime. Rusty, in his wife-beater T-shirt and too-tight jeans, his face nicked by thorns, looked like he'd just lost a bar fight. Without thinking, I wiped my eyes with the sleeve of my t-shirt, then cursed, expecting that half of my Stevie Nicks eyeshadow and mascara would be transferred to the shirt. But they weren't. Donna-Lynn was right—the waterproof make-up she used was heavy duty. Nonetheless, I knew better than to blot the *trompe l'oeil* grapevine tattoo that climbed from my neck up over my right ear, applied by my Italian muralist friend, Fabrizio.

I had packed myself, braless, into one of Cleet IV's undershirts. After I ripped off the bottom third of the T-shirt, I had sliced, with a straight razor, horizontal slits across the remaining fabric. I looked like one of those gals lying flat on her back on a bar. The bartender pours liquor from four bottles at once into her open mouth, the liquor streaming down her chin.

Rusty gazed down at my chest. My nipples, hardened by sweat and the cool rainwater, peaked through my wet, white shirt. "This is an anti-sex sex cult you say?"

Ahead was the compound—fixed in the center of the bowl, about ten minutes' walk inward. Although I'd been here once before, I had been too distracted by the thought of meeting my daddy to take more than a cursory gander at the structure. It was plain, made mostly of wood, and rectangular—like a gigantic log cabin. The windows out front, from which pointed many a rifle during my previous visit, were square, evenly set, and modest in size. At one end of the building was a trampoline.

Twenty yards from the metal front door we stopped.

"Let me do the talking," Rusty whispered.

Just then a window opened, and a figure appeared. Same drill as last time.

"Put your hands up!" Brother Boaz shouted.

"We come for help," Rusty shouted. "Heard this is a place for the God-fearing and forlorn!"

"Keep 'em up!" another fella shouted as more windows opened and rifles appeared.

"We are sinners," Rusty said.

"Or you're ATF," said Brother Boaz.

"We're not ATF. We're just at the end of our ropes."

"How'd you get in here?"

"On foot. We walked."

I heard the crackle of the bullhorn being turned on. "She walked all the way here in those shoes?" broadcast a man's voice. It was Euple Grymes's voice.

I looked down at my vintage Candi's platform wedges,

courtesy of some former jailbird Donna-Lynn Deneen had made over. Yes, my feet hurt. But I'd done ten-mile runs in boots—uphill, with a fifty-pound pack on my back.

"She did indeed, sir," Rusty said.

"Why are you here, son?" Daddy pressed.

"This morning I woke up next to this girl. I wiped the grit out of my eyes and looked around the room, which I didn't recognize. Then I looked down upon my naked body, where I saw about an eight-ball's worth of cocaine smeared on my privates. I rolled over and tried to rouse this perfect creature, because I'm at my best during the morning. But she turned to me and said things had to change—for me and for her, too. In the middle of the night the Lord came to her and told her—"

"—The Lord Himself?"

"Indeed."

"And just what did He say?"

"He said—"

Daddy cut Rusty off again. "—Girl, you answer the question; you're the one He spoke to."

I stepped forward, paused, and collected my thoughts. The voice of Director Loehr echoed in my ears: *Don't let your emotions cloud your judgement.* I put on the thickest West Virginia accent I could summon. "He said, 'Harlot, it is time to change your evil ways.'"

There were some affirmative grunts among the disciples. Euple Grymes shushed them. "And just what exactly were you doing when the Lord came to you? Did He visit you in a dream?"

I cleared my throat and glanced at Rusty, who made a not-so-subtle hip-thrusting gesture.

"I was fornicating, sir. With this gentleman—and three of his friends from the restaurant he works at."

Rusty gave me a subtle nod of approval.

"You and four men." Daddy said judgmentally. "Fornicating. Last night. Smearing cocaine on each other's genitalia."

Actually, me and three men. The fourth person was a woman. She's the new fry cook by the name of Krista, I think."

"Krissa," corrected Rusty.

"I've heard enough!" Daddy said.

The silence lasted for several moments. I heard the breeze blow through the tops of the trees. A rifle cocked and Rusty, on soldier's instinct, stepped in front of me.

"Rusty," I whispered, as soft as can be, "stand down." I worried his innate sense of chivalry would give us away—or betray his military training. Men who wake up after orgies with cocaine on their genitals, I reckoned, are not inclined to take a bullet for a woman.

"Not a chance," Rusty whispered.

There was another crackle from the bullhorn. I stepped out from behind Rusty.

"Sir, it is your prerogative who you accept or decline into your ministry," I said. "But we ain't got nowhere else to go, and while I can't speak for my companion, I can tell you that if you do not grant us acceptance into your fold and help us change our ways, then I'm—then I'm going to take my own life!"

I gasped, bringing my hand to my mouth and quaking my shoulders like I was holding back a torrent of tears. Once again, silence from inside the building. Finally, there was a stir somewhere up on the second floor. The bullhorn's mic was still hot, and I heard Euple Grymes mumble into the ear of one of his disciples. Seconds later, the big metal door opened and the young fella from last time—the six and a half footer—came out and marched up to us. His thin, white tunic flapped in the breeze, hugging his muscular physique.

"Empty your pockets."

We turned them inside out.

"You got any weapons under there? Guns? Knives?"

"No," we said in unison.

He began to pat us down.

"Beneath our garments is only lustful flesh," Rusty said.

"We'll fix that soon enough," Daddy's disciple said before turning to the compound. "They're clean," he shouted.

One by one, rifles were withdrawn from windowsills. The would-be shooters disappeared from view. The windows were lowered. Dark shades were pulled down over each pane.

"Are we going inside?" I asked.

The young man looked me up and down. "Your clothes stay out here. Nothing from the outside comes in. We start clean and natural."

Rusty began to peel off his shirt.

I froze.

"What are you waiting for?" the young man asked. "Remove your evil garments."

I was overcome by anxiety. Euple Grymes may not have known it was his daughter standing before him, but I did.

When the young man, who was walking ahead towards the main door, was out of earshot, I whispered to Rusty "I can't do this."

Rusty looked straight ahead as he mumbled out of the side of his mouth. "You can stand naked 500 yards away from that man up there. Besides" he added, "the old devil probably can't see anything past the end of his nose."

"He's not that old," I whispered.

Hugging myself, pretending like I was chilly, I pleaded with my eyes. "Sir, Mr. Pastor, sir!" I called out to Euple Grymes.

"He's not there," our escort grunted. "It's almost time for the holy service he has daily with his Angels. He went to take a ceremonial bath."

"Oh," I said.

I smiled both demurely and seductively at him, seeing if it would have an effect. But this tall, well-built young man was all business.

Licking my lips, I peeled off my wet half-shirt, then slowly wiggled my way out of my jean cut-offs, until I stood naked, except for my Candi's platform wedges. I could hear Rusty breathing heavily and did not dare look at him.

"Those, too," said our escort as he pointed at my shoes.

I turned around slowly, jutting my hip just a bit as I twisted. Then I bent over from my waist, unbuckling the leather straps.

From between my knees, I could see his eyes were on me, but he said nothing. I needed to take charge of the situation, as I was trained to do; I needed to get the target reacting to *me*. Had I entered the compound in my usual undercover fashion—as a socialite who spoke in an affected "Anglo-Swiss-Hungarian-with-a-dash-of-Bombay" accent—I might have clutched my pearls and been compelled to accuse this disciple of Euple Grymes of being unseemly, or coarse, or ungentlemanly. Instead, because I was, on this particular mission, undercover as an "inarticulate-West-Virginia-white-trash-slut-with-a-dash-of-opiod-addiction accent," I cocked my chin, flipped my hair, and said in a syrupy Southern drawl, "So what do you think?"

"About what?" the escort said.

"Me, sailor. Like what's on the menu?"

"Harlot!"

"Sure you wouldn't be willing to give me one last go? Because once we walk through those doors, I never get to sin no more." I licked my lips and glanced down at his gear, around which his tunic was all bunched up.

"Temptress!"

He turned his attention to Rusty. "Your turn."

Rusty stepped out of his boots, then removed his shirt and tossed it on the ground.

"Pants off."

Rusty removed his trousers.

"Britches, too."

Rusty stepped out of his underwear, and I looked upwards, making sure to keep my sights squarely on his head and shoulders.

"Turn around."

Rusty obeyed.

"Okay. Both of you approach. Slowly!"

"Take a deep breath," Rusty instructed as we made our way to the front door.

21.

Just before stepping inside, we heard a half dozen deadbolts twist. Katy bars were unthreaded, the iron bars clanging as they tumbled to the floor. We entered and stood in the vacant entry, which was as rustic as the exterior: Wood floors, a tin ceiling and a large stone fireplace with a raging fire. I was grateful for that, being as I was naked as a jaybird.

"Step forward," said the tall, young disciple.

We obeyed.

On the opposite side of the foyer, a door swung open. It was Bosley. She stepped into the foyer. On her crown, above orange hair arranged in an unfashionable bowl cut, she had pinned a white nurse's cap. Her eyes were the size of peas. Instead of the Pennzoil t-shirt I had seen in photographs, she wore the sex-cult version of a nurse's uniform: a white tunic that fit snugly, revealed a too-thick middle and too-short legs. In fairness to her, her breasts were pert and perpendicular. I suppose everyone, if you look closely enough, has at least one redeeming feature, and Nurse Bosley was clearly proud of hers; she glided across the room with the confidence of a fashion model—one holding an Oscar in her right fist, and a Nobel Prize in Chemistry in her left.

"Welcome," she purred in a deep, gravelly voice.

I did not see her arm move, although it must have, because I felt the sting of a needle in my buttocks. Almost immediately, my vision started to blur, and my arms and legs weakened; I felt like an *al dente* noodle. I looked over at Rusty, who was already swaying. Two of the male disciples were in the process of keeping him propped up. Presently the disciples ushered Rusty towards the door through which the nurse had arrived.

The nurse surveyed me. "She's perfect," she said. "She'll make a wonderful Angel."

When I awakened, my head was pounding, and my mouth was dry. My eyes blinked open to a blur of light, but as things came into focus, I could at least make out my surroundings.

The first thing I saw were two big eyes staring down at me from the wall. His image was contained in an ornate picture frame—carved wood, painted gold. The picture had a 3D effect, like those velvet Elvis paintings. Only it wasn't The King of Rock-n-Roll depicted, it was my daddy, Euple Grymes. The head was oversized in the portrait—improperly proportioned, as my late husband Gonzalo Fernandez, who owned an art gallery in Palm Beach, would have been quick to point out. Daddy's deep blue eyes were fierce and penetrating. He wore a white suit that practically glowed against the black velvet background. He stood with his arms wide in welcome.

Still groggy, I scanned the room. The black velvet in Daddy's portrait, and the gold frame that surrounded it, presented the only flash of color in the room; everything else—the ceiling, walls, a single long counter, and a row of cabinets—was gleaming white, like his suit. My nose began to itch, and I went to lift my hand to scratch it, only to discover my arms and legs were restrained. My wrists and ankles were bound, and there was an additional strap of white leather across my midsection. Lifting up my head as best as I could, I was able to ascertain that I was lying on some sort of gurney. I noticed that my backside was not sticking to cool vinyl, or a cheap polyester hospital sheet, but to a comfortable, bordering on luxurious fabric, a swatch of butter-soft white suede.

The room was deadly quiet. When I cleared my throat, the sound echoed.

Presently I heard the tumblers on a lock click. The door on the opposite side of the room opened. Its hinges squeaked. In came two of the most beautiful girls I had ever seen. Identical twins, they were dressed in white silken robes and had long, wavy blonde manes that stretched midway down each girl's back. Even their pencil-thin eyebrows were matching. Their remarkable hair looked as though it was being blown by a gentle breeze. The sisters' matching eyes, a shade of crystalline blue, had something of a thousand-yard stare to them. One carried a white leather satchel; the other sister carried a white porcelain bowl and a plastic tub.

"We will make you presentable for Pastor Grymes," one of the twins said.

In silence, the girls went to work on me, removing one item of jewelry at a time: the cigarette earrings Mama had given me, the fake septum horseshoe sticking out of my nose, the metal tongue stud, which was *not* fake, and which I was all too glad to be rid of, the black-beaded necklace with the miniature ceramic penis pendant, the chrome rose pedal crammed in my navel.

They daintily placed all my accessories into the plastic tub.

My two-inch-long, lacquered acrylic nails, each styled into points, were inspected. "A certain kind of man likes these inserted into his bottom," I said, in keeping with the wanton character I was portraying.

The girls ignored my comment.

After clipping my nails, one of the sisters applied nail polish remover and scraped away the layers of dirt packed beneath the remaining nails with a cuticle.

"You're really good at this," I said to Twin No 1. "Did you work in a nail salon before you came here?"

Silence.

"Do you have a name?"

"I am Sister Jill," Twin No. 1 said.

"That's a nice name. And what about you?" I asked her sister, who was at work on my toes, applying nail polish remover.

"And I am Sister Jill," said Twin No. 2.

"Twins with the same name? That's unusual."

Silence.

"You two been here long?"

More silence.

"I like your names. Would you like to know mine?"

"The pastor will assign you a new name once you have completed your sacraments."

"Sacraments?"

"Quiet, please," murmured Sister Jill No. 1.

After they were finished with my nails, each twin grabbed a sponge and plunged it into the bucket of water, which contained no soap—only salt. Misshapen salt chunks the size of golf balls. I recognized the formation and color: sourced from the Dead Sea, that salt was.

Sister Jill No. 2 kicked a lever, making the cot to which I was strapped flip up, putting me nearly into a standing position.

The girls scrubbed me head to toe, except for my private parts. Sister Jill No. 1 unbuckled the leather strap on my wrist and instructed me to wash those parts myself.

I did as she instructed. After resecuring the restraints, the girls blotted my skin with towels. Dipping their fingers into a white porcelain bowl of emollients, they massaged the warm, oily goo into my skin—from face to foot. Sister Jill No.1 then clapped her hands, and almost immediately one of the muscular male disciples entered the room. He was carrying a rifle, which he pointed directly at me.

Sister Jill No.1 told me to turn around and asked me to lean stomach-down on the cot, which I did. They did not strap me in this time, and merely rubbed down my backside the same way as my front.

"Thanks, girls. Is it now time for me to meet the pastor?"

"We must complete your grooming," said Sister Jill No. 2, who snapped on a pair of surgical gloves. She made the cot lie flat again. She then began running a fine-toothed steel comb through my hair, bit by bit.

"I don't have lice."

"Quiet, please."

After she inspected the comb, and declared me lice-free, they made me turn around again. Her sister performed the same procedure on the nest of dark hair above my privates, then tossed the comb in the tub. "She's clean."

Next, Sister Jill No. 1 removed from the satchel a pair of styling shears, a round brush, a hairdryer, and squeeze-bottle of honey blond hair dye. For the next ninety minutes, I was dyed, dried, curled and primped, all while staring down the barrel of a shotgun. Even the hair that concealed the zipper tattoo mama inked onto my *mons pubis* as a teenager was colored and styled, but left unsheared, in contravention to contemporary grooming trends.

"Put this on," said Sister Jill No. 2. She handed me a folded white tunic.

I obeyed.

"Follow us," said Sister Jill No. 1.

"Where are we going?"

"To chapel," said Sister Jill No. 2.

We walked in silence down a white corridor that must have been a half mile long. There were several doors along the way, only one of which was open enough for me to see what was inside. The room was piled high with a stockpile of supplies: five-gallon jugs of water, buckets of Macaroni & Cheese whose labels boasted twenty-five-year shelf lives, crates filled with matches, glow sticks, and medical supplies, dozens of rolls of toilet paper, spools of extension cord, rolls of duct tape, balls of twine.

And ammo: box after box of rifle bullets, shotgun shells, jacketed hollow point bullets.

At the end of the corridor painted on the wall, was a mural. It was a disconcerting image, that mural: Euple Grymes, dressed once again in a white suit, stood triumphantly in the midst of what appeared to be a depiction of the world on fire: all done up in red and orange, with fire in the skies, and angels playing trumpets at his feet. Little devils, dressed in paramilitary uniforms—police, ATF, etc.—flew around them, brandishing scythes.

"Do you girls reckon the Pastor can redeem me?" I asked the twins.

No reply came as the girls ushered me past the mural, through a pair of white doors with golden door knobs the size of cantaloupes.

While it contained rows of long pews, it resembled no chapel I had been in previously. Up front and center, where one would expect to see an altar, was an antique wooden desk—the fancy kind my first husband, Cletus Bland III, had in the library of his Virginia farmhouse. The desk stood on an elevated plywood platform covered in plush brown shag carpet. The desk was uncluttered: no computer or monitor, no desk pad, no pens, no papers, no bric-à-brac—only a circa 1970s avocado-green, multi-line, rotary-dial telephone stationed next to a rectangular steel box that looked like some sort of intercom. There were stuffed leather chairs on the side of the desk, the kind you'd see in the offices of a semi-retired lawyer in his seventies who no longer felt obliged to keep up with contemporary decorating trends.

In the chapel, no religious iconography was on display. No lectern. Alongside the wall, where one might have expected to view a tabernacle, or a cross, were shelves stuffed with leather-bound books.

Suddenly, the phone rang. The door next to the bookshelves opened, and in strode a parade of beautiful young women. About thirty of them total, and all of them wearing form-fitting pink dresses of various cuts. There were blondes and brunettes, all coiffed to perfection, sporting assorted hairstyles that seemed to adhere to a theme. Brunettes with shoulder-length hair wore sleeveless mock turtleneck dresses, all in matching pink, that flowed past the knees. A second group of brunettes, who wore their hair longer, to mid-back, wore dresses that went just above the knee. The blondes with long, wavy, extravagantly blow-dried hair like lionesses' manes—like the twin Jills—were the prettiest of the bunch. There were fewer of those girls than the brunettes, so they really stood out, and wore dresses with plunging V-shaped necklines that went well above the knee.

Only my Jills wore an alternate outfit—the silky, white robes that made them look like they worked at a heavenly spa. The Jills flanked me at the back of the chapel, while the rest of the ladies filed into the pews.

During the procession, the phone continued to ring. And ring. And ring.

Finally, one of the brunette congregants in a sleeveless mock turtleneck dress sashayed up to the desk, sat on it, and casually, yet elegantly, crossed her legs. She lifted the phone from its cradle, set it on the desk, and pressed a button on the speaker.

"Good morning, Angels," Euple Grymes's voice purred through the speaker.

"Good morning, Pastor," the girls said in unison.

"I hope each and every one of you young and appetizing Sister Kellys, Sabrinas—and especially you lovely Jills—are rested and ready for your next assignment."

22.

The congregants' blank eyes fixated on the little metal box.

"It looks like one of my Sister Sabrinas skinned her knee," Daddy said.

A quick scan of the room revealed four security cameras, one mounted in each corner.

One of the Sabrinas, a spunky little brunette, blushed. "It's just a burn, pastor. Got it on the trampoline."

"I know, Sabrina. I was watching you bounce from my quarters. That was some flip you attempted. Come see me after chapel and I'll rub some Neosporin on it."

"Yes, pastor."

"Yes, pastor," the other Angels repeated in unison.

"I see we have a new Angel among us."

"We do, pastor," the Angel sitting on the desk replied as she uncrossed her legs. She signaled the twin Jills who escorted me to chapel. The girls led me to the desk, although not up onto the platform on which it stood.

"Well, well, well," intoned the disembodied voice inside the speaker. "She certainly looks angelic now that she's been groomed."

"Yes, pastor, she certainly looks angelic now that she's been groomed," the angels parroted.

"Bring this young lady forward, closer to the desk, so that I might have a better look at her."

Jill No.1 guided me up onto the platform, nudged me forward, and instructed me to rotate full circle—and do so as slowly as possible.

I obeyed.

There was a long pause on the other end of the speaker. "Just as I suspected." A brief silence ensued, followed by the sound of a crown being popped off the top of a bottled beverage. "Our newest angel is the rarest of them all: a Sister Jill. And possibly the finest and Jill-est of any Jill that's ever graced our heavenly compound."

There was a gasp amongst the Angels.

"Um, excuse me," I said. "My name's not 'Jill.'"

The telephone line went dead. Sister Sabrina restored the handset to its cradle and clicked off the speaker.

"As I was saying, my name isn't Sister Jill. My name is—"

"—The pastor decides which Angel you'll be," Sister Sabrina said curtly. Then, catatonically, she chanted: "He is everything. He is the spirit and the trinity."

He is everything," the congregants repeated. "He is the spirit and the trinity."

"He is everything," Sister Sabrina said.

"He is everything," the girls in the pews repeated.

"Everything will be illuminated," said Sister Sabrina.

"Everything will be illuminated," the chorus repeated.

"And when will that be?" I asked.

Sister Sabrina raised one of her sculpted eyebrows. "In time. Right now, it's time for your cleansing."

I pointed at the twin Sister Jills. "Those gals already cleaned me up."

"Your flesh is clean, but your soul is polluted," said Sister Sabrina.

On cue, the Fanta-haired nurse strode through the door next to the bookcases.

Sister Sabrina at the desk looked at me and smiled. "I believe you have already met Bosley, Sister Jill."

"Yes, we've met." I girded myself. I wasn't about to let that gargoyle who pretended to be a "nurse" inject me unawares again. "And for the third time, my name's not 'Sister Jill.'"

"Sister Jill, Sister Jill, Sister Jill, Sister Jill, Sister Jill," chanted the congregants.

The Fanta-haired woman approached. This time, I did see her hand move, and was prepared. I squeezed my glutes just as tight as possible as she attempted to stab me with the hypodermic needle. I say "attempted" because, this time, the needle broke in half as it encountered hard muscle.

Bosley growled.

"I don't like needles," I said. "It's why I won't shoot heroin. I only do drugs I can smoke or snort."

Bosley puffed up her chest. "Take her to the cleansing room," she said to the twin Sister Jills.

The Jills, both of them twiggy and fine-boned, grabbed my wrists. I could have put them both on the floor, with broken necks, in five seconds had I wanted to. But I chose not to resist. Best to see what the next phase of indoctrination looked like. I allowed them to guide me through the doorway behind the altar, into an anteroom, where three additional doors appeared on the rear wall. Bosley followed. The girls ushered me through the first door. Inside, it was pitch black. Bosley soon entered and flipped a switch. A single, bare lightbulb, which dangled like a noose from the ceiling, crackled and fizzed, emitting a dull glow. A cement staircase was revealed. Bosley pointed towards it. The Jills guided me down a staircase that led to another plain room, one with no furniture, only a drain on the floor.

"Ok, Angel, strip," Bosley said.

"I have to be naked to have my soul cleansed?"

"Strip!"

I pulled my tunic off over my head. One of the Jills handed me a white hand towel that barely covered my torso as Bosley then retrieved from the utility closet a cylindrical tank that looked like a fire extinguisher. Attached to it was a long-necked spray hose.

"Open up," Bosley demanded.

"Open what?" I asked.

"The towel. Open up your towel."

I did as I was told.

Though not attracted to women, I knew how to be alluring to them when the mission demanded it. Rather than jiggle, I opted for a more subtle approach, jutting out a hip.

"Stay still," Bosley commanded. A fine spray coated my breasts, belly, pelvis and legs. I recognized immediately that it wasn't just water; something had been added to the liquid. I cocked my head and sniffed, like an English Springer Spaniel on point. "I know that smell," I said. "That's Lucky You Body Mist."

"Shut up."

Bosley next sprayed my face. I coughed, having involuntarily taken in some of the mist, but made sure to inhale no further. In this clash of wills, I was confident I would prevail: Once, in Bamyan Province, Afghanistan, I held my breath for nine minutes while disarming a bomb concealed in a fuel delivery tanker truck.

I was nonetheless feeling woozy, which I reckoned was not simply the result of holding my breath. The spray, I surmised, contained more than water mixed with Lucky You Body Mist: I recognized the astringent aftertaste of Scopolaminea, with which I had become familiar on my military tours of duty. Also known Devil's Breath, the drug, an alkaloid, interfered with a subject's capacity to exercise free will. It was also an efficient memory-eraser. This "truth serum" was administered by the United States military to coax terrorists into making confessions. It was, alternatively, administered by terrorist organizations to new recruits, to facilitate the process of jihadist brainwashing. In the civilian world, the drug was reportedly popular among criminals, occultists and cult leaders—including, apparently, Euple Grymes.

Lucky me, I thought to myself.

23.

"You girls leave now," said Bosley.

The twin Sister Jills bowed and retreated, walking backwards. After the door was shut, it was locked from the outside.

"Wrap the towel around you."

I obeyed.

"Do you know your scripture, Sister Jill?"

I made a puzzled face. "Who's Jill?"

"—You're Sister Jill, dear. Let me ask again: Do you know your scripture?"

I had been in this situation before: The interrogator asks open-ended questions about broad-ranging subjects to determine to what extent, if at all, the drugs are taking effect. As this was not my first experience with Scopolamine, I knew to calibrate my behavior, to make her believe I'd gotten the full dose. I needed to be highly suggestable, prone to hallucinations, and uninhibited in my speech and actions.

"Huh?" I covertly exhaled the breath I'd been holding.

"Everything in the present is rooted in the past, Sister Jill," said Bosley. "Everything we think we're doing for the first time—whether that's sinful or saintly behavior—was done by those before us. Millions of times, by millions of people, over millions of years."

"Millions," I repeated.

"Jill, do you know the story of Oholah and Oholibah?" Bosley asked.

I rotated my neck, feigning sleepiness.

"Ezekiel 23:1-21," Bosley said.

"Ezekiel Gibson went to my high school."

"There's a story in Ezekiel about two sisters. The older was named Oholah, and her sister was Oholibah. Both of them prostitutes. But these girls weren't in it just for the money, Sister Jill. These girls were randy. Sluts. They were having *fun*. Oholah, the older sister, was hot for Assyrians—'warriors clothed in blue, governors and commanders, all of them handsome young men, and mounted horsemen, who caressed her virgin bosom and poured out their lust on her.' And get this, Sister Jill: Her sister Oholibah was even more depraved. She hooked up with studs 'whose genitals were like those of donkeys and whose issue was like that of horses.' Do you know what 'issue' means, Sister Jill?"

"Sports Illustrated," I mumbled. "Swimsuit issue."

"No, Sister Jill. 'Issue' as in seminal emission."

I grinned. Wantonly.

"What do you reckon happened to those sisters, Sister Jill?"

"I have a sister."

"The girls were eventually punished, Sister Jill. I won't get into the gory details. But swords were involved. Let's just say they came to an unhappy ending."

"Bad girls."

"Did you know that we have an Oholah and Oholibah in our midst?"

"Mist?"

"The twins. Sisters Jill & Jill. The girls who just left us. They're straight out of the Good Book. About thirty seconds after they turned eighteen, they became pornographic actresses. Known to millions of drooling men as 'The Smithers Twins.'" A lusty leer came over Bosley's face, one at odds with the stated purpose of the Before the Fall Ministries. "There are about two hundred videos of the girls on the internet, where dozens of men—and almost as many women—'handled their virgin bosoms and poured out their lust upon them.' They come from a town called Smithers, which is how they got their name. It's a shithole. Like most of this Godforsaken state." The West Virginia accent in Bosley's speech pronounced itself.

"I love West Virginia," I said dreamily. "I don't ever want to leave."

Bosley smirked. "You might just get your wish."

Bosley returned the tank and spray nozzle to the closet. She turned her back to me, likely believing that I was too impaired by the Scopolamine to threaten her. From inside the closet, she asked: "Are you feeling relaxed?"

I furnished no spoken answer. Instead, as she emerged from the closet with a walkie-talkie, I twirled—in a mystical, trancelike fashion—like the Sufi dancers I once saw in Egypt performing a whirling dervish.

Bosley depressed a button on the two-way radio, "She's ready, Brother Boaz."

"Change into this," Bosley said, handing me a pile of

clothes that included a pair of tight, bell-bottomed blue jeans, a light blue cotton blouse, and a simple pair of slip-on loafers.

"Tuck in the blouse and leave the top three buttons undone," she commanded. I complied.

"Perfect," she said. "I think you're going to be His favorite."

"Is it time to see the pastor?"

"Not yet, dear."

That same muscular disciple who escorted Rusty and me into the building entered the room, pushing a gurney.

"I think you've already met Brother Boaz," Bosley said.

Brother Boaz strapped me in. Bosley placed a burlap sack over my head. I let her do it. It wasn't my first time wearing a bag over my head as I was taken by the enemy from one location to the next, and I had been trained to use my other senses to determine my surroundings: hearing, mostly, plus smell and touch, when possible. Bosley led the way, her squishy nurse's shoes making farting noises on the concrete floor as she strode. After walking a good fifty yards, we stopped. I heard a set of keys jingle as Bosley opened a squeaky steel door. Wherever we were, the room was big, spacious and carpeted—and graveyard silent.

The gurney came to a halt. Its brake was applied. The sack over my head was removed. Which did no good: The windowless room I was in was pitch black.

"Where am I?"

"It's showtime," chortled Bosley. She mumbled something to Brother Boaz, who exited hastily.

Suddenly, a very dull red glow began to appear. As the objects in the room came into relief, it was soon evident I was in some sort of movie theater—one with movie screens on each of the walls and affixed to the ceiling. There were about twenty rows of plush recliners, separated by a wide aisle.

"Did you like to go to the movies in high school, Sister Jill?" Bosley asked. "To the cinema with your 'special beau'? A bucket of popcorn perched on your lap?"

"I don't like the movies."

Bosley's laugh bore a trace of malevolence. "Oh, I think you'll learn to. The movies, you see, are central to our missionary work here at Before the Fall Ministries. Watching them. Learning from them. And *starring* in them."

24.

The steel door in the rear of the theater squeaked open.

"If I'm not mistaken," Bosley said, "your future co-star is just arriving."

Brother Boaz pushed a gurney down the aisle and rolled up next to mine. After the brake was affixed, the burlap sack covering the head of the individual on the gurney was removed.

"Rusty," I whispered.

"No talking during the film," barked Bosley.

Rusty looked over at me, dreamily; I was uncertain if he was able to recognize me. I wanted desperately to hold Rusty's hand. Not an option, as we were both secured.

"You two just lay back, relax, and enjoy the show," Bosley said as she and the Brother Boaz headed towards the door.

Not a second after it was sealed and locked, I heard a hissing sound commence. A fine yellow mist—this one different than the Lucky You formulation—began to puff out from a series of overhead vents that ran the length of the ceiling. I held my breath again, taking in only the slightest sniff and taste of the substance. Banisterine Baradanga this time, no doubt about it. It was sour and fungal simultaneously. There was another substance in the mist concoction as well, probably a psychedelic similar to LSD, if they were following classic brainwashing protocol.

I could hear Rusty beginning to struggle next to me. Exerting himself was only going to make him breathe in deeper, taking in more of the drugs. "Stay still, Rusty!" He was struggling so violently that the gurney was bouncing up and down off the floor. He ranted and raved for another minute or two, becoming increasingly incoherent as the drugs took hold.

Suddenly, the room exploded in light, a kaleidoscope of colors and shape-shifting images. Next, the disco-tinged opening theme music to the old "Charlie's Angels" television show began. On the ceiling a big burst of orange fire appeared. In silhouette, an image of three young women came into relief, the middle one holding a rifle, the other two karate-chopping the air.

Daddy's narration followed: "Once upon a time, there was some very naughty young men and women who did some very naughty things. They pole-danced in strip clubs. They cooked meth in trailer parks. They drank themselves into oblivion every night. But I took them away from all that. My name is Euple." The theme music was scratchy and skipped at times as the screen cut to crudely-filmed images of Euple's Angels—the various Sabrinas, Kellys, and Jills inside the compound—as they performed light stunts: Angels on the archery range; Angels doing judo; Angels throwing knives; Angels kicking up dust as their pickup trucks burned rubber in the basin.

What followed were a series of "episodes," all of them presented back-to- back. They weren't hour-length, like on the TV show, but about ten minutes each. The plot, and even the set, was the same in every episode: The Angels infiltrated the world of high fashion to investigate the deaths of models who were strangled with rag dolls. In each episode, the cast of angels and costumes changed, as did the villains, who were portrayed by

Brother Boaz and several of the other muscular young male disciples who lived on Daddy's compound. No crime was ever solved, either: Ninety seconds into the angels' "investigations" everybody started having sex. At the end of each episode, Daddy, clad in his white suit, imparted "the moral of the story" by spouting Biblical verses of the strangest variety, many of them chilling bordering on grotesque: "No one whose testicles are crushed, or whose male organ is cut off shall enter the assembly of the Lord.—Deuteronomy 23:1"; "When men fight with one another and the wife of the one draws near to rescue her husband from the hand of him who is beating him and puts out her hand and seizes him by the private parts, then you shall cut off her hand. Your eye shall have no pity.—Deuteronomy 25:11-12."

It was a shrewdly conceived production, one meant to infiltrate our minds, Rusty's and mine, with themes that were at once bizarre, tantalizing, and terrifying. Images intended not to condition our minds to serve God, but to serve one man: Euple Grymes.

To those gurneys we remained strapped for two days as the violent and pornographic images were seared into our minds. We were never allowed off the gurneys. At four-hour intervals Bosley and Brother Boaz returned, at which time the disciple loosened our straps just enough to be able to shove bedpans beneath us.

We were starved, Rusty and me, as the drugging continued, forcing me to hold my breath longer each time as another batch of yellow mist seeped out of the vents.

I warned Rusty for the tenth time: "Close your eyes and your mouth!"

Rusty did a respectable job of keeping his mouth shut

and breath held, but despite his best efforts to keep his eyes screwed shut, he kept squinting through them. I could tell the drugs—and the film's messaging—were doing a number on Rusty. I can state without fear of contradiction that Rusty was wildly aroused. While I studiously avoided looking in Rusty's direction, his labored breathing—which at times bordered on outright gasping, panting and moaning—betrayed his condition.

Though I'd consumed very little of the misty concoction myself, I was feeling its effects, too: I was becoming frisky, and was forced to execute a series of resistance strategies, which required supreme mental discipline. Eyes clinched shut, I re-seized control of my mind by disassembling, then reassembling, the engine of my El Camino by memory while silently humming *The Army Goes Rolling Along*.

Finally, on the third day, the lights went up. Bosley and Brother Boaz returned to check on us. Rusty lay next to me in a drug-induced stupor, while I pretended to be confused, hysterical, joyous—and not a little lustful. While I have never thought of myself as a prude, I never understood why people wanted to watch others engaged in sexual congress when there was no prospect of the encounter culminating in True Love. Any moments of friskiness I encountered in that cinema were not the result of being stimulated by what I saw—and studiously attempted to avoid seeing on screen—but by the movie that played in my head of me and the men I'd loved: my husbands Cletus, Jack, and Gonzalo. Some of these were memories of encounters we'd shared as men and wife, while others, I admit, were fantasies of the four of us having a go together in heaven one day. I saved any imaginings of me and Rusty consummating our feelings for one another on the fine cotton sheets at his condo in Lewisburg, for after this ordeal was over.

"What's your name?" Bosley said through her gas mask.

"I am Sister Jill."

"Did you have a name before you came to us, child?"

"I was always Sister Jill. I am Sister Jill forever."

"That's right," Bosley purred. "*Who* is He?"

"Pastor Euple."

"*What* is He?"

"He is Everything!"

"And you," Brother Boaz said to Rusty, "What's your name?"

"I am Brother Er."

"Did you have a name before you came to us?"

"I was always Brother Er. I am Brother Er forever."

"*Who* is He?"

"Pastor Euple."

"*What* is he?"

"He is Everything!" Rusty said mechanically.

I was faking. I was not so sure about Rusty, though.

25.

Burlap sacks recovered our heads. Brother Boaz pushed Rusty's gurney up the aisle. Bosley pushed mine. Outside, in the corridor, I asked "Are you finally taking me to meet the pastor?"

"Soon—very soon—you will earn your Angel's wings," Bosley chuckled. She rolled the gurney forward, then stopped. "Where do you think you're going?" I heard her say to Brother Boaz.

"With you and Sister Jill," he replied.

"No, you're not. Look at him," Bosley said. "You think he'll be giving testimony? He's catatonic. Bring Brother Er to the studio and put him to work. Filming starts in fifteen minutes."

"You think he can . . . *perform* . . . in his condition?"

"Come here, Brother Boaz." I heard Boaz's shoes slap on the floor. "Peel his tunic upwards, over his torso." I heard the rustle of fabric. "See that?"

"Yes."

"It's the only part of him that's conscious. Toss him on a mattress and let the Angels work their miracles."

"Right," said Brother Boaz. As he passed my gurney, Boaz brushed my strapped-down forearm. "Good luck in the waters, tadpole," he mumbled.

"So where are you taking me?" I asked Bosley. "To the river, for a dunking?"

"There's no river here, Sister Jill."

The gurney rattled down the corridor. Bosley opened a door and rolled me into a room. "Welcome to the Garden of Eden," Bosley said as she removed the burlap sack. I took in the scene. The room was painted forest green, including the floor. Plastic vines dangled from the ceiling. Some two dozen oversized pots, in which stood fake trees with shiny red plastic apples, were scattered throughout the room. A bubbling hot tub in the center of the room issued an inviting gurgle.

"How many baths do I have to take before I'm ready to meet the pastor?" I asked.

"There are three phases to the ritual, Sister Jill. First, I will unstrap you, at which time you will rise from your gurney. Next, you will strip naked. After which time you will enter the healing waters. But you will not lower yourself into the waters; instead, you will stand motionless. At this point, I will summon our witnesses to your testimony. And once your testimony is rendered, the witnesses will enter the waters and dunk you three times. Do you understand?"

"I do."

"There's one more important detail, Sister Jill," continued Bosley, "so listen closely. You will not make any attempt to assault me, or the witnesses, or try to escape, because I will have this trained on you at all times." Bosley flipped open a switchblade and twirled the weapon in an impressive formation. "Do we understand one another?"

"We do."

"Let us proceed."

I removed my bell bottom jeans and blue blouse, and

handed her my clothes, which she folded and placed on the gurney.

The door opened. "Ah, our witnesses have arrived," said Bosley.

Two men, naked except for the plastic fig leaves they held over their gear, approached. Were it not for my training I would have fainted. For there before me stood my two best friends from high school: Ricky Ray Jeeter and Scooter Skinner.

Given that my mind had, supposedly, been erased over the previous seventy-two hours, I knew better than to admit recognition. Nonetheless, I looked at them intently. They betrayed no hints of recognition. I was convinced they were not faking, as they stared not at me, but *through* me.

In fairness, I must have been as unrecognizable to them in my transformed state as they almost were to me. The boys were still tall and lean but *extremely* worked out, the scrawny skin and bone of their youth replaced by layers of sculpted muscle. The mullets I remembered from high school were gone, exchanged for short haircuts that made them look almost handsome. Only their tattoos confirmed their identities: On Ricky Ray's lower abdomen, inked just below the belly button, were the words WARNING: CHOKING HAZERD, beneath which was an arrow pointing downward. On Scooter, the image of a reclining, flower-haired, flat-chested prostitute—Scooter's nipples standing in for hers—was clearly inspired by Manet's "Olympia," though I doubt Scooter knew the image's art-historical backstory. That one read HOT MAMA.

I eyed the boys slowly, and lustily, from head to toe, in keeping with the protocols of my mission. Biting my lower lip suggestively, I said, "I am Sister Jill."

Unthinkingly, Scooter Skinner said, "I am Gad, Jacob's

seventh-born son and forefather of the tribe of Gad, one of the twelve tribes of Israel."

Mindlessly, Ricky Ray said, "I am Phut, third son of Ham, one of the sons of Noah."

Normally, it would have been awkward to introduce myself to two naked men when I was myself naked. Nonetheless, I extended a hand.

The boys looked at me impassively.

"Before we hear your testimony Sister Jill," said Bosley, "Brothers Gad and Phut will recite scripture."

Ricky Ray Jeeter—the one Bosley called Brother Phut—quoted Exodus: "Whoever lies with an animal shall be put to death," he said.

If that prophecy was true, then Ricky Ray was lucky still to be alive: One time, when we were teenagers, he guzzled a quart of Southern Comfort mixed with Dr. Pepper and "interfered" with a calf on the Smallwoods' property.

Scooter Skinner—or Brother Gad as Bosley referred to him—told a story about Solomon's bride, who had "breasts like two fawns."

I wondered if he recalled that I was a lot like Solomon's bride in my early life. For it was at Beryl's Hole, the freshwater spring near our homes in Thurmond where, as a teenager, my "two fawns" were for the first time exposed, and groped—one by the hand of Ricky Ray Jeeter, the other by Scooter Skinner.

I fixed my eyes upon them as the rote-memorized passages of scripture poured off their tongues. I attempted to rekindle our previous connection. I batted eyelashes. I cocked my shoulder. I flipped my hair. I did everything I could do short of standing up and shouting, "Ricky Ray! Scooter! It's me, Tami! I know you remember me! Snap out of it!" All to no avail.

When they finished their recitals, Bosley instructed the boys to remove their fig leaves, which they did, without shame. Then, she turned to me. "The time has come for you to give your testimony, Sister Jill, after which time you'll be anointed in the purifying waters, such that you may always and forever henceforth live 'Before the Fall.'"

"What is it, exactly, that you want me to testify about?"

"Your sins."

"Which ones?"

"Sins of the flesh."

Bosley instructed me to enter the hot tub and stand in the middle.

"How far back am I supposed to go?"

"Where else?" replied Bosley. "To the beginning."

I collected my thoughts. "My first sexual encounter occurred at a place called Beryl's Hole, near Thurmond, West Virginia," I began, glancing down at the boys' privates to see if I was stirring up memories.

The boys remained unstirred.

Bosley nodded, indicating for me to continue.

"It was hot as blazes that day in July, ninety-nine degrees. I was alone at the swimming hole. I stripped and jumped in, because the spring-fed water was ice cold—and as clear as a just-washed window. I swam back and forth across the pond, like a dolphin. When, after my last plunge, my head surfaced for air, two friends of mine, Ricky Ray Jeeter and Scooter Skinner, were standing on a rock, pointing at me, laughing."

I locked eyes on the boys. Again, neither of them registered any form of recognition—either of me or their own names.

"Go on," Bosley said.

"The boys pointed over my right shoulder. A big trail of

blood was following me in the water, like spilled oil behind a tanker. I had just gotten my period. Ricky Ray Jeeter said I was gonna get eaten by a shark. At first, I was humiliated. Then I was mad as a hornet. So, I got out of the swimming hole and shook my fist in their faces. It was then I noticed they were staring—leering, to be more precise—at my breasts."

"And?"

"I told Ricky Ray and Scooter that if they got to see me naked, I had a right to see them naked, too."

"What happened next?"

"They stepped out of their jorts and t-shirts, and tighty-whities. We all jumped in the pond. I suppose one thing led to another."

"Yes, I suppose it did. And that was your first sexual encounter?" Bosley pressed. "With two boys?"

I bowed my head.

"Continue."

While I had not before that day ever thought of myself as "wanton"—I was just a girl in search of True Love, a girl keen to break a curse that had plagued the women of her bloodline for centuries—Bosley gasped, grunted, and invoked the names of various biblical characters as I chronicled my romantic history. Because I was undercover, impersonating a lower-class harlot who'd never been out of West Virginia, I was careful not to disclose names, exact dates, or the overseas locations where most of the encounters occurred, when I was deployed. For example, when describing the goes I had in Afghanistan with Ed Earl and Luis from the motor pool, I described them simply as "two automotive mechanics I met several years ago."

"Did you engage in sexual congress with them both at the same time?" Bosley queried.

"No. Separately."

"Go on."

Over the next forty minutes or so I shared the details of my various romantic encounters: My go with a supply chain logistics officer in Iraq, a translator from the French news agency, a public affairs officer, a telecoms engineer, Private Second Class McKim, an optics technician, a one-armed small-arms technician, Director Loehr's budget analyst, an electrician, an Army base fuel manager, a radio systems engineer, Captain Delmar Jorn, a cyber operations specialist with eagles tattooed on his shoulders, a C-12 pilot who wore his baseball cap backwards during our go, a Special Forces intelligence sergeant major, Command Sergeant Major Moellering, a food safety officer, a biomedical equipment specialist who talked to me in Italian, Colonel Cletus Bland, the Crabtree brothers, Jack Capers, Argentinian pop singer Coqui Crespo, Gonzalo Fernandez, and, most recently, Jeremiah Tibbs.

When I completed my testimony, Bosley shook her head. "That was some testimony," she said.

"Thank you."

"It wasn't a compliment."

"I beg the Lord's forgiveness."

"You'll need it." Bosley cleared her throat. "Before you exit the ceremonial font," Bosley continued, "Brothers Phut and Gad will now plunge your head below water. When you emerge, you will no longer remember your past sexual encounters, although you will retain all of the sexual skills you acquired in your previous life." Bosley waved a finger and the boys dutifully stepped into the hot tub. Each grabbed one of my biceps, gently and respectfully, and steered my upper body downward.

They dunked me three times.

When I surfaced the third time, Bosley was on her walkie-talkie. "Yes, pastor, I'll come right away." She turned to Ricky Ray and Scooter: "I have to leave. Brother Phut, get Sister Jill a towel so she may dry off. Brother Gad, if Sister Jill starts ranting and raving like some of y'all do at this point, just hold her down. Do you both understand?"

"Yes, Bosley," they said.

"*Who* is He?"

"Pastor Euple," the boys said.

"*What* is he?"

"He is Everything!" they chanted.

"You're good boys," Bosley said as she headed towards the door.

26.

Bosley exited the Garden of Eden, locking the door behind her. I turned to Scooter and Ricky Ray. Time to go to work. As I wrapped a bath towel around my torso, I asked, "Could I trouble one of you fellas to fetch the oil?" I pointed at a cabinet, where stood a soap dispenser, a bottle of baby oil, and a pile of washcloths and towels.

Scooter looked at Ricky Ray. "Is that okay?"

Ricky Ray, who even in this godforsaken place was still the senior partner in the friendship, nodded his approval.

Scooter fetched the oil, then squirted some of it onto a washcloth.

"I'm just so sore after being strapped to a gurney for so long. I can hardly stay standing. And I think He would want me to be able to stay standing, don't you?"

The boys looked at each other and shrugged that yes, they supposed so.

"The washrag will drink it all up. Put some in your hands and rub it all over me. It's what He'd want you to do, and He is Everything."

Scooter looked to Ricky Ray for re-authorization.

Ricky Ray once again shrugged and nodded. "He is Everything, so, uh, just do her legs, below the knees."

I sat down on the edge of the hot tub and lifted up my leg, pointing my toes. Scooter started to rub the oil into my foot, and I moaned. Scooter stopped cold.

"Maybe you ought to do it," Scooter said to Ricky Ray, handing him the bottle.

Ricky Ray gave him a side-eye and Scooter resumed.

"Calves next, please" I murmured.

Scooter went on rubbing, and it brought up memories of my own—sweet first times with these two boys as we frolicked naked around Beryl's Hole, having go after go. I knew it wasn't True Love, of course, but I wanted to get in as much practice as I could so that when the real thing did cross my path, I would be ready. I would know how to be good to my forever man.

"A little higher, please," I told him. "My thighs are aching."

Scooter kneaded his thumbs into my thigh muscles. The grunts and sighs emitting from me were authentic. I truly was stiff as a board from lying on that gurney for three days, watching brainwashing movies and holding my breath for long stretches. As for Scooter, his reaction was true as life, too: His breathing became increasingly audible, and was matched by Ricky Ray's, in whom I could detect early signs of arousal. There was no doubt a certain member was struggling, against the directives of Before the Fall Ministries and Euple Grymes, to remain bendy.

"Stop, Brother Gad!" Ricky Ray shouted. "We're in the Garden, being tempted by Eve, who visits us in the form of Sister Jill! Just as He said would happen. 'You will have many temptations,' He told us. 'But only in my name can you have your release.'"

"My name isn't Eve," I said. "Nor is it Sister Jill. I'm Tami. Tami Vaduva."

The mention of my name did nothing. Both Scooter and Ricky Ray were too preoccupied with trying to be good congregants. Obeying the orders, accepting the new identities given to them during a terrible, drug-fueled protocol. One poor Rusty was still suffering through.

Time was running short, and I needed to give this all I had. Either I would have to kill them or conscript them in my effort to intercept daddy. The stakes were too high to be sentimental. But the prospect of having to hurt these two still broke my heart. We had history. We were dear friends once, these boys and me—albeit many years prior. Further, despite the fact that I could have effortlessly outmaneuvered and escaped them, such a move might have spelled doom for them both anyway. Were these boys fools? Lost sheep who had never done much with their lives? Yes and yes. But Scooter and Ricky Ray didn't deserve to die.

What I needed on this mission, at this moment, was a sherpa—or two. First, to bring me to Rusty. And next to show me where the guns and brimstone were hidden. Helpers who could help me corner and trap Euple Grymes, so I could subdue him and get him out in one piece.

I removed my leg from Scooter's lap and stood. "I'm not here to tempt anybody, so you fellas needn't oil me up any further. Just hand me the oil and I can take care of myself."

Scooter and Ricky Ray looked relieved.

I poured the oil all over my abdomen and began to rub slowly as I spoke to them. "Before I came here, uncleanliness was a way of life for me. Now I've been reborn and want to stay on a straight and narrow path. In order to do that, I must purify not only myself, but others. Will you permit me, Brothers Gad and Phut, to wash your feet?"

The boys looked at one another.

"It's what He would want," I said in as reassuring a voice as I could muster.

"He is Everything," the boys said in unison.

"Take your seats on the rim of the tub," I said as I fetched the liquid soap dispenser from the shelf.

Scooter looked over at Ricky Ray. "S-s-seems like what He would want," Scooter said.

"Alright. But we should do it fast," Ricky Ray commanded.

"You always have," I said.

The boys took their seats.

I pumped some soap into my hands and made up a good lather. "This soap is heavenly. It smells like peaches. Fresh, fuzzy, juicy peaches. I bet you can smell it too?"

They grunted in the affirmative.

As I went to work on Ricky Ray's feet, I said, "I don't know what's going to be going on here over the next few days, but there sure seems to be a lot of talk about Angels and endings."

"I don't know nothing about that."

"I'm just glad we're all here together," I continued as I lathered Scooter's foot. "I want one last chance to repent before the End arrives. Meet my Creator in as pure a state as possible. Grant me that wish, won't you, Brothers?"

"Y-y-yes, Sister Jill."

"Good. Now relax," I said, with one of the boys' feet in each of my hands.

"Do you mind if I softly sing a little spiritual while I cleanse you two?"

"Do you know 'Peace in the Valley'?" asked Scooter.

"Or 'Let the Heavens Open'?" asked Ricky Ray.

"I do. But I have a different hymn in mind. And I know

you've heard it before, because we listened to it years ago, in a previous life, on an old cassette tape player, when all three of us went swimming at Beryl's Hole. Ready to hear it?"

Puzzled, the boys nonetheless assented.

"The hymn was made famous by a band named Molly Hatchet," I continued, as my hands roamed further up their legs, above their knees, and towards their inner thighs. "It's called 'Flirtin' With Disaster.' Does that title ring a bell?"

They indicated it did not.

My hands slid up the highest point on their respective inner thighs. "It's going to, fellas. Because we're about to take a trip down Memory Lane."

27.

Thirty minutes later, the three of us were splayed on the floor like starfish, in a puddle of warm water, next to an overturned plastic-apple tree.

Ricky Ray unscrewed his eyelids. "Where the fuck am I?"

Scooter, who opened his eyes a split second later, grinned as he looked over at naked me, down at his depleted loins, then over at naked Ricky Ray. "We're in fuckin' heaven, dude."

After Ricky Ray and Scooter high-fived each other, Ricky Ray said, "Tami? Tami Vaduva?"

"In the flesh."

"Damn, girl, you growed up different. *Good* different."

"You fellas were brainwashed. I had to snap you out of it."

"Darlin,' you can snap me anytime you like!" Ricky Ray looked around the Garden of Eden room. "What the hell is all this?"

"We're up in Tucker County, in the Alleghany Mountains, in a place called the Canaan Valley."

"Huh?"

I told them about Before the Fall Ministries.

"How long we been here?" asked Scooter.

I told him I didn't know. "Do you remember how you got here?"

"No," said Scooter.

"Maybe," said Ricky Ray. "But the details are blurry."

Ricky Ray recounted, as best he could, the boys' path to the Before the Fall Ministries: It was like any other Monday night in Beckley, he began. He and Scooter had spent the day, and the evening, and the early hours of the next morning eating chicken wings and drinking Busch longnecks at a gentlemen's club just off Kanawha Street.

Scooter's eyes twinkled. "Fonda Shaft!"

"Huh?" said Ricky Ray.

"The stripper. Her name was Fonda Shaft. We did cinnamon schnapps shots with her."

"Right!" exclaimed Ricky Ray, who re-assembled further pieces of the story: "When the bar closed, we were too wasted to drive. This hot girl, Sabrina Somebody, gave us more beers and offered us a ride home. She had a big Tahoe. And her own driver, this dude in a Pennzoil t-shirt—"

"—I think the driver was a woman, Ricky Ray," said Scooter.

"Bosley," I said.

Scooter blinked and scratched his head. "Next thing I know, me and Ricky was here, strapped down onto some cots and these orange puffs of smoke was coming out of some vents above our heads."

"Are you telling me you didn't come here of your own volition? To clean up and better yourselves after a life of debauchery?"

Ricky Ray chuckled.

"Better myself? I had a beer in one hand, Fonda's ass cheek in the other. What's better than that?"

Bosley was due back any minute. I needed intel. And

promptly sourced it: Yes, they were drugged, starved, sleep-deprived, strapped to gurneys and made to watch porno movies. Though, the boys added, they did not necessarily object to having to watch the films. "Them girls was hotter than any girls I ever seen—except you, Tami," Scooter said. "And whatever it was they was spraying out of the vents made them double hot." The boys were also subjected to weeks of intense PT: running, weightlifting, sit ups, and obstacle courses, they reported.

I looked Scooter and Ricky Ray over; they were truly in the best shape of their lives. I'd have never applied the term before that day, but the boys were . . . *alluring,* as my mama would say. "Do you know if there's a film studio here?"

They looked at each other.

"I think so," said Ricky Ray.

"What do you mean 'I think so'?"

"By a few weeks in, we were in a permanent state of high," Scooter said. "I can't remember what was real or a what was a dream."

"So did you *dream* about a film studio, or were you *in* a studio?"

"I dreamt about a fashion show," said Ricky Ray.

"I had the same dream, dude!" said Scooter.

"Sounds like it wasn't a dream, fellas."

"A runway. Hot models everywhere," added Ricky Ray. "Running."

I had to chase the girls with a scummy old Raggedy Ann doll."

"Me too!"

"Cut to the chase, boys: Were they filming sex videos in that studio?"

"I think so," said Scooter.

"Were there twins in your dream, Ricky Ray?" Scooter asked.

"Yes! Two of the most smokin' hottest identical twins I've ever seen," replied Ricky Ray.

"It wasn't a dream, boys! Those girls—you might have known them as 'Jill'—are the Smithers Twins. They're all over the internet."

"So are we, I think," said Scooter.

"How do you know?"

"I had a go—or twelve—with those girls. And every time we had a go, it looked to me like we was being livestreamed."

Ricky Ray nodded in agreement. "Didn't think nothing of it at the time, but there were gigantic monitors on the set. We saw people on the other side of the camera. The dudes watching from their basements, or wherever. They were always typing comments, which came up on screen, telling us what positions to get into." Ricky Ray smiled wistfully.

Now I understood how Euple Grymes was able to afford this place—the food, the weapons, the sophisticated electronics and video equipment, industrial-grade PsyOps drugs. The vast majority of it funded, presumably, by the Smithers Twins' OnlyFans account, which must have been generating a million dollars income per month.

"The man I came in with, Rusty Riddle—they now call him Brother Er—do you know where he is?"

Scooter looked to Ricky Ray and shrugged. Ricky Ray just shook his head.

I described Rusty, but the boys had absolutely no recollection of him.

"Okay, you don't know Rusty. But you know this place. There's a cache of weapons hidden somewhere," I said. "I saw a room with boxes of ammunition, but no guns."

"Huh?" said Scooter.

"Try to remember! You've got to help me find Rusty. And the guns. And the sulfur."

"Sulfur?" Ricky Ray asked.

"Sulfur. Yellow rock crystals. They're hidden somewhere on this compound. Three tons of brimsto—"

The lock on the door clicked and the three of us froze. "Put a blank look on your faces and just repeat after me," I commanded.

"Repeat what?" whispered Scooter.

"He is everything."

"He is everything," the boys repeated.

I was expecting Bosley. Instead, it was Brother Boaz that appeared.

"Everything will be illuminated," I continued.

"Everything will be illuminated," the boys repeated.

Boaz approached. "Looks like the tadpoles jumped out of the pond," he said. He looked around. "Bosley's been detained. She sent me to fetch you, Sister Jill. Put your clothes on."

I began to dress. Something was just . . . *off* . . . about this guy, Brother Boaz. He spouted all the right scripture, but he had an edge to him, a hint of cockiness that the drugs and brainwashing should have erased by now. I looked him up and down: the lantern jaw, the ramrod straight posture, the rock-hard physique. This guy was ex-military, I was sure of it.

And while he didn't quite have the attitude or clear-headedness that Bosley woman seemed to have retained, I sensed he was more than a brainwashed helper. Brother Boaz, if I wasn't mistaken, had been chosen as a member of Daddy's "senior leadership team." Which in my mind begged the question: Would all of these so-called true-believers be willing to self-immolate in some End of Days cult—or might there be a bigger play?

Brother Boaz fielded a call on his walkie-talkie, then addressed us. "Y'all stay put. I've got to go see Bosley."

"He is everything," I said.

"He is everything," the boys repeated.

Brother Boaz re-locked the door from the outside.

Once he was gone, I applied heavy pressure to Ricky Ray and Scooter: "Boys, you're in mortal danger here. They're not just going to let you waltz out of this compound. Euple Grymes—the pastor—is planning something big. It involves blowing up this whole place and everyone in it. The ATF is going to come down on this place any time now. Probably in the next forty-eight hours. You've got to help me stop him or we're all going to die!"

"What do you think we should do?" Ricky Ray stammered.

"That tall fella, who just left, Brother Boaz, you know him?"

"Seen him around a lot," Ricky Ray said. "I think he's been here for a while."

"Well, I think he's a SEAL. Or at least he was before his brain got all scrambled."

"Huh?" said Scooter.

"SEAL stands for Sea, Air, and Land. Special forces. U.S. Navy."

Scooter scratched his chest. "What makes you so sure?"

"I've met Navy SEALs. Once you've been in the armed forces for a while, you get a sense for these things. He called me a 'tadpole'—twice."

"So?" said Ricky Ray.

"In the SEALs you're called a tadpole until you make it through training. And a tadpole, well, that's a BUD/S student.

That stands for Basic Underwater Demolition/SEAL. Got it? After training a tadpole becomes a frogman."

"When he called us tadpoles, I reckoned he was talking about sperm," said Ricky Ray.

"He wasn't. He also has a 'mighty fine' haircut. A mighty fine is an induction haircut. It's the shortest possible hairstyle without using a razor—unlike the buzz cuts most of the men here sport. All Navy SEALs get mighty fines."

Ricky Ray and Scooter both nodded, but I could tell they didn't fully understand.

"Bottom line, we need to get this Navy SEAL on our team."

"You gonna 'snap him out of it,' like you did to us, Tami?" grinned Ricky Ray.

"Something like that."

Scooter and Ricky Ray elbowed each other.

"And, if we get out of here alive, I'll buy you two cases of Busch beer and hire Fonda Shaft for a private dance."

"Deal," they said, and high-fived each other once more.

28.

Brother Boaz re-entered the Garden of Eden. He looked at Ricky Ray and Scooter, who in unison chanted, "He is everything. Everything will be illuminated. He is everything. Everything will be illuminated."

"Where's Sister Jill?" said Brother Boaz.

I leapt out from behind the door, slamming it shut. "Frogman!" I barked.

Brother Boaz jerked.

"Attention!"

He spun around, looking me up and down. "I told you to stay put and I would be right back."

I stepped right up to him and went face to face. "You don't tell me anything! I do the telling around here! Do you understand, Frogman?"

"I—"

"That's 'Yes, Ma'am!"

He blinked his eyes hard. "He..is—"

"Do I look like a 'He' to you, Frogman?"

"No—"

"That's 'No, Ma'am!'"

"No, Ma'am!"

Involuntarily, he stood ramrod straight, like a panicked fifth grader who encounters the school principal at the shopping mall. He was visibly flummoxed, confused, intimidated and, based on my experience, in that moment highly suggestable. I had to work quickly. I got nose to nose with Brother Boaz, then pointed at Ricky Ray and Scooter. "Do those two look like BUDS/S material to you?" I shouted.

Brother Boaz shook his head. "He is Every—"

"—Answer the question! Do those two look like BUD/S material to you?"

"Everything will be illumin—"

Spittle flew off my lips. "I asked a simple question: Do they look like they have the mettle to complete Basic Underwater Demolition/SEAL training? Or are they Non-Quals? Yes or no?"

"Um . . ." Brother Boaz looked down at my shoulders, presumably in search of some sort of insignia that would indicate the superior rank I had assumed.

"'Um'? Are you talking to me or my shoulders, frogman? Eyes forward!"

He snapped back to attention. Out of the corners of his eyes he appraised Ricky Ray and Scooter. "They look like Non-Quals to me, ma'am."

"Wrong! They're brave patriots! When you disparage these men you insult them and you insult me. Drop down and give me fifty!"

Brother Boaz heeded my command, dropped, and performed some of the most impressive push-ups I'd seen in my military career. "Good job, Frogman. Keep it up."

"Thank you, ma'am," he grunted.

"Those boys over there *will* qualify. And *you're* going to turn them into Navy SEALs. The kind of pipe-hitters we need.

Because we need every able-bodied man we can get. Do you understand, frogman?"

"Yes, ma'am."

"And you're going to dig down deep in your guts and make sure those tadpoles don't ring out on me!"

"Yes, ma'am."

"Now tell me, frogman: Who is everything?"

"He is every—"

"Wrong! Country is everything. Duty is everything."

"Yes, ma'am!"

"Say it!"

"Country is everything. Duty is everything."

"Do you know who 'He' is?"

"He—" His push-ups remained flawless, but his face got all pinched up like he just drank his own urine.

"Who. Is. He?"

"Who, ma'am?"

"'He is Uncle Sam."

"Yes, ma'am!"

"Say it, frogman!"

"He is Uncle Sam, ma'am!"

"If you understand what I just said, give me a sign."

"Booyah!" he yelled as he clapped between each repetition. His temples throbbed and I could feel the heat coming off his body, seeping through the thin tunic he wore. His sweat was making it stick to him like a thin, fresh layer of paper mâché.

"Are you going to turn those tadpoles into frogmen?"

"Yes, ma'am!"

"Are you going to follow the instructions of a senior officer?"

"Yes, ma'am!"

"Give me a sign."

He gave two claps in between his repetition that time. "Yes, ma'am."

"Louder!"

"YES, MA'AM!"

I had been in this situation before: He was breaking, albeit slowly. My capture of his attention was still fragile, and I had to make it stick.

"People sleep peacefully in their beds at night only because rough men and women are ready to do violence on their behalf."

"Yes, Ma'am," he grunted.

"That means you, too, Ricky Ray and Scooter."

"Yes, ma'am," they replied in unison.

"All of you must be your very best in your darkest moments. You're here to survive this, you're here to take charge of it."

"Yes, Ma'am," all replied.

"Now, you repeat after me: I will never quit."

They did as I commanded.

"I persevere and thrive on adversity."

Once again, they did not let me down.

"If knocked down, I will get back up every time."

Ricky Ray gave a "whoop-whoop" after that one.

"Individuals play the game, but teams beat the odds. Are we here as a team?"

"Yes, ma'am!" they shouted.

"Do you understand me, frogman?"

"Yes, ma'am!"

"Give me a sign!"

The Seal started switching up left and right, doing one-handed push-ups.

"Are we going to save every single soul in this compound from hellfire or die trying?"

"Yes, ma'am!"

"Are we going to stop Euple Grymes from carrying out whatever twisted scheme he's got cooking?"

"Hell, yes, ma'am!"

"Attention!"

The SEAL jumped to standing, stood at attention, and looked me in the eyes.

"What's your name, frogman?"

He hesitated for a moment, and I held my breath in anticipation. But then a smile crept up on his face. Strong and clear, he furnished it. His *real* name. He was no longer "Brother Boaz." He was Bryan Dean Blankenship from Parkersburg, West Virginia. Proud Navy SEAL and proud patriot.

"At ease."

I summoned Ricky Ray and Scooter and we formed a scrum.

The SEAL looked judgmentally at nude Ricky Ray and Scooter. "Would you two mind putting your tunics back on?" After they did, the SEAL told his "induction story," which was similar to the boys'. It all started at a bar in Charleston, a joint called The Second Time Around. I knew the place. It was where frisky divorced women who hadn't had a go in a while were known to congregate. Bryan said he'd never been there before that evening, but an acrimonious break-up with a Navy gal named Shelley had brought him to the depths of despair. The last thing he remembered before waking up here was that a super pretty girl with long, wavy blonde hair bought him a pilsner, then asked if he wanted to go out to her Mustang and have a ride—the kind you take horizontally in the back seat.

His brainwashing protocol was particularly grueling, he recalled, as he was so resistant to it.

"It was like Hell Week in BUD/S, but over and over again, and with wacked out drugs and movies with hot girls and Bible verses," he said.

I winced, thinking of Rusty.

"They broke me with a particularly strong cimora mixed special just for me—at least according to that Bosley woman."

"Cimora. I don't know what that is," I said.

"It's a psychedelic cactus," said Ricky Ray. "My hippie brother took some at some desert music festival. Says it's used mostly for shaming purposes and comes from Peru."

"I think he meant *shamanic* purposes," I told him.

"Didn't we get some from that dealer in Beckley we used to buy meth from a few years back," Scooter asked. "That dude who worked at Pizza Hut before he went to jail."

I turned back to Bryan the SEAL. "What about the Angels?" I asked. "All those Sabrinas and Kellys and Jills?"

"They're mostly just here for his amusement. He rotates them in and out of his bed. Nightly. Orgies and role-playing scenarios. He loves to play Charlie," the SEAL said. "But they are strong and well trained. He doesn't take any chances and made sure everyone around here was prepared to fight."

"'He' as in the pastor, I assume?"

"Who else?"

I expected, as I learned more and more about Daddy's decadence and depravity, to grow increasingly numb to it. Instead, each time I was overcome with an even deeper sense of shock and sadness. I put my emotions in my imaginary Tupperware container, sealed tight the lid, and steered the conversation back to the mission. I needed to learn what was *really* happening in Daddy's world—the world outside his bedroom.

There was a strict, military-style hierarchy in the compound, said Bryan. Euple at the top. The next layer down was comprised of hand-selected senior henchmen—and one particularly fearsome henchwoman, Bosley. The next layer down in the ranks was represented by a platoon of obedient strong young men, many of them veterans, tasked with protecting the compound from infiltrators, ATF and police. Below them were the grunts—people like Scooter and Ricky Ray—unskilled worker bees harvested from West Virginia's rural communities who, after they were done servicing the Smithers Twins before the video cameras, were slated to become the first wave of 'soldiers' sent out into the basin to defend the compound against ATF.

"So, he expects to be raided by the ATF? Sounds like he almost wants it," I said.

"There's no almost about it," the SEAL confirmed. "He and Bosley want a fight bad, and they expect to win."

None of this made any sense. I explained to Bryan what he must already have surmised, given how long he'd been here. That Euple Grymes was no soldier. He had never spent a single day in the military and wouldn't have the slightest idea how to train a commando force.

"He's not the one doing the training," he explained.

"Then who?"

"Bosley is the military strategist."

"Bosley? She's an *accountant*."

"She may have enrolled in some sort of jobs skills training program when she was in prison, basic accounting or whatever."

"Prison?"

"We'll get to that. But accounting is not the career she originally trained for, trust me."

Bosley had a certain way about her that indicated she was

no stranger to command and discipline. I nonetheless had my doubts that she ever spent a single day in the United States Armed Forces. To Bryan I said, "I know the branches—Army, Navy, Marines, Air Force, Coast Guard—each has its own distinct vibe. A distinct personality is forged by the experience."

He appraised me. "You're Army, right?"

"Army, active duty. Command Sergeant Major Tami Vaduva," I extended a hand. "Nice to meet you, sailor. Now back to the mission: Tell me about Bosley. She doesn't give off any distinctive military vibes."

"She may have once," said the SEAL.

"When?"

"For the approximately two weeks she served as a private in the U.S. Army."

"She's a vet?"

It didn't seem possible.

"About five minutes after she completed basic, she boarded a C5-M to Habu Halab prison in Iraq," the SEAL told me. "There, she tortured and sexually humiliated inmates, was dishonorably discharged, court marshalled, and sentenced to nine years in a military prison."

"That doesn't explain all this."

"You're right about that. It only explains her love of paramilitary kink. To be honest, I don't know how she learned to do what she did here. I can only tell you she's damned good at it."

The SEAL could tell something was puzzling me. "Why are you shaking your head?"

"Motives," I said. "If Bosley is getting to live out her sick fantasies and Euple Grymes has got the Smithers girls bringing in a ton of cash every month, and all of his pretty Angels are fluttering around him, why would he want to blow the place up?"

"His motive is the same as Bosley's," said the SEAL. "Revenge."

29.

"Revenge against who?" I asked.

The SEAL ran his hand through his finely-shorn, honey-colored hair. "'The Government'—whatever that means. And all of West Virginia, given the way Grymes talks about this place. Whenever he's not screwing his Angels, he's in front of the TV, usually with Bosley, watching cable news shows, one after another, back-to-back. The two of them scream and rant and throw beer cans at the TV, spouting off one crazy conspiracy theory after the other: The main one is about how 'The Deep State'—which includes everybody from the IRS and the CIA to every police department in the country to college professors and corporations—has joined forces under a cabal of both Republicans and Democrats to form a new world order."

"That's right," Ricky Ray said. "Pastor Grymes told us all the fighting between the liberals and conservatives is pretend, rigged like a wrestling match. They're all slapping each other on the back behind closed doors, he says, using the media to keep Moses busy."

"The *masses* busy," the SEAL corrected him.

Bryan the SEAL went on to say that my daddy's grievances against authority of any kind dated back to his boyhood. "When the pastor preaches to new recruits, he always mentions the 'wanton days' of his youth" the SEAL explained. "But those days are always downplayed. He tells the new inductees that he got into minor trouble a few times as a young man—'mix-ups'—to use one of his favorite words—that were blown way out of proportion by 'the demonic forces in charge,' as he calls them. Grymes actually seems to believe that he's been targeted specifically for persecution all of his life and didn't deserve any of it. He's got delusions of grandeur, Command Sergeant Major."

The SEAL watched as I continued to shake my head in disbelief.

"It still doesn't add up."

"What?"

"Luring ATF onto the compound, then blowing them up makes sense as an act of revenge. But the pastor has to know there's no way he'll get out alive. And blowing everybody up—himself included—sounds like a really reckless and self-destructive act of revenge," I said. "Kamikaze missions aren't acts of vengeance; they're acts of desperation."

The SEAL shook his head. "He has no intention of blowing himself up," he said. "I've overheard him on a few occasions, when he's kibbitzing with Bosley. He talks a lot about 'when this chapter of the story closes and our new one opens far, far away from here. Someplace warm and sunny.' In my brainwashed fog, I always thought he was talking about heaven, but now it's obvious to me that he's got an exit strategy."

"Which I intend to thwart. If I can borrow from my commanding officer, a man who's been like a father to me—ATF Director Peter D. Loehr—'You've only got three choices in life: give up, give in, or give it all you've got.'"

"I'm giving all I've got as long as you're fighting by my

side, Command Sergeant Major," said Bryan. He scanned me head to toe, starting with my light blue mostly unbuttoned cotton blouse, then heading south, pausing on the thighs of my skintight bell-bottomed blue jeans. "If we get out of here alive, maybe you'd let me take you to dinner?"

He was my type, there was no doubt about that. But I was determined it was going to be Rusty and me that did the celebrating. "I'm flattered by the invitation," I said, "but I'm sort of in a relationship at the moment. Or at least trying to be. It's a long story."

"Shame on me," the SEAL said. "Women like you don't ever spend the night alone."

If only he knew. But now was not the time to tell him about the family curse.

"So, here's the plan, gentlemen: You, me, and Rusty Riddle, who you're going to help me find, are going to get everybody out of this compound. Safely. Scooter and Ricky Ray, you will take your place among the congregants, and when you get the signal from either me or this here SEAL, you will begin to herd everyone you can towards the entry to the compound."

"Got it," Ricky Ray said, then turned to Scooter and repeated my instructions.

I turned to the SEAL. "You need to find Rusty Riddle—the man who came in here with me. He's a good soldier and a man of character. Hopefully the drugs will have worn off enough by now to make him want to help to us. If not, I ask that you subdue him, so that we can return for him on our way out of here. Then, I ask that you, and hopefully Rusty, get as much weaponry and ammo as possible from your store, and lock it up tight, so no one else can get to it. Meet me in Euple Grymes's quarters after that. I expect to have restrained him by then, hopefully alive. If all of that goes as planned, you can take me to where those bombs are hidden, before taking Pastor Grymes out of this compound and delivering him to the authorities."

"You can't face him on your own, Tami," said the SEAL. "He's heavily armed, and no one to be trifled with. He may have been a petty criminal in his past, but I can assure you, he's learned and leveled up like a pro."

I placed my hand on the SEAL's muscular forearm.

"Neither Euple Grymes, his henchmen, or that Bosley woman, scare me. What does scare me is the thought of the innocents in this compound being blown to bits."

"I have no doubt that you can get to Euple Grymes," said the SEAL. "Even if his quarters are guarded day and night. It's the bringing him to justice peacefully part I'm not so sure about. The man is as single-minded as any enemy I've ever encountered in my service."

He placed his hand on top of mind, and I gently removed it, placing it at my side.

"And so am I. You boys listen to me and hear me good: We're going to complete this mission successfully!"

"Yes, ma'am!" they shouted in unison as the door to the Garden of Eden burst open.

"I thought I was the one who gave the orders around here," said Bosley. She stood there in her same tunic and nurses cap, but with a black fanny pack strapped across her waist, stuffed full, and looking like a pair of bull's balls.

"He is everything," I chanted. "Everything will be illuminated."

"He is everything," the fellas echoed. "Everything will be illuminated."

30.

"I see you've earned your wings, Jill," said Bosley. "Now that you're all fresh and clean, I will finally have the honor of presenting you to the pastor for . . ." she paused and chuckled, ". . . *inspection.*" She looked skeptically at the others. "All of you, come with me."

No plan survives first contact with the enemy. This old military slogan has been proven to me time and again in combat. But even this seasoned battlefield veteran will admit that I didn't expect our plan to unravel quite so quickly.

It unraveled even further the moment we stepped out of the Garden of Eden.

About halfway down the corridor, Bosley stopped. "Did you really think it was going to be this easy?" she said. She was standing spread-legged, the little red cross on her nursing cap staring us down like a third eye. She unzipped her fanny pack and retrieved what looked like a grenade, her index finger poised on the pin. "All of you stay right where you are. Don't move one inch."

"In my training, the only easy day was yesterday," I told her.

Bosley's laughter was equal parts bitter and loving every minute of this. "My trainers told me the same thing."

"So now what?" I said to Bosley.

"*This* what," she said. Bosley pulled the pin, and rolled the grenade towards us, at which time she removed from the fanny pack a gas mask and affixed it to her face. A thick, dark orange mist, similar to the one Rusty and I were subjected to in the infirmary, began to puff out of its top.

I wasted no time, giving a roundhouse kick to Bosley's jaw. As she bent forward, I executed a handstand move, wrapping my legs around the woman's head. "Hold your breath fellas!" I shouted.

But Bosley was no easy target. She did a twist and roll, losing her entire nurse's tunic in the process, like a wrapper coming off a candy bar. I've seen a lot in battle, and am rarely distracted, but even I had to do a double take. Bosley's entire body, neck to toe, was covered in tattoos. It started with the number thirteen just above her clavicle. Her arms and legs were done up with skulls, daggers lugers, and lots of swirly gang writing, while the detailed face of a moderately attractive young man was inked between her fake, pointy and admittedly spectacular breasts. On her belly was the granddaddy of all her tattoos: An image of the dome of the U.S. Capitol exploding. Humvees running over people. Hooded men in ponchos standing atop milk crates, their fingers connected to electrical wires.

"Help me pin her down!" I screamed to the SEAL.

Bosley struggled and swatted at my nose, trying to force inhalation.

I heard Scooter and Ricky Ray start to cough.

"He is Everything," Bosley chanted through her mask.

"He is Everything," Scooter and Ricky Ray repeated in unison.

"Hold your breath, fellas!" I shouted.

The boys' voices were fading. "He is Everything," Scooter and Ricky Ray repeated in unison.

Great. Now, we were down two—just me and the SEAL.

With my legs I locked Bosley's head in a scissors hold, then ripped the gas mask off her face and affixed it to mine. She wasn't going anywhere. With my hand I knocked the smoking grenade down the hall and instructed the SEAL to evacuate Ricky Ray and Scooter and find Rusty, but the SEAL didn't respond.

"Did you hear me?"

The semi-catatonic SEAL's eyes were wide and his nostrils were flaring. "He is Everything," he said.

Bosley pounced. "Kill her!" she screamed to the fellas. Any moment, my three comrades would turn against me. There was no time to waste. I released my hold on Bosley and leapt to my feet. Putting Scooter and Ricky Ray out of commission was easy. A hard kick to each of their chests, and a one-two knockout punch as a follow up, left them both on the ground and incapacitated. Under normal circumstances I would have killed them in order to get them out of the way, but these were my best friends from high school. If I could manage to keep them alive and drag them out later, I'd snap them out of their trance again. One way or another.

The SEAL and Bosley were going to be another story.

"Two is one; one is none," I called out to the SEAL, hoping some proper Navy SEAL lingo might reset him.

"Your stupid jargon is nothing compared to my cimora," Bosley said through a cough. "Brother Boaz, take the mask off of her and give it to me. NOW!"

Mechanically, the SEAL punched me in the gut. I doubled

over, but managed to inhale some good, clean air before he removed the mask and handed it to Bosley, who stood and reaffixed the mask to her face.

He'd be coming back at me for the kill any second now. Without another word, I took a running start up the wall, flipping backwards and landing a kick to the SEAL's chest. It sent him into the wall, where he slumped to the floor. I had thirty seconds if I was lucky before he revived. I dropped to the floor, cupped my mouth, and sucked in bit more of the clean air down there as Bosley thrust her knee into my buttocks, hitting my tail bone hard. I sprung up and tackled her. She was able to roll me over, the two of us bowling down the hall, and thankfully further away from the orange mist of her cimora. At last, I was able to take a deep breath.

This woman was nothing short of a rattlesnake, and in the half-second it took to fill up my lungs, she struck at me, trying to bite my neck and rip open my carotid artery. I twisted. She sunk her teeth into my shoulder, and I cried out.

"Pain is good; extreme pain is extremely good," I shouted, hoping to shake the SEAL loose from his stupor with more Navy directives. He was no longer slumped, but standing in the mist like a zombie, engulfed by the cimora. I was dizzy from breathlessness as I dug my fingernails into Bosley's breasts, squeezing as hard as possible as I twisted one clockwise, the other counter-clockwise.

"Brother Boaz!" Bosley squalled. "Pull her *perfect* hair out, rip her *perfect* head off!! KILL HER!"

31.

I was reaching for Bosley's mask when, from behind me, the SEAL grabbed me by the hair and dragged me off Bosley. I gripped him at the wrists, hanging on tight and kicking my legs up, landing one on his jaw. It was good enough to get him to let go of my hair, but not enough to disable him for more than a second or two. He came right back after me and I maintained my distance, trying to stay moving. I knew that if a guy as strong and well-trained as the SEAL could land one clean hit I stood a good chance of getting knocked out cold, making it game over for me.

"There are two ways to do something," I said to the SEAL: "the right way, and again." I crouched for leverage and lifted my leg, bearing straight down on his knee joint, then slid away. He growled like a jungle cat, but shook off the pain. I needed to keep at him, take my chances, but steer clear of his advances.

He swung a right hook, which I barely avoided by ducking under his arm and coming out around his back. He spun around, giving me no more than a second. But that was enough. I jumped forward and head-butted him, convinced I had cracked my skull in the process. I ran my fingers across my forehead. No blood, thankfully. "I persevere and thrive on adversity," I told the SEAL, loading on more jargon. "If knocked down I will get back up every time."

He came at me, giving me the back of his hand hard, stunning me, then side-kicked me in the shoulder, which sent me reeling.

"That's more like it," Bosley sneered as she massaged her tender breasts, whose swollen, blood-red nipples seemed to stare at me like the eyes of little devils.

The SEAL took a couple of swings, but I ducked them. I was running out of energy. I needed to take the SEAL out or take him with me, and I needed to do it double quick. He charged me. I gave him an ear slap, one on each side of his head, giving him quite a ring. He actually stumbled backwards.

"You going to ring out on me, SEAL, is that what you're going to do? You going to ring that bell?"

I sprung forward and gave him another ear slap, but this time he grabbed my wrist and flung me to the floor.

He jumped on me, pinning my arms down with his knees. His big hand wrapped around my throat. He brought his face close to mine. His teeth were bared, his eyes locked onto mine like lasers. "I don't ever, *ever*, ring the bell," he said.

"Bryan," I croaked as his hands clenched tighter.

Behind him, I heard a cackle. Smug and bitter. "Goodbye, Angel," Bosley said.

Though she was close, she sounded far, far away.

The SEAL came in even closer, eye to eye, just inches from my face. Then all of a sudden, he smiled and winked at me. "Booyah!" he mouthed.

In a flash he spun around and knocked Bosley out cold. She slid down the wall and plopped down hard on her rear end, legs splayed and eyes closed, but that thin mouth of hers hung open in surprise. I yanked the mask off her face and handed it to the SEAL. "Inhale deeply!"

I sat up, keeping my breath held and rubbing my neck.

He handed the mask to me. "Your turn. You okay?" he asked.

I nodded, getting up and on my feet. I took a couple of deep, deep breaths through the mask.

"Sorry I roughed you up, but I was out of it for a couple minutes there. When I came back to my senses, I had to make it look real," he said.

"Sorry I roughed you up, too. But I had to stop you. Still friends?"

We shook hands.

"I thought you were never going to snap out of it," I told him.

The SEAL exhaled and shook his head. "Once, during Hell Week, I was doing pushups while getting a hose sprayed in my face. It was a tough stream, and it hurt. I'd hardly slept in days, and every single muscle in my body hurt."

"Been there," I said. "Not at BUD/S, obviously, but in similar situations."

"My commanding officer came up real close, that hose right in my face, and said, 'We're not going to stop until we get at least one quitter. You going to be that guy? You gonna quit?' Just now, you said, 'Are you going to ring that bell' and that rung my bell, if you know what I mean."

"That cimora didn't stand a chance."

"Hearing my name—my real name—on your lips didn't hurt either." Bryan looked down at Bosley. "What do we do with her?"

Bosley was still out for the count, so I ran back into the

Garden of Eden and pulled down some of the plastic vines hanging from the ceiling. I tested them, and they were indeed strong. I returned to the corridor hall.

"These'll work," I told Bryan the SEAL. "Go back in there and see if you can find some duct tape while I secure our prisoner here."

As I was hog-tying Bosley, I gasped with joy at what I saw. But almost instantly, that joy melted away.

"Stop right there, Sister Jill."

Standing before me was Rusty Riddle, holding an Uzi, which was pointed at me. His eyes were black and vacant, like a shark's.

"Rusty," I said. "It's me, Tami."

I heard a chuckle from beneath me. Bosley spat out a wad of blood and saliva, then proceeded to unwind the plastic vine at her wrist with her teeth.

"Your Rusty is gone," she grunted, her jaw clenched tight. "And he ain't never coming back."

32.

He had dark circles under his eyes. He was pale. His skin looked cold to the touch. I wanted to hug him, tell him he would wake up from this nightmare—only there was an Uzi between him and me, and there was no telling if he was far enough gone to pull the trigger.

Bryan the SEAL reentered the corridor from the Garden of Eden. He was eager to advance, but I held out my hand for him to stand down. Last thing we needed was for him to get himself killed defending me.

"Rusty," I said. "Do you remember the night we met?"

His face was immobile, distant, like a drawn picture—something that resembled him but could not capture his essence.

"Your friend, Jeremiah Tibbs, made us some of the tastiest goat sliders I've ever had the pleasure of eating. It was at your restaurant that you worked so hard to build. I drank all your flavored moonshines, though I myself am not a drinker. But your concoctions were so good. Bologna moonshine, pizza roll moonshine."

Nothing.

The SEAL looked over at me as if to suggest I should give

him a turn at talking Rusty down. I indicated that he needed to keep quiet and let me continue.

"There's something special between you and me, remember? I don't know what it is or why. I don't know what we're going to do about it. Actually, I do. We made a deal. Do you remember? There's a go in your future, Rusty. Between you and me. Let's have that go. It'll be beautiful. We've both saved ourselves. Let's not spoil it. Because it can't end like this. It can't end with you pointing an Uzi at me, and me having to take you out or die trying."

Bosley rolled out from under me and writhed up to a seated position with her back against the wall. She was panting heavily and rubbing her forehead. There was a big goose egg on it, right above her left eye. Her nursing cap, the only piece of clothing on her, was askew.

"Shoot both of them, Brother Er," she instructed Rusty. Pointing at me, she said, "Start with this little wild cat. She's been a thorn in my side since I was twelve. 'Watch after Tami,' that old bitch Gladys was always saying. 'Play dolls with her, 'cause she's all sad'. 'Don't be a hog, save some of that deep-fried squirrel for Tami.'"

I looked over at Bosley, my deepest memories stirring and recognition slowly dawning on me. Was this Po? I knew a Po during my brief time as a girl at daddy's church. A redhead, like Bosley, but there the resemblance stopped. The old Po was a chubby girl with bad acne and a flat chest. Her teeth were tiny and all twisted up in her mouth, except for a big gap between the front two. It was not a fond memory. Po—her full name was Parlene-Ola—was a few years older than me, and always in trouble: with her mama, with daddy and his mother, with the other congregants. Sour girl. Nasty mean streak. She tortured animals. Skinned alive a chipmunk we all loved to play with. We'd named him Tobias and I cried for a week after she'd dropped his skinless form on me from a tree she'd been hiding in. The adults mostly let it go; at least the congregation could eat the critters that she killed. She was almost as cruel to us little ones, although she saved her worst high jinks for the other kids, as she was afraid of my mama. And now she was back with her old pastor, helping him run a cult even more sinister than his snake-handling operation, putting her sadistic kills to good use.

"You're Po from the Pentecostal Tabernacle of the Holy Ghost's Testimony Church?"

"In the flesh," she grinned.

I looked that flesh up and down, focusing on some of her older tattoos—namely the prominent ones with the swirly gang letters and big number 13s.

"So, how did a West Virginia gal like yourself end up as part of the Mara Salvatrucha criminal operation, if you don't mind my asking? Those are official MS-13 tattoos you got there, if I'm not mistaken."

"How does a woman like you or me end up anywhere?"

"True Love?" I said. "I suppose in your case, you fell in love with a man who shares your passion for torture and murder?"

Bosley smiled, baring those now Angel-perfect teeth of hers. "What can I say? Some couples like to play tennis and watch rom-coms."

She laughed again. "Unfortunately, our love wasn't meant to last."

"Aw. He leave you for a leggy blonde? Or leggy brunette?"

I could tell by the pucker of her lip that I'd struck a nerve.

"He left me for hell," she hissed. "He's a pile of ash in a river of molten lava now. I gave him a hot bath one little toe at a time. Then one foot at a time, then up to the knee, and so on."

"How romantic," I said.

It was a gamble, but I decided I had no choice but to roll the dice. "Before you have me shot, can I tell you what they used to say about you down in McDowell Country, when we were kids? I think you'd find it of interest."

Her lip curled up on one side like a smear."Knock yourself out," she said. "I've granted last wishes tougher than that."

"Po," I said, all sing-songy. "Po, as in Po-faced, Poo-faced, No-Po-no-way, rather-die-than-have-a-go-with-Po."

Her smeared-up lip started to tremble.

"Meaner than any of the snakes they was handling," everyone said. "Even uglier on the inside as she was on the outside."

"Shut up!" Po susurrated.

The SEAL reached over and brushed my forearm, as if to say, "That's enough, Tami."

"Back off," she instructed him. "Or I'll kill her slow and make you watch."

The SEAL gritted his teeth but obeyed.

"Just you wait until the pastor has me all fixed up," Po continued. "He's already done my teeth. Bought my boob-job. And as soon as we're out of here, he's going to have the best plastic surgeons in the world fix up the rest of me—eyes, lips, a new nose. Then we're going to the Bahamas together. Just him and me."

"Are you saying my daddy is your . . . boyfriend?"

"Almost," Po grunted. "He doesn't want to spoil things between us by having a go with me, but that'll change."

She looked down at her perfect breasts with a mixture of pride and hope.

I shook my head.

"Making your outside look nice isn't going to change what's on the inside of you. I promise you that if anyone could have stomached your . . . *personality* . . . you would not have found yourself alone with a body full of bad tattoos and a dead boyfriend."

Po stood up and walked behind Rusty. "I've made the acquaintance of several beautiful girls in my time here, and plenty of them are shallow and vapid and petty. Still, I don't see anyone turning them down."

"Hmmm," I said. "Any of them torture animals? That's usually a line-crosser with quality men. That, and murder, and brainwashing."

I looked over to Rusty, hoping against hope that I would see a glimmer of his old self. His hand was firm on the Uzi, his finger held gently on the trigger. His face expressionless.

"But there are still two other problems that you got, Po, and they're big ones."

"Really?"

"See, I don't believe for one second that Euple Grymes plans to take you with him to wherever he's planning to go, after he lures in the ATF and blows up this place, taking most of our 'wild and wonderful' state down with it. That's assuming it even gets that far. See, I happen to know the director of the ATF—very well I might add—and you picked the wrong man to tangle with."

"I picked exactly the right man to tangle with," she spat. "Peter D. Loehr had me put in prison for nine long years, and I'm going to put him out of commission forever."

The venom in her voice nearly compelled me to take a step backwards. It all made sense now. Of course, General

Loehr—back when he was still with the Army—would have presided over such a high-profile court martial. The press had had a field day with the female private who'd sexually abused the prisoners in her charge.

"Director Peter D. Loehr is the best man I know," I told her. "And you're lucky he didn't make sure you got put away for the rest of your natural life. Because that's what I would've done after you disgraced yourself and the United States Army. You should've fallen to your knees and thanked the man for his mercy, but instead, you ended up with Euple Grymes who most certainly will not be showing you any compassion."

Po took a step towards me and put her hands on her hips. "You dressed up, fixed up, ho," she grunted. "I don't need mercy from nobody. Who do you think made those bombs, set those timers, controls every part of what we're going to do here?"

Po licked her lips with her short, pale tongue.

"I can have your friend Rusty plug you full of holes and still have plenty of time to meet Pastor Euple and get the hell out of here. And he will be waiting for me. Unfortunately, you won't be around to see that part of it."

33.

I reached up to the buttons on my prison blouse and began to undo them slowly. Then I angled a bit so that Rusty could get the best view. In one jerk, I tore the blouse open, revealing my bare breasts.

"I've fed three of my children with these, and never once had to have them lifted. They are one hundred percent real. No pastor needed to buy me a set, like he bought yours."

Po squinted at them and shrugged. "So what?"

"I know a little bit about what a great plastic surgeon can do and what he can't do. See, after my mama took two bullets that were meant for me, I purchased for her a full upgrade, head to toe, including a vaginoplasty."

"Your point?"

"My point is that my mama had something to start with. She had good bones and lovely skin, despite years of smoking and a poor diet. She had good genes that gave her a thick head of hair and a shapely figure. But most of all, my mama's the kind of woman, who despite her many flaws, would take a bullet for her little girl. Not on purpose, exactly, but nevertheless she took them like a champ. And you can't buy that kind of beauty."

I looked down at my breasts. Then I looked over at Rusty, who had begun singing gently.

"In fact, if I had a choice between these, between my body, my face, my hair, and a good character, a good heart, I would choose the latter two. Because that's the only way you can ever entice someone to truly love you. I think deep down you know that whoever's face is tattooed between your breast didn't leave you because he found a hotter girl."

"Actually, that's exactly what he said. 'Po, you're ugly and she's not. I'm outta here.'"

"Then he was just as ugly as you are. On the inside. And the two of you deserved each other."

Po put her hand on Rusty's shoulder and leaned in to his ear. "Brother Er," Po said. "I think it's time we give this bimbo what she deserves. Shoot her. Shoot her in the hands and the feet. Shoot her in the shoulders and the thighs. In the stomach, in the buttocks, and most of all, in both of her perfect, *real* breasts."

I saw Bryan the SEAL jerk away from the wall and quickly shot him a look that said, "not yet, not now." Once again, he followed my orders and stood down, but wasn't happy about it.

Then I looked into Rusty's face and swallowed hard. He stood still as a statue and continued staring off into space. There was a serenity to his gaze, almost an otherworldliness. The hum coming from his throat was barely audible, but sweet and clear.

"Did you hear me?" Po growled. "Quit that weird singing. *He* wants you to kill this bitch and *He* is Everything."

Rusty's lips started to move. His eyes rolled back into his head once more, revealing only the whites. At first it was just like he was mouthing something, but after a few moments, the words started coming out. "When you pass through the waters, I will be with you; and when you pass through the rivers, they will not sweep over you. When you walk through the fire, you will not be burned; the flames will not set you ablaze."

"What the hell you quoting scripture for?" scolded Po. "That's not what He told you." But as she spoke to Rusty, he seemed not to be paying any attention to her at all. He was still pointing the Uzi at me, and his finger was still on the trigger, but it was like he wasn't there at all. He gazed at the ceiling. The verse kept tumbling out of his mouth, getting louder with each recitation. I could swear there was a glow about him.

The SEAL mouthed *what's going on?* Clearly this was not part of any brainwashing regimen he'd experienced or witnessed at Before the Fall Ministries.

"Rusty?" I said.

Po started berating him. She smacked his head, but he just kept reciting the verse. His hands were still firm on the Uzi, but I took my chance. I figured there wasn't going to be a better one.

Jumping up from my left foot, I executed a crescent kick with my right, landing my heel right in the middle of Po's forehead. She flew backwards, her arms whooshing in circles. I slid and twirled to the right of Rusty, wrenching the Uzi out of his hands. He did not protest. Instead, he continued to recite verse.

"Put your hands up," I said.

"Or what?" snorted Po as the SEAL spun around and joined me. "You'll kill me? I don't think so. Your Daddy will kill you if you kill me. He needs me to get out of here in one piece with his money."

I cocked the Uzi and repeated my order. Po's hands went up to her nurse's cap as she approached me.

"Shoot her!" said the SEAL.

I don't know what made me hesitate. Perhaps it was the knowledge, deep down, that that evil place in McDowell County helped transform a girl into a monster. I should not have hesitated. From beneath the cap, she pulled out a Shuriken and whipped that five-pointed blade right at me, aiming for my eyes. I tilted my head to the side, the blade nipping the top of my ear. It lodged itself into the wall behind me. As I recovered from the surprise, Po reached back into her cap. I wasn't going to wait to see what was coming at me next.

I unloaded the Uzi on her.

She died quicker than she deserved, with a foul grimace on her face. Her upgraded teeth clenched and gleaming.

34.

I put the safety on the Uzi. As I was rebuttoning my blouse, I realized that Rusty wasn't reciting Bible verse anymore. He was staring at me. Not through me, like before, but really looking at me. At first, he appeared remorseful. On closer inspection, though, he was calm. Almost . . . *blissful.*

"You okay?" I asked.

He smiled. "Better than okay. Blessed."

"Why are you crying?"

"Tears of joy."

"Look," I said, "I'm sure we've got a lot to tell each other, but it will have to wait. Daddy's planning to blow up the compound, plus a good chunk of West Virginia."

"I know."

The SEAL approached. I re-introduced the men. "He's the one they called Brother Boaz, the one who wheeled you in and out of the cinema, Rusty."

Rusty didn't remember Brother Boaz.

The three of us searched for a stairway or elevator to Euple Grymes's quarters on the second floor. Congregants clogged the corridors: vacant-eyed young men in tunics, primped Angels. All seemed to be anxiously, if not a little cluelessly, milling about. The whole place appeared to be mobilizing.

We couldn't find a staircase or elevator.

"It's too late," Rusty mumbled as we passed a window.

"What's too late?" I asked.

"The end is near."

"How do you know, Rusty?" asked the SEAL.

Rusty pointed out the window. The fading orange sun hovered above the top of the Allegheny Mountains. "Armageddon. After sunset," Rusty reported.

Concern crept into my voice. "Who told you? Bosley—or should I say 'Po'?"

"No."

"One of Euple's Angel's?"

"No."

We entered the chapel. "Then who?" asked the SEAL. Rusty paused, in front of the bookshelves, reflected for a moment, then said, "The Holy Ghost told me."

In Rusty's tone I detected none of the snark and sarcasm he deployed on that first night we met, on the walk from HOOCH to Jeremiah's loft, when Rusty quoted some passage or another from Genesis about people getting drunk and "laying uncovered" in tents.

Bryan the SEAL and I looked at each other skeptically. The SEAL bit down on his lip. "Um, did the Holy Ghost tell you where the bombs are planted?"

Rusty looked up at the ceiling, then lowered his eyes and directed his gaze at the SEAL and I. "The men's dormitory. The women's dormitory. The cinema. The infirmary. The barn."

Rusty began to swoon.

"What's wrong?" asked the SEAL.

"Dizzy," mumbled Rusty. He leaned against one of the bookshelves, which swung open to reveal a hidden staircase.

"No talking," I said as we slithered up the stairs.

At the top was a reinforced door with an electrical panel next to it. Entry required a code.

"This is it," Rusty said. "Euple Grymes private quarters."

"The Holy Ghost didn't by any chance give you the number sequence that would get us in there," the SEAL asked.

"No."

I ordered Rusty and the SEAL to stand back and unloaded the Uzi. Sparks flew. The door vibrated gently, then opened.

I stepped in cautiously, fanning the Uzi.

No sign of Daddy.

We surveyed the room. My first thought was that it was both everything I imagined and nothing I imagined. The floor was covered in a white shag carpeting so thick and fluffy that it felt like we were walking on clouds. In the center of the room was a crescent-shaped white leather sofa.

"Get a load of that skylight," said the SEAL.

We looked above the sofa. The light cast upon it by the sun was golden and perfect, almost holy. The clear plastic dome, which rivaled a European cathedral dome, must have been twenty feet high and just as wide.

"What's hanging off the skylight?" I asked.

"Trapeze?" said the SEAL. "Or some sort of harness-and-pulley system. Something kinky, from the looks of it."

"Oh, Daddy," was all I could muster.

One entire wall contained a series of built-in television monitors, above which were mounted speakers. Both FOX News and MSNBC were on mute. Behind the sofa, against another wall, was a blinking neon Budweiser beer sign featuring three smiling frogs: "Bud," "Wei" and "Ser." Next to the neon was a series of tin signs: *Girls Welcome*, *Game On*, *Cigars*, and so on.

On the opposite side of the room, below a rotating disco ball, was a dance floor that was all lit up like it was Christmas.

Adjacent to that was a hot tub that could easily accommodate ten, a pool table covered in red felt and fitted onto the bottom half of a red Ford Mustang—it had the headlights on—a foosball table, and an arcade: Pac-Man, Galaga, Space Invaders and even a *Charlie's Angels* pinball machine. A series of blips, beeps and electronic chimes emitted from the machines.

"The world's largest man cave," the SEAL noted as he surveyed the Farrah Fawcett poster gallery: Farrah on a skateboard; Farrah in a rust-colored one-piece bathing suit tilting her hair back and flashing her pearly whites; Farrah, along with her *Charlie's Angels* costars, standing side by side, their hands in prayer pose. In the center of the *Charlie's Angels* poster gallery was a seven-foot-tall image of Daddy, shirtless and in jeans, perched above a blood-red-and-black custom Harley Davidson Night Rod. Orange flames were painted on the gas tank.

The SEAL took one last look around the hermetically-sealed room, or, more precisely, five-star fortress . . . as envisioned by a frisky teenage male. "You think he might've turned himself in? Fled the scene? What?"

The picture of daddy on his Harley swung outward. "Neither," Euple Grymes said as he emerged from behind yet another hidden passageway—this one leading from his bedroom, I presumed. He stood before us in a red velvet robe, aiming a .357 Magnum at me. "Drop the Uzi, girl. Put it on the floor. *Slowly!*"

35.

I obeyed.

"Y'all step back," commanded Daddy.

We did.

He fetched the Uzi and laid it on the *Charlie's Angels* pinball machine. "This thing's a bit much," he said. "For a man who needs to overcompensate if you get my meaning. As for me, I prefer the clean, simple power of a Magnum."

"I've been waiting for you, Daddy," I said. "Not just now—my whole life."

"I've been waiting for you . . . Tami. But only just now."

He pointed to the fancy gold cursive letters above his left breast. "And call me Euple, like it says on my robe."

I raised my chin and defied him. "I think I'll keep calling you Daddy," I said.

"Suit yourself." He grinned. The seductive, boyish grin I'm sure he'd deployed a thousand times to get a girl to do his bidding.

"How many girls you got tied up back in your bedroom, Daddy."

He shook his head and shrugged. "Maybe none. Maybe one. Maybe a dozen. It don't really matter much, does it?"

"It matters to me," I said. "It matters that I share blood

with a man who could kidnap all these young people, brain-wash them, and make them have sex with him. It matters worse that you intend to sacrifice them all, to make them party to the death and destruction you're planning."

"I didn't make nobody have sex with me who didn't want to—didn't beg to in some cases." He raked his fingers through his lavish, jet-black-with-just-a-hint-of-gray-at-the-temples hair. "The ladies, they've always liked me. And nobody here ever got tied up who didn't ask to be."

Rusty and the SEAL looked at Daddy: Rusty judgmentally, the SEAL strategically. I could almost see the cogs turning in Bryan's mind. How would he disarm him, maybe get his hands back on that Uzi?

"Let me get a better look at you, girl." Daddy retrieved a remote from his pocket, pushed a button, and the lights went up. He looked at me like I was a meal. "I was right, you know. Always am. You *are* the best Jill I have ever seen. Better than my Smithers Twins. Five times as good as the Jills who come to chapel. Hell," he said as he pointed at the posters of Farrah Fawcett, "I'd venture to say you're even better than the original, and that's saying something." He picked up the Uzi and ambled over to the white leather sofa, sitting down carefully, with the Magnum trained on us as he lowered himself. He set the Uzi down at his feet and scanned me head to toe. "Looks like apples don't fall too far from trees, darlin'."

"What do you mean, Daddy?"

"Looks to me like you could get a man to do anything for you. Assuming I am your daddy, you might just have me to thank for that."

"And my mama," I said. "You remember her, don't you? Dark hair, smokey eyes, goes by the name of Velvet."

"Not an easy one to forget, your mama," he said. He leaned back into the sofa and gazed up into the skylight. "Y'all like my dome? Better than the Sixteenth Chapel's."

It was not the time to correct him. "We were talking about Mama, Daddy."

"Every stretch of my time in prison was different, but one thing was always the same," he said, making it clear that he would be shaping the contours of the conversation. "I couldn't see the sky, except for when they walked us around the yard on leashes—like dogs. Hardest part was I couldn't see the stars at night. I missed starlight something fierce. That's when I always had my quiet time. My thinking time. Missed so many years of stargazing I can't even count. That's why I put that dome up." Daddy pushed a button on the remote. The top of the dome retracted, welcoming in the fresh air. "It's bright at midday. Too bright." He shrugged. "But only for a couple of hours. That's when I go to my sleeping chambers. Pass the time with pleasing female company. A Jill here. A Sabrina there." He arched an eyebrow and grinned like a mischievous little boy. "Or maybe a Jill, Kelly and Sabrina all at the same time." He pushed his shoulders back and stretched. "A 'siesta,' I think it's called. At least that's what all them MS-13 gang fellas I served time with called it."

"We could have been a family, Daddy. *Should* have been a family."

He looked down for a moment, then back at me. He seemed a little wistful. "Velvet Vaduva." He grinned again. "Man, she was somethin'."

I peered into his piercing blue eyes. Cheekbones high and lips full, his face looked like it was carved out of marble. So did his body, to which the robe clung like cellophane wrap. Unlike my mama, Euple Grymes appeared to be nothing short of a workout fiend. “Daddy,” I said. “Look around you. Seems to me you’ve got everything you’ve always wanted. You’re a free man. This ministry of yours is a successful small business.”

“*Big* business,” he said, correcting me. “We got subscribers from Finland to Hong Kong.” He aimed his remote at one of the monitors, pushed a button, and a map of the world came up. Subscriber countries were indicated in red; there must have been fifty of them.

“Then why do you want to go and destroy it? This scheme of yours will land you in either one of two places: prison or a graveyard.”

“I ain’t going back to prison,” he said. “Never.”

“You’re prepared to die?”

“I am, girl. But ain’t nobody taking Euple Grymes’s life. I’m the taker in this situation.”

Through my military training and experience, I knew how to lay it on thick, to get the man I was trying to cajole, usually an enemy combatant, to stand down or, as Daddy said, “do my bidding.” In this instance, though, what I said next came straight from the heart. “I can make sure you get out of here safe, alive, and with a good deal, Daddy. You haven’t killed anybody. You’ve released no sulfur into the atmosphere. As you just noted, the sex here—while unseemly—is among and between consenting, legal-age adults. Nobody’s going to put you in jail for squatting on public land. A good lawyer will argue that all the drugs have been used for religious purposes.” I took a deep breath. “ATF Director Loehr is a good, fair man. He’ll listen to whatever I have to say.”

“The director of the ATF? A ‘good man’? Not according to my Bosley.”

"Your Bosley sullied the good name of the United States Army. She was lucky she was ever let out of prison at all. As for Peter D. Loehr? I know him a lot better than she ever did. He's been a mentor to me. Almost like the daddy I never had."

Daddy's lip curled up. "Almost, huh?" He rose and walked over to the bar area. Next to the Budweiser neon was an industrial-sized refrigerator. Daddy plucked the remote from his pocket again and clicked a button. The door opened automatically, like a vault. Daddy procured a Pabst Blue Ribbon.

"It's going to be dark soon. The place is surrounded. Tell us how to disarm the bombs, Grymes," said the SEAL, "before ATF lights this place up like the fourth of July."

Daddy cocked the Magnum and pointed it at the SEAL. "Shut up, Brother Boaz, lest I shut you up permanent."

The SEAL crossed his arms over his chest and stared Daddy down.

Rusty approached Daddy slowly, but fearlessly, stopping just a few feet away from the barrel of the Magnum.

"We can have hate and death. Or we can have love and peace," Rusty said. "I feel the presence of love. Right here, right now. It hovers above us. Will you pray with me, pastor, that that love will come down and fill this room?"

"Shut up, Brother Er, lest I shut you up permanent, too."

Rusty began to vibrate.

"What's wrong with you, boy?" Daddy asked.

The SEAL looked over at me.

Daddy waved his hand dismissively. "Nice try, boy. But don't waste your time. Or mine. I know all the same tricks. Used them myself to good effect on more than one occasion. So, save your 'I saw the light' bullshit for some other fool."

"Do you hear that?" whispered the SEAL.

"Chopper," I whispered.

"There ain't no God," continued Daddy. "They're ain't no Angels. There ain't no afterlife with trumpets and—"

Daddy stopped mid-sentence and looked up.

We all did.

Just then, the whole room began to shake. We could not see the chopper, but could hear its swirling, menacing blades. Then, like an eclipse, the sun's rays were blocked by what I can only describe as a UFO.

36.

The UFO's underbelly, descending gradually into the open dome, was fashioned out of dark gray corrugated metal, pocked with rust and gouges. A long, rectangular object—one that looked like it was made of scrap metal parts of various shapes and sizes—was affixed to it at the center. Slowly, methodically, the hovering assemblage lowered itself in through the dome. Daddy ran for cover behind the bar.

Rusty, his eyes rolled back again, looked up at the UFO as if it were some sort of Divine Intervention, like a burning bush. While Rusty stood there, frozen, Bryan grabbed Rusty by the forearm and yanked him out of the drop zone. The metal contraption was now inside the room, dangling from a wire, hovering over Daddy's conversation pit. From high above, someone in the chopper released the magnet. The gigantic glob of metal crashed with a thud, squashing the sofa. The suspension wire retracted with a whip and a zip, the way an unlocked tape measure returns to its case. The chopper took a sharp right turn, over the top of the building, and disappeared from sight.

"What the devil?" shouted Daddy.

The SEAL looked over at me, then back at the lime-green pile of dented steel. "Is that a . . . *Pacer*?"

"No," I told him. "It's a Gremlin. A '73. Made by the same company, though—American Motors Corporation."

A grave silence fell over the room.

From where we stood, we could not make out exactly what was going on inside the vehicle, but whoever—whatever—was in there was moving around. Then, from inside the Gremlin, country music began to blast.

"What is this, some sort of PsyOps trick from the ATF?" asked the SEAL.

"It's Conway Twitty," Daddy said. "'*Hello Darlin*'," he added as he cautiously approached the vehicle, whose hood and windshield were missing.

The driver's side door opened unhurriedly. We saw the bare feet and painted pink toenails first. Flashes of white leg followed: One long, fleshy, uncovered leg after another slowly swung out and made contact with the floor.

"Velvet," murmured Daddy.

Once Mama stepped out of the car, she tugged on the seat of her frayed, way-too-tight-on-her Jordache jean shorts. They were visibly creeping up in the rear. She adjusted the tube top she was wearing—a pale yellow number with the words *Foxy Lady* spelled out in glitter; a tube top not designed to accommodate Mama's new, enormous breasts. Leaning back against the vehicle, Mama looked like a lady of the evening resting against a lamppost. An Eve Ultra-Light Menthol 120 dangled from her pink-painted lower lip. From her back pocket, which she could barely get her hand into, she retrieved a Bic lighter, lit the cigarette, and said to my father: "Remember the last time you saw me dressed like this?"

"I sure do," Daddy said as he looked her up and down.

"I had on this exact same outfit the day we met." Mama

blew the smoke from out the side of her mouth without even taking the butt from her lips. "Remember what we did in a car exactly like this one?"

"Oh, I do indeed," Daddy said. "Every second of it."

"So do I."

Mama pointed at me, then at Daddy. "We made my baby."

"You followed our baby here to track me down?" asked Daddy.

Mama's sultry vixen character was retired; the real Mama came on stage: "You fool. Your face is splattered across every TV screen in America. There's TV trucks out there. And tanks. Choppers. Fire engines and ambulances. About a thousand ATF agents. Everybody knows you're in here."

"Just as I planned."

"And I got some more news for you, Euple. I'm your last line of defense. I convinced the ATF director to let me come in this way as a last resort, before them government boys come in *their* way. And it was no easy sell convincing the director, I'll tell you that. We had to fish that Gremlin out of a junkyard in Roanoke and chopper it all the way over here. But he knew Tami was in here. I promised I'd bring you and my girl out alive. And I intend to do just that."

"What makes you so sure, Velvet? You think I'm gonna ditch all my plans just because you show up and stir up some old memories?"

Mama pulled two pieces of Juicy Fruit gum out of her front pocket, which was even harder to get into than the one in back. She put one stick in her mouth, then walked over to Daddy and unwrapped his stick, all seductive. I didn't know it was possible to undress a piece of gum, but that's what Mama did. She held up the gum. "Come and get it."

Daddy inched forward and reached for the stick of gum.

"No, that's cheating. Come and take it like a fish nibbling on a line." To my amazement, Daddy did just as Mama told him to, albeit while keeping the Magnum trained on her the whole time. She dangled the stick over Daddy's gaping maw. She dropped it in. "That's a good boy."

Daddy began to chew. His nose scrunched up and he leaned in closer to Mama, taking a deep sniff.

"Recognize my scent?"

I swear Daddy shuddered. "Lucky. You. Body. Mist," he said.

Mama's tone grew even sultrier. "That's right, lover. It was like knockout gas the first time you smelled it on me, at the Swirli King. Remember?"

"I remember."

Mama started to dance around. "Recognize that Conway Twitty song playing in the car?"

"I do," he said as he sipped his beer.

She danced over to Daddy, shaking her bottom.

"Look what I brought." She reached behind her and produced a half pint of Virginia Gentleman whiskey that she'd jammed into the waist of her shorts.

"It was our drink," Daddy said.

Mama nodded in tune to Conway Twitty. "I used to get it from Harby's Liquors for free. Didn't even have to show my titties. Just got it for a wink and a smile."

"I'll take some of that, and whatever else you've got to offer."

Daddy put his beer down on the bar, grabbed the pint and unscrewed the lid. Mama scanned the penthouse. "You got a nice place now," she said. "But so do I. You see, Tami here, she's rich. I mean *real* rich. And whatever she's got is mine, too."

"Well, I wouldn't say that, Mama," I said.

"Take a good look at me, Euple." Mama made a yummy sound. "Do I look like your average gal from down in McDowell County?"

Daddy took a long drink from the pint of whiskey, and an even longer look at her.

"You never did, baby. You was always a class above everyone else."

"Still am."

"Daddy! Mama!" I called out. "Have you forgotten that the ATF is going to be here any time, and that there are bombs set to go off all over here taking a big part of West Virginia with them?"

Mama stepped back from Daddy. "Bombs?"

"Yeah, well, you know." Daddy smacked his gum and threw the whiskey to the floor, shattering the pint. He picked up his beer off the bar counter and shrugged.

"What the hell are you doing looking to blow up the Wild and Wonderful. Best place in the 50 states!"

Daddy kicked a glass shard with the toe of his slipper. Anger flashed across his face something fierce.

"Best place in the 50 states? I hate West Virginia and everyone in it. I hate the little towns! I hate the big towns! I hate cities! I hate the countryside! Most of all, I hate the way this place has kicked me when I'm down, and then held me down!"

"And so you want to blow it up and find yourself on death row?" Mama shouted. "See, this is exactly why it was never going to work between you and me, Euple. You're not a far thinker. You do whatever you want to do in the here and now!"

Daddy chuckled.

"I thought it was because men ain't worth a damn, and your family was cursed or something. At least that's what you told me—not that I believed a single word."

"If I'd known you were capable of building a racket like this, I might've stuck around. And now that I am here, you want to blow it all up!"

Daddy stepped up and pointed his finger in Mama's face. "Well, I didn't know you was ever coming back!"

"Well, you don't know nothing!"

Daddy grabbed Mama and pulled her close. He plucked the cigarette off her lip, took a drag, then threw it on the shag carpet.

Mama pushed her breasts into his chest.

"First time I saw them, in the Gremlin, I thought: Them's the finest set of twins I ever saw," Daddy said, looking down at Mama's chest. "I never reckoned I'd see a better set, but these new jumbo models you now got are even finer, Velvet."

"I got 'em for you," Mama purred.

"Still a lying snake of a woman," Daddy grunted. He then pressed his lips to hers and pressed them hard, kissing her like they were in a Hollywood movie. He bent her body back, all while keeping his Magnum trained on her temple.

The SEAL whispered to me. "What's she going to do? She got a needle on her or something A hidden blade?"

I honestly didn't know. I never expected to see my mama and daddy in the same room, let alone pawing each other like a couple of frisky teenagers. Especially after hearing from Mama what a good for nothing man my daddy was all these years, and how she would move all of heaven and hell just to keep us away from the likes of him. She never even told me his name; I had to find that out myself.

It was like Daddy heard my thoughts. All of a sudden, he pushed away from Mama, training the gun on her cleavage. "You just hold on a second. I'm not that easy a mark, Velvet!"

Mama licked her lips and moved in towards Daddy again, but he was having none of it.

"I touched that hot stove once and got burned in the third degree." The smile on Daddy's face twisted into a malevolent grin. "I got me a harem of girls now and not one of them over the age of twenty-five. Ain't no fossil like you going to lure me into a go."

Mama made an obscene gesture.

Daddy snickered. "I notice that index finger on your right hand is still missing."

"Thanks to you," Mama snorted.

Daddy and Mama had now officially entered—or based on the stories I had heard, *re*-entered—rumble mode.

Bryan the SEAL was growing impatient. He pointed up to the darkening sky. "This place is going to blow any minute. How long do we let this play out?"

"Try to sneak out now," I whispered. "She's distracted him."

"What about your friend?" he said, pointing down to Rusty, who lie prostrate on the floor, praying.

"Leave him be."

Bryan eased his way back to the door.

Daddy fired a warning shot, which ricocheted off the doorknob.

It stopped Bryan in his tracks. A second later he shot me a look that suggested he wouldn't be stopped for long.

Daddy took a long pull off his can of PBR. Bryan's would-be rebellion put down, he re-engaged Mama in conversation. "When I was in prison, all the men around me found Jesus. All day long they'd chant the same prayer, a thousand times each. Chaplain taught it at Bible-study class. I couldn't get five minutes of peace before I heard yet another fool chanting, 'Lord Jesus Christ, Son of God, have mercy on me, a sinner.'"

"You never said a prayer in your life," Mama said. "At least not one you meant."

"I came up with my own prayer," Daddy continued. "Didn't chant it, though. I sang it. Every day, all day, to drown out them Jesus freaks. A song from Saint Mary Robbins about a no-good girl from way out in the West Texas town of El Paso. Nasty piece of work named Felina, who looked like you, Velvet."

Daddy began singing: "Blacker than night were the eyes of Felina. Wicked and evil while casting her spell."

I could tell Mama was flattered by the praise. She was a spell-caster, my Mama was—and she knew it.

"So, you know what the first thing was I did when I got out of prison and went into the snake-handling trade?" Daddy didn't wait for an answer. He fidgeted with his remote control as he continued his story. "I bought my very first rattler. And named her Felina. I don't believe in God. Never did. Never will. But if there is a God, Velvet, he surely intervened on my behalf when you showed up in McDowell Country looking for money and my very own wicked Felina took your finger." Daddy laughed heartily as he pushed a button, then dropped the remote into the pocket of his robe.

The sound of the blast was so intense I reckoned I was back in Ghazni Provence.

Everybody ducked.

"What was that?" panted Mama.

"And so it begins," grinned Daddy.

37.

From outside the compound, a voice blasted through a bullhorn. "Euple Grymes, this is Peter D. Loehr, Director of the Bureau of Alcohol, Tobacco, Firearms and Explosives."

Daddy ran back to his bar and retrieved a walkie-talkie from a holster affixed to the wall. "Euple to Po. Come in, Po!"

"It's no use, Daddy. Po's dead. I killed her."

"Good," Daddy grumbled. "Saved me the trouble."

He aimed the remote at the television. A few clicks later, the entire outside of the compound was visible on the screen, which was split, showing everything from the air and the ground. ATF agents and firefighters, all in gas masks, rushed towards the men's dormitory.

"Daddy, you don't have to do this. Stop now!"

"We're just gettin' started, darlin'."

Mama came up behind me. "I told you he's no good, child." She lit up another cigarette and looked disdainfully at my father. "What are you going to do now, genius, the whole place is surrounded."

Director Loehr's voice boomed. "Grymes, you have one of my people and her mother in there. Let them go and you'll survive this."

"Daddy, please," I begged. "He means it."

"Pastor Grymes," Rusty entreated, "heed Isaiah: 'No longer will violence be heard in your land, nor ruin or destruction within your borders, but you will call your walls Salvation and your gates Praise.'"

"I already told you once to shut your pie hole, Brother Er," he said to Rusty.

"It's over, Daddy. But it doesn't have to end in tragedy. We can still be a family. I've got three boys, and a daughter, Augusta. She's the daughter of my first husband, but she feels like my own. You'd love them, Daddy, and they'd . . . learn to love you, too."

Mama stepped forward. She put her hand on her hip and shook her head. "It's no use child. He's never been a forward thinker, and he's not going to start now."

Daddy cocked his head and spat out his gum. "You know what, Velvet?" he said. "You never did believe in me."

"You'll never get out of here alive, Daddy. Surrender now."

Daddy looked over at Mama. "You think you're rich, Velvet? I got more money than the both of you. I'm fixin' to buy me an island in the Bahamas when I leave here, like that Epstein fella. Find me some new Angels to cavort with."

"Daddy, you'll never see a dime of the Smithers Twins' earnings. They'll find your bank accounts, no matter how well hidden you think they are. They'll freeze them. Then what will you do?"

Daddy laughed. "What kind of fool do you take me for, girl? You think I'd let the government control my money?" He fetched a backpack from behind the bar, then approached the fridge, opening it up again. He gestured for Mama to come toward him and she sauntered over, eyeballing the contents.

"You hungry now of all times?" she asked him.

"Slowly—and I mean slowly—put the sacks in the backpack," he commanded her.

There were five shelves inside the fridge. The top shelf was stocked with beer. On the other shelves, row after row of Hardee's paper bags were impeccably ordered, their tops crisply folded and stapled shut.

"You're brining your Monster Double Thickburgers with you, Daddy?" I asked him. "Ready-to-eat meals to sustain you while you're on the lamb, on the way to your private island in the Caribbean?"

He patted his washboard abs. "Girl, you know how many calories are in one of those burgers? Fourteen hundred. I don't eat that shit." He procured a bag from the fridge and shook it in Mama's face. "Hear all those sweet little rocks shaking? Diamonds, rubies, emeralds, jade, pearl, topaz, turquoise, amethyst. Picked up at estate sales, plucked out of old wedding rings and earring settings, or bought wholesale at those little jewelry stores in Charleston and Beckley and Huntington whose books my Po does. Or used to." He instructed Mama to sweep the Hardee's sacks into his backpack.

Mama snorted. "That's chickenfeed, Euple. Me and Tami got our very own a Cartier necklace. Diamond-and-rubies. *Burmese* rubies, at that. Three layers of strands. The rubies are the size of marbles, separated by little slivers of diamond. A million dollars' worth of jewels. I just wore it out on a date with my new beau."

"New beau?" Daddy asked, looking like he swallowed a bug.

"Mr. Harlan Stuhl, who just happens to be an associate manager at the Dollar Store," Mama said.

"Well, I'm the all-supreme, five-star General of Managers

in this joint!" He zipped up the pack, strapped it across his shoulder, and blew Mama a kiss. Winking at me as he kept the Magnum trained on Mama's head, he walked backwards over to the wall where the monitors were installed. After affixing a gas mask, he unplugged each power cord from the electrical sockets on the floor. "And now, sinners, it's time for Pastor Grymes to make his exit."

Daddy took the remote out of the pocket of his bathrobe and pressed a button, then tossed the remote aside. The panel of wall on which the monitors were installed rose, like a garage door, revealing the night sky, which, near the women's dormitories, glowed blue with burning sulfur.

He jumped out the window.

"Daddy, no!" I cried.

Me, Mama and Bryan ran to the window as Rusty, who was prostrate again on the floor, continued to pray.

The trampoline was about twenty feet below. At Daddy's age, I'd have not been willing to risk the impact on the knees. But his landing must have been smooth, because by the time we arrived at the opening, I reckoned he had already had at least one bounce, possibly two. Gunfire rang out. But bouncing targets are difficult even for well-trained snipers. "Cease fire!" I shouted, but no one heeded my command.

As I continued to call out, waving my hands and trying to deep Daddy from getting killed, he executed a front flip off the trampoline, landed, then rolled under its long skirt.

"Damned vermin might just get away with it," Mama intoned. "Family lore has it that twenty-five generations back there was an old man in Petrești, our little village in Romania, who could walk between raindrops. Maybe your daddy's got some Gypsy in him after all."

Amidst the screeching sirens, discharging weapons, and blaring bullhorns, I saw shrieking congregants of the Before the Fall Ministries fleeing every which way across the basin. A door beneath us burst open and a flock of Angels in red bikinis emerged from the billowing smoke, coughing and staggering.

"Run to the officers, ladies! They're here to help you!" I called.

What we heard next was somewhere between a very loud growl and a roar. When he heard the noise, Rusty's trembling hands covered his skull. His eyes rolled backward again. "Behold the great red dragon, having seven heads and ten horns, and seven crowns upon his heads," he quivered.

"It's not a dragon, Rusty," I said as I watched Daddy's Harley, which came out from beneath the trampoline, blast forward with a loud screech of the tires.

More gunfire rang out. Mama ducked as bullets hit the frame of Daddy's escape window. I heard a popping sound. I watched as he zig-zagged across the basin at ninety miles per hour, dropping smoke bombs from his backpack until he was completely obscured. "Don't shoot!" I shouted as I heard Daddy's bike roar up the side of the mountain, into the forest.

"Tami," Bryan called. He was on the floor, kneeling next to Mama, who was flat on her back, clutching her chest.

"I been shot!" Mama cried. "Again!"

38.

I went to Mama and examined the wound. "Where's the blood?"

"Looks like one of her . . . uh, you know . . . is gone," Bryan said, pointing at her breast.

"One of her *fake* breasts has been popped; it's an implant," I said. "Or was."

I heard choppers overhead, along with repelling ATF officers landing on the roof. Another chopper hovered just above the open wall. The Bell 212's rear door slid open. Two Colt M4 carbines were aimed at us. A third agent issued orders through a bullhorn. "Director Loehr's on his way up. Stand down!"

I affirmed.

"Get this buckshot out of me! It burns something fierce," cried Mama.

Three ATF agents entered the penthouse, followed by the director, a Glock in one hand, a bullhorn in the other. He saw that Mama was down. "You're going to be okay, Ms. Vaduva," the Director said. "It's just rock salt. That's all Justice would authorize." The director knelt before Mama. He retrieved a monogrammed handkerchief from his trousers and blotted Mama's wound. He looked over at me. "She's lucky those implants are so big, Command Sergeant Major. They absorbed most of the impact and only left superficial wounds."

Director Loehr stood and approached the open wall. Through his bullhorn, the order was issued: "Cease fire! Cease fire!"

I had never experienced—nor welcomed—absolute and utter silence as I did in that moment. The ATF agents hoisted Mama off the floor and laid her on the pool table. "My whiskey is a goner, but I noticed there's some Peach Schnapps behind the bar over there. Get me a sip of it, son."

The ATF agent fetched the bottle, then poured a few drops on her tongue.

"Ah, that's better," she said.

"Director Loehr," I said, "we have to get Mama and the folks in this compound out of here fast. I know we can contain the fire in the men's dorms, but—"

"—We already have, soldier."

"More bombs are coming, sir. Five or six more. The women's dormitory. The cinema. The infirmary. The barn. And when they blow, which I expect to be any minute now, you won't be able to contain the toxic fumes. The winds will carry them out of the basin, over the mountain, and—"

"—through West Virginia, into Virginia, and ultimately into the District of Columbia. Yes, I know."

"You brought bomb experts?"

The director nodded. "I've got fifty of them outside."

I bit down hard on my lip, almost drawing blood.

"I've got an idea, sir."

"Long as I've known you, soldier, you've generated ideas. I'm all ears."

"My Daddy seems to like gadgets an awful lot." I went

across the room and fetched his remote. "This is the brains of the outfit. My hunch is that somewhere in this building is some sort of mainframe or central command center."

"Your idea, please, Command Sergeant Major. We haven't got all night."

"Just before the men's dorm blew, Daddy hit a button on the remote. Seconds later, boom! Maybe we fight this battle on two fronts. You send the bomb boys into the buildings to look for chargers. We'll stay here, in the main building, and look for the mainframe."

"Who's 'we,' soldier?"

I introduced Director Loehr to Bryan the SEAL. "He's a demolitions expert, sir."

Director Loehr spoke into a mic on his lapel, ordering his men to start doing a sweep of the compound and a full evacuation.

From the pool table I heard moans. "I'm dying, child."

"No, you're not, Mama."

"Rub my feet."

"There's no time, Mama. I have some bombs to find or we're all going to die!"

"For the time being, you'll stay here with your mother," the director said. "The SEAL and my men can search the building."

"But sir!"

"That's an order, Command Sergeant Major." The director executed a half turn and summoned more men from his microphone.

"I'll start in the cinema," Bryan said. "Come find me when you can, Tami."

The director spoke into his mic again. "Get me medics. Send them to the penthouse." He looked over at Mama. "We're going to get you out of here ASAP, ma'am." The director headed towards the door.

Rusty drizzled bottled water over Mama's head. He looked deep into her eyes, giving her the attention she deserved.

"You're a kind boy. What's your name?"

"Russell," he said. "My friends call me Rusty."

"Fine name. Where are your people from?"

"Doddridge County."

"I know it well," Mama said. "Tell me some stories. Start with your parents. It'll keep my mind off the pain."

Rusty nodded and cleared his throat. "Both my biological parents and my adoptive parents have passed. I'm an only child."

Mama took a deep breath. "That breaks my heart. Where'd y'all live in Doddridge County?"

"Big Isaac, Smithburg, Ashley, Blandville, and about a half dozen other places."

Mama stared at Rusty. "You got some set of eyes on you. Like coal."

I rolled my eyes and squeezed Mama's hand. "Mama, this is no time to flirt with my friend."

Mama smiled warmly at Rusty. "What do you do for a living? You in the military, like my Tami?"

"I was." Rusty explained that he was a veteran, a restaurateur, and an artisan pot-and-pan maker.

"Copper? Tin? Metal? What's your material?"

"All of the above," Rusty replied.

"Pot-making is a Gypsy trade," Mama said approvingly. She brushed Rusty's hand and asked to know more about the people who raised him.

I gave Rusty a look, but he signaled for me to be patient.

It was hard, as I was desperate to be out there helping Director Loehr. Rusty then put his hand over Mama's and my conjoined hands and began explaining that his adoptive papa, Clyde, had been a dog groomer, and his adoptive Mama, Glodene, was part of a team the police brought in to clean up crime scenes.

Mama turned white. Her injury was well-contained, so it couldn't have been from loss of blood.

"You ok, Mama?" I asked.

She swallowed hard and stuttered out her next question. "What's your last name, boy?"

"Riddle."

Mama's lips began to quiver.

"Mama, what is it?" I asked her.

Tears welled up in Mama's eyes. Rusty attempted to blot them with part of his tunic, but Mama sliced through his open arms and clutched his face in her hands.

"It's you!"

"Who?" Rusty asked.

"It's you!"

Rusty was spooked. He tried to break free. "I'm just Rusty Riddle, ma'am."

Me and Rusty's eyes locked, two sane people in the presence of an insane person.

Mama noticed our eye contact. Her eyes widened. "Oh, no. No, no, no, no, no."

"What, Mama?"

To Rusty she spoke sternly, in a mother's voice. "Just tell me you didn't have a go with my daughter!"

"Mama!"

"Answer me, boy!"

"No, ma'am."

"Nothing dirty between you two?"

"Mama!"

"No, ma'am," Rusty repeated, this time emphatically.

"Swear to God?" she demanded of Rusty.

Rusty put his hand over his heart. "I swear to my Lord and Savior, Jesus Christ that I speak true words."

"Praise Jesus," Mama said.

I looked out at the smoke and fire and all the ATF agents running about.

"Mama, you've never praised Jesus in your life. But given the situation we're in, I do think it's right that you're making your peace."

Mama reached out with her other hand and piled it on top of our conjoined hands. I wanted to pull away, as time was ticking. "What's the *matter* with you, Mama?"

Mama asked for another shot of Peach Schnapps. Rusty obliged, tilting her head up a bit. After she swallowed and gave an "ah," she looked at us both. "Rusty is your half-brother, girl. I bore him."

Then she passed out.

39.

The medics arrived, ushered in by Bryan. "We've turned the building upside down. Combed every room. Nothing."

Despite the startling news about Rusty, this was no time for emotional indulgences. I stood up from Mama's side and told the SEAL that Rusty and me would join him for a second look after Mama was evacuated.

"It's useless, Tami," Bryan said. "If there was a mainframe downstairs, we'd have found it by now.

I took a deep breath and searched my gut for what I knew of my daddy: his habits, his interests, his talents, and his obsessions. My eyes flickered around his man cave—over the games and posters, the humidor and the beer fridge, all the TVs. No, it wouldn't be here, either.

"I want my boy with me," Mama slurred, as the medics picked her up and began moving to the door. Rusty ran to her side.

"Stop!" I ordered.

"Get me out of here before I die!" shrieked Mama.

"You're not going to die of salt pellets inside your popped fake boob, Mama!"

I summoned Rusty. "You were an Atheist when you walked in these doors, became a brainwashed believer after that, then became a true believer again—or so it would appear. I don't know what you really believe and maybe you don't either. What I believe, however, is that we're out of options. And though I am not much of a believer myself, I believe in you, Rusty. And at this point, anything's better than nothing. So, I ask you to pray, Rusty. Pray to God. Ask for a sign. Ask Him where Daddy's hiding the command center for all these bombs."

Rusty nodded his agreement.

"Somebody fetch me some Schnapps!"

"Quiet, Mama!"

Rusty reassumed his prostate position on the floor.

I understood the first thirty seconds or so of his prayers, but his praise was soon drowned out by the sound of choppers. "Pray, Rusty!"

Rusty prayed.

"Where's the mainframe?" the SEAL demanded.

Rusty, determined to maintain his concentration, waved the SEAL off.

Rusty's prayer and intensity increased.

A chopper was nearing. "Where?" I impatiently shouted.

Rusty, perspiration pouring off his forehead onto the floor, waved me off.

"Pray harder!" I shouted.

The Farrah Fawcett posters began to rustle as a fierce, howling wind entered the penthouse. From above the roof, I heard the chopper descend. It was outside Daddy's retractable wall. "Take cover!" shouted the SEAL. We all dove—except for Rusty, who remained prostate. He was screaming now, borderline hysterical.

The chopper angled its nose into the penthouse. A spotlight shone on us, about 15,000 watts of white-hot light. Rusty stood.

40.

Inside the chapel the SEAL and I overturned bookcases, upended pews, searched under the riser for a trapdoor. He ran down the corridor and returned with two axes. We began chopping through the plank wood flooring, looking for a secret bunker. "Nothing but dirt below," he lamented.

"We're chopping through every inch of this flooring."

Three-quarters of the floor was ripped up. "Some good the prayers did," groaned Bryan.

"Are you going to tell me you didn't hear the same singing I did? The crowds chanting? The animal howls? The applause?"

"How do you know they weren't all sound effects Rusty was—"

The telephone on Euple's desk rang.

"What do we do?" the SEAL asked.

What else was there to do?

"We answer it," I said, punching Line One on the phone. No one was there. I punched Line Two, Three, Four. No one was there either. The phone kept ringing. Finally, I pushed the intercom button.

"Well, hello, Sabrina. I was expecting you to pick up on the first ring. Did someone pluck the feathers off your wings and delay your flight to the chapel?"

I took a deep breath. "It's not Sabrina, Daddy. It's me, your daughter, Tami."

I heard fumbling at the other end of the line. Then silence.

"Daddy? I know you're there. Quit pretending you're not. Talk to me. It's not too late."

I heard the tab atop a beer can crack open. I listened to him gulp then swallow. "You're a very determined young woman, Tami."

"You don't know half of what I'm capable of."

"Oh, you might just be surprised, my dear. I've spent the last few days reading about you in *Stars and Stripes.* Most highly-decorated female combat soldier in U.S. Army history. All those medals you won in battle: stopping an attack on the Empire State building, killing that Corned Beef Hash terrorist fella, and so on." He chuckled. "You're very cool under pressure."

"The more you sweat in training, the less you bleed in battle," I said.

"Don't I know it, darlin.' I did a lot of sweatin' too—before judges, in prison, building my business, planning my getaway. 'Apples and trees,' darlin,'—just like I told you."

"A poison apple, in your case, Daddy."

"I reckon you must be wondering what *I'm* capable of?"

"There's a central command center here, Daddy," I said. "Where is it? Just tell me this. I promise to visit you in prison. I'll bring food. My boys will come, too. Cleet IV, my oldest boy, will bring his guitar. He'll sing you Conway Twitty tunes, that Marty Robbins song you like, the one about—"

"—Goodbye, Angel."

The line went dead.

The SEAL stroked his chin. "Well, I guess Rusty was right,"

he said. "We heard 'his voice.' Not sure what good it did us, though."

I looked down at the intercom and pointed. "Which came through there."

I picked up the intercom and inspected it. "We've got to remove the casing."

"Which is probably rigged to blow," the SEAL said, "assuming the brains of this outfit are even housed in there."

"We need a screwdriver." I reached for the lap drawer of the desk. "Maybe there's a letter opener or pen—"

"—Stop!" shouted Bryan. "Shimmy it gently. *Very* gently. It might be wired."

I eased the drawer open. No evidence of wires. Nothing in the lap drawer, except for a half dozen or so decades-old, tattered copies of *People* magazine, each with a picture of Farrah Fawcett on the cover.

I checked the vertical drawers on the sides, stacked three deep. *Slowly,* as the SEAL recommended. All were empty. Finally, I opened the sixth and final drawer. Jackpot: a junk drawer. I went fishing through the contents: a stapler, a calculator, a toenail clipper, fountain pen cartridges, ballpoint pens, and a Ziplock bag full of paper clips. "This will work," I said as I unzipped the baggie and reached for a paper clip.

Then I heard a click. Followed by a hiss. The SEAL looked up. Orange mist poured through the vents.

"The cimora!" he said.

"Take a deep breath and hold it!" I told him. "Before it floats down into our air space."

I, too, did as I'd advised him. Though the phone didn't ring, Line Three on Daddys desk lit up, then blinked three times.

"Well," croaked the SEAL through his held breath, "are you going to answer it?"

But before I could press the button, we heard the explosion.

Reflexively, the SEAL tackled me, and we rolled under one of the pews.

"It's not inside the building," I said.

"Sounds like it came from the women's dorms."

Outside the chapel windows, fire and brimstone was enveloping the basin. Again. The air out there was getting thicker with smoke by the second. Inside the chapel the orange mist, filled with tiny, poisonous snowflakes, fell down towards us. "No talking," I whispered before crouching down and sucking a sip of clean air close to the floor. I handed the SEAL a paperclip and fetched a ballpoint pen from the desk drawer. We turned the intercom face down, as soft as a feather. Then each of us went to work on a separate corner of the speaker. The casing popped off after about thirty seconds' effort. Inside there was a jumble of colored wires. Yellow and red button lights glowed. A quartz wristwatch with a thin wire inserted into its crown served as the timer.

Bomb dismantlement was not my specialty. I had done it before. But only on crude bombs constructed by insurgents, bomb-makers who learned their dark art from YouTube videos. Po had clearly been given superior training from her MS-13 boyfriend and his cronies. The SEAL pointed at a thick grouping of multi-colored, crisscrossing wires—all of them bundled together with twist ties, with a small, round metal dial under that. Normally, a bomb like this could be dismantled in six or seven minutes, assuming those doing the dismantling knew what they were doing. "There's a color-coded order to the wires," the SEAL said. "We need to cut them in the right color order. If we get it wrong, it's game over."

We studied the bomb. I was suddenly struck by the beauty of the apparatus. An explosive, before it detonates, can be an elegant piece of work, a neutral tool that can be used to blow holes in mountains for trains to pass through or to kill, maim, and devastate. My Daddy had chosen the latter, which filled me with sadness and a level of shame I feared I would never get over, assuming I survived the next few minutes. If I didn't, Daddy would likely die along with us. Nowhere near time for him to get over the mountains on his Harley and go in the opposite direction that the winds would carry the poisonous fumes. Assuming, that is, that he had not been taken into custody already.

Not a forward thinker, as Mama said.

"There could be thousands of different color combinations here. Maybe even millions," I told Bryan.

The SEAL nodded. "There could, but I think this is a Roy G Biv formulation."

"A what?"

"Roy G Biv. It's the colors of the rainbow in order. Red, orange, yellow, green, blue, indigo, and violet."

The SEAL pointed at the red-coated wire, indicating that should be cut first. I fetched the toenail clipper from the desk drawer and obliged. The timer ticked down another thirty seconds, which seemed like an hour. With all this stress and exertion, my lungs were already starting to give me trouble. Next, it was time for orange. That wire was tangled up under one of the bundles, which the SEAL had to loosen with the ballpoint pen. I completed that task. We watched the timer. Next, the SEAL pointed to the yellow wire. Done. Finally, the time came to clip the green wire. The red-faced, oxygen-deprived SEAL was beginning to exhibit signs of dizziness. Sweat coated his forehead. I pointed to the stairwell door and indicated that he should go have a breath. He started to shake his head, but I insisted, and he knew I was right. But he didn't even get to the door before it was kicked open, sending him reeling backwards, hitting his head on the edge of the desk, and falling limp to the floor.

In burst the Smithers Twins.

They weren't dressed in the silky white robes they had on before, but wore lacy, red thongs and push up bras, plus matching stockings and pumps—the costumes they wore during their OnlyFans live video performances. Both wore gas masks.

Po had apparently trained them well enough that they knew not to be shooting guns in a place that was ready to blow, so they came armed with more practical weapons—each with one machete, and one push dagger.

I didn't want to have to kill these girls, as they'd been brainwashed into their evil doing and were just carrying out their programming. I told them as much, making sure to use their names—not their first names, as I didn't know those . I reminded them that Euple Grymes had been taking all of their OnlyFans money for himself.

The girls started laughing.

"I know exactly who I am and always have. My name's Clover Smithers."

"And my name's Clementine Smithers. This time tomorrow, we're going to be in the Bahamas with Euple and all our jewels, plus some gold bars Euple got hid away. You, on the other hand, will be dead."

I guess I did want to kill these girls after all.

I dove down to the floor, next to the desk, taking a micro-breath of air. It was smokey, and I could detect a slight taste of the drugs, but overall, a little wouldn't do much to me. I took a second micro-breath, holding that one, and positioned myself on my back as the girls came at me. Holding on to the underside of the desk, I kicked up in a scissor chop, knocking the machete out of Clementine's hand, and kicking her sister in the push dagger hand, making her cut her own shoulder.

"You fucking bitch!" Clover shouted, looking down at her wound.

I rolled in a backwards somersault to a standing position, taking Clementine's fallen machete with me.

I advanced towards the twins, butterflying the weapon. Clover ducked down, trying to attack my calves with her push dagger. I saw her coming and jumped up, tucking my legs and grabbing a fistful of her hair. I brought the machete down onto those blonde waves, cutting them clear off on my way down, then rolled over the desk to get some space between us. I took another small breath from the better air at our feet.

"That Jill cut my fucking hair!" Clover cried.

"Listen, ladies," I said. "I don't know what Euple told you, but I can promise that he had no intention of taking you with him. At least not last time I saw him, when he was hightailing it out of here on a Harley, leaving you to die with everyone else here."

"Lying, bitch," Clementine spat.

"I'm not lying, and I would appreciate it if you would watch your language."

"We've still got time to get out of here before this place

blows and meet Euple on the banks of the river," Clover informed me. "And I'll use any fucking language I want!"

Her sister came at me with her machete, trying to take my head clear off, but I ducked behind the desk again. The blade landed right on the edge of it, taking off a hefty sliver of wood.

"Ladies, on this desk is a bomb. And it's not just one bomb. It's the brains for a whole sequence of explosive devices. If I don't dismantle it in the next few minutes—you, me, and the folks between here and the District of Columbia will be history."

"Bullshit," said Clementine, bringing her machete down onto the middle of the desk to make her point. She watched me wince and duck on instinct. For the first time, a light went on in that head of hers.

But I couldn't wait for her to connect the dots.

Seizing my opportunity, I grabbed her head, thrusting my knee into it and dropping her unconscious to the floor.

Clover didn't miss a step. She jumped over her sister, swept down, and took the machete from her hand. Then she came after me.

She chased me around the desk several times. Having to run while holding my breath definitely weakened my position. I would have otherwise been able to take care of these girls in under thirty seconds. Their training had been good, but not good enough.

"Clover," I said. "We don't have much time. I've got to disarm this bomb!"

She watched me wobble and shake off my wooziness. I needed a breath, a deep breath, to be able to take her out, but I was starting to see double.

As she came at me, I stumbled backwards, tripping over the

SEAL's arm. She dove at me, aiming to shove the push dagger into my temple and sink the machete into my torso. At least that's what I would do. But she ended up doing neither. Because Bryan rose up, knocking her sideways with a kick. Clover slammed into the desk, her dagger getting stuck in its side.

The SEAL shook off what must have been a monster of a headache, then did a kip up from his supine position. He landed a punch to Clover's stomach.

The girl slumped but didn't collapse. Instead, she girded herself, then swung the machete, cutting across Bryan's breastplate. He hit the floor hard.

I kicked the machete from her hand, caught it, then lunged at the twin, beheading her. I chased the head as it rolled across the floor, and when it stopped, I removed the gas mask and put it on. Twin No. 1 was beginning to stir.

"Get out! Now!" I ordered. "Before I take your head off, too!" The girl became hysterical at the sight of her fallen sister.

"Git!" I repeated. "Run as fast as you can or it's over for you inside of one and half seconds!"

Twin No. 1 rose and fled the chapel.

I ran towards Bryan, who was still breathing. There was a good deal of blood on his tunic, but it didn't look like he'd been cut too deep.

"Frogman!" I said. "Bryan! Wake up."

He groaned and his eyelids fluttered, but he wasn't anywhere near ready to rally. I got up from his side and went back to the bomb.

Three wires remained: blue, indigo, and violet. But to me, they were just blue, royal blue, and purple blue. I wasn't sure which was which. The plain blue one was obvious to me and I cut it, but that left me with the last two, and it wasn't at all clear which could be called indigo and which would be violet. They both just looked like different gradations of purpley-blue to me. I sucked in on the mask and snipped the lighter one first, for no other reason than that was the color I liked best. It was the color of a pair of sapphire earrings my late husband Cletus Bland IV had given me after I had given birth to our son. That I was still standing was a good sign. Praying my luck would hold, I went ahead and clipped the last purple wire, the one that seemed closest to the color Mama had always said was her favorite. Then I froze. The red light inside the intercom started blinking and beeping. I didn't know if that was good or bad. Seconds later, I heard what sounded like a serpent's hiss. I waited. And waited. And waited. Sixty seconds later, I was still alive, and I knew it was over. The intercom was smoking, but even that was petering out.

"Thank you," I said to no one in particular.

I returned to the SEAL, crouching next to him. He grunted, then started to cough.

"Can you get up?" I asked. "You're bleeding pretty bad."

"The bomb?"

"Looks like we're all going to live, sailor."

42.

Outside, the basin was illuminated in firelight in addition to all the white spotlights. In the melee, congregants were still running in every direction. Those intercepted by the ATF were being herded into convoys. I stopped a passing medic and told him about Bryan's machete wound. Then I spotted Director Loehr and rushed to him.

"The bomb's disabled, sir!" I said.

"Are you certain, soldier?"

"I snipped all the wires and nothing has blown, sir."

"Nothing has blown *yet*, soldier."

"If it was going to, it would have by now, sir."

The director greeted my insubordination disapprovingly. "That's not your call to make, Command Sergeant Major Vaduva; it's *mine.*"

"Yes, sir," I said sheepishly.

He pointed at a bay of ambulances. "Your mother's in that medical transport with that young man. Go and join them, then get your family out of here."

"Thank you, sir. But I need to see the mission through. My duty is here."

"You've done your duty Command Sergeant Major Vaduva.

Get in that transport. Your duty now is to your family. Go. That's an order."

"Yes, sir." I looked around and reckoned he was right. The situation was calming down. The area was secured. I ran to the medical transport, which was crammed with congregants who had been exposed to the sulfurous fumes. Everyone was coughing and hacking. Industrial fans rotated, ventilating the area. The medics flushed the eyes of the injured with distilled water, poured ice water into throats, and administered analgesics to those who complained of headaches.

"We're back here," shouted Rusty when he spotted me.

I ran to Mama and my half-brother. I grabbed my mother's hand. "How you doing, Mama?"

"I'm dying, baby."

I placed my hand on her cheek. Her eyes were clear. Her breathing was regular. Her lips were moist. "No, you're not, Mama."

"Keep rubbing my feet, boy."

As he kneaded her foot, Rusty said, "Mama's about to tell me about my daddy."

At length Mama explained the situation she'd gotten herself into with another ne'er-do-well, a man with whom she had had a one-time encounter. She claimed not to remember his name, but coincidentally, her encounter with him had also occurred on the Swirli King parking lot inside a vehicle—an orange, 1972 Dodge van with fringe on the windows.

Mama told Rusty about the curse of single motherhood in our lineage, and the tradition of keeping the girls, and training them in the Romani arts, although she used the word gypsy—and her family tradition of giving up the boys. The women in our bloodline had been taught never to make contact with their sons again, Mama told Rusty, for the only thing more painful that not seeing their sons was to see them—and want them back. Which was not an option.

Rusty asked why he was turned over to such old caregivers, people in their 60s unfit to raise an infant.

"I was in a jam. And Clyde and Glodene was in my debt."

"How do?" Rusty inquired.

"Let's just say they owed me a favor. A big one," was all Mama would say.

Rusty had a tear in his eye.

Mama squeezed his hand.

Rusty, a soldier like me, pulled it together.

"Were they kind to you? Clyde and Glodene?" Mama asked.

"No." He did not elaborate either.

"I'm sure it made you tough."

Finally, the dam broke, and tears streamed down Mama's face. "I'm sorry I broke your heart, boy."

I could tell she meant it.

Rusty struggled to control his emotions. He looked up into the ceiling of the medical transport and smiled like he'd just seen a friend.

Then he looked at me and Mama. "Did you hear that?"

"What?" asked Mama.

"That singing."

"Huh?"

"Ain't nobody singing," Mama said. She passed the water bottle to Rusty. "Drink this, boy. You're mind's playing ticks on you."

43.

The following Sunday afternoon, me, Mama, Cleet IV, Little Jack, Maximo—and the newest member of the family, my half-brother, known to my boys as "Uncle Rusty"—were crammed into a booth at the Swirli King.

"Stop fidgeting, girl," Mama said. "She'll be here soon enough."

"You know better than anybody what it's like to be separated from your kin," I said to Mama. "I'm aching to see my daughter."

Mama sniffed. "Last time I saw Augusta was down in Palm Beach, at that party you threw—and got me shot at."

Oh, please, I thought to myself: Is she really going to bring *that* up again?

I saw Augusta step out of her vehicle. "There she is now!" I jumped up and ran out to the parking lot, where I greeted Second Lieutenant Augusta Bland.

After what seemed like a five-minute hug, I escorted her to the booth. She had a warm reunion with her siblings, applied a kiss to her step-grandmama's cheek, and shook hands with her new step-uncle Rusty, who, clad in his black suit and thin black tie over a white shirt, greeted her with a somewhat imposing, newfound formality.

"They've got a Matterhorn sundae here," I said. "Five scoops of ice cream, five different sauce toppings—butterscotch, caramel, chocolate, strawberry and pineapple—plus pecans, peanuts, chocolate chips, and gummi bears."

Augusta, whose crisp, creased unform looked like it had been welded onto her frame, patted her rock-hard stomach. "I'd have to P.T. for a month to work it off. No thanks, Mom."

"Killed anybody yet?" Little Jack asked his sister.

Augusta smacked her baby brother playfully. "I just got my bars, Jack. Give me a few weeks." She inquired after Little Jack's silat training, which he described, incomprehensibly, as he shoveled ice cream into his maw. Then she turned to Cleet IV. "Are you still playing Gypsy jazz guitar?"

Cleet IV told her he was migrating towards bluegrass and country.

"'Bout time," Mama said as she attempted, with her fingernail, to liberate a chunk of peanut stuck in her teeth.

"Will you play something for me?" Augusta asked.

Cleet IV reached for the guitar leaning against the back corner of the booth. "You like Willie Nelson?"

"Who doesn't?"

"Me," said Little Jack.

As I nursed Maximo, Cleet IV strummed and sang the first few lines to "I'm My Own Grandpa."

After the conclusion of Cleet's musical recital, Mama rose and exited the booth. Augusta stroked Maximo's fine black hair as he nursed. When Mama returned from the counter with a sundae refill, she saw the disapproving look on my face. "Dairy is healthy for the bones," Mama said. Then she pointed at Maximo. "Besides, if he gets to have seconds—and thirds, and fourths, and fifths—then I'm entitled, too."

"I didn't say a word, Mama."

"You didn't have to!"

About halfway through her sundae, Mama took a break from her binge and said, "This is where it all began." She swept her outstretched arms over the restaurant, like she was the matriarch of a ten-thousand-acre ranch in Wyoming. "This is where my family started."

"In here, grandmama?" Little Jack asked.

"Out there, technically" Mama said, pointing to the parking lot.

"I thought our family started five centuries ago, Mama. In Petrești, Romania."

Mama shooed me away as she plunged the plastic spoon back into her sundae. "That's ancient history, child," Mama said. "You people around this table are alive. You're my family. My present and future."

"I hear *your* future is about to change dramatically Uncle Rusty," said Augusta.

Mama looked over at Augusta. "Your new uncle is going to snake-handling school," she snorted.

"That's not nice, Mama," I scolded. "A religious seminary isn't the same thing as snake-handling school, and you know it."

Mama shrugged.

"The people who ended up at the Pentecostal Tabernacle of the Holy Ghost's Testimony Church were lost souls," said Rusty. "That place strayed from the original intention of the Protestant Charismatic Christian movement. Its congregants represent one percent of one percent of the faithful—a misguided offshoot of the faithful, for sure. But most of their churches have closed down, thankfully; most state laws now prohibit the handling of venomous serpents." He appeared deep in thought as he took a sip of decaf sweet tea. "True Pentecostalism emphasizes direct personal experience of God through baptism with the Holy Spirit—and you don't need to have rattlesnakes wrapped around your forearms to experience that."

Augusta, who was raised in the Episcopal tradition, but rarely attended services, was keen to know more about Rusty's religious conversion.

Rusty grew increasingly passionate as he described "The Call" that compelled him to enter the Pentecostal Theological Seminary in Fairmont, West Virginia.

"Is it true that an angel spoke to you?" Augusta asked.

"Angels," Rusty said. "Plural."

"They told him how to find—and dismantle—the bombs," I said.

A pickup truck rolled onto the lot. Scooter Skinner and Ricky Ray Jeeter emerged, looking like their former selves: Scooter in plaid flannel shirt with the sleeves cut off; Ricky Ray in camo, wearing a backwards baseball cap.

Rusty continued. "I'm the last guy on earth who should have heard or, frankly, heeded 'The Call,' but I can't pretend that what I experienced on that compound in the Canaan Valley wasn't the Lord sending me a message."

Augusta looked pleadingly at her grandmama. "Velvet, can I ask a question about the Canaan Valley?"

"No! I don't want to hear another word ever again about that place and I don't want to talk about that fool. I'm going out for a cigarette."

Mama was furious that Euple Grymes had not been apprehended by the ATF or any other authorities.

Augusta remained respectfully silent as she watched her

grandmama head for the door. She then turned to me. "I've been meaning to ask you something, Mom."

"Shoot."

"When you talked to my Daddy at that séance, you said he—"

"—I shouldn't be party to this conversation," interrupted Rusty. He rose from the booth.

"You stay put," I said to my brother in a tone that was bossier than I intended.

"Under the tenets of the Pentecostal Church, this kind of talk qualifies as blasphemy."

I softened my tone. "I listened respectfully when you discussed your beliefs, Rusty. Afford me the same courtesy. You're family now, and you need to be up to speed about family matters."

Rusty demurred.

"Go on, Augusta. You wanted to know about something Cleet III said."

"You told me that he told you that if you found your daddy, and forgave him, and allowed him to love you, and you loved him back, maybe it would heal your heart—and lift your curse with men." She took my hand in hers.

"I think the only thing more heartbreaking than never knowing my daddy was finally getting to meet my daddy—and having my heart broken by him a second time," I told Augusta.

What I didn't tell her—what I had told no one—was that a bouquet of flowers had come to my office at the University. It was a beautiful bouquet of red roses with a card that read, *"I never in a million years reckoned I'd see my little girl again. I'm glad we met. We'll never likely see each other again but I want you to know I'm proud of you. Love, Daddy."*

I fought back the tears welling in my eye as I looked out the plate glass window, onto the parking lot, at my cursed mother. She was alone, lighting up an Eve Ultra-Light Menthol 120. She had always been alone. She would always be alone, I reckoned.

"You didn't answer my question, Mama?" Augusta pressed.

"Which one?"

"Do you think the curse has been lifted?"

I shrugged. "I was asked out on a date," I said.

"What? You haven't said a word!"

"Well, I'm telling you now," I said to Augusta.

"Who is he?"

"His name is Bryan. He's a Navy SEAL. Nothing serious, mind you. I'm not ready for that and don't know if I ever will be. Anyway, we're going to Rusty's restaurant and having goat sliders."

"My soon-to-be *former* restaurant," corrected Rusty, who intended to exit the moonshine-slinging business.

"So maybe this one—this Bryan—he'll lift the curse?" Augusta inquired hopefully.

I stirred the melted ice cream in the plastic cup before me. Clockwise, then counter-clockwise. I set the spoon on the table and squeezed my daughter's hand. "Only time will tell, child. Only time will tell."

A Humble Request

V.J. Fitz-Howard would be grateful if you'd publish an honest review of *Next of Kin*—even if it's just a sentence or two—on one or more of your favorite platforms.

Tami's Next Stop:

NEW ORLEANS!

In *Garters & Guns*, book five in the series, Tami "never the bridesmaid, always the bride" Vaduva has just arrived in The Big Easy for the social event of the season: her step-daughter's wedding! But despite the sweet smell of magnolia that perfumes the air, things are never easy for Tami. In the company of old friends and familiar enemies, the most highly decorated female combat soldier in U.S. Army history must confront a seductively deceptive threat—to both her country and her family.

Book 5 of the series, *Garters & Guns*, is coming soon.

www.ingramcontent.com/pod-product-compliance
Lightning Source LLC
Chambersburg PA
CBHW020745190726
48285CB00006B/1887

9781955039116